# SECRETS OF OUR HEARTS

# SECRETS OF OUR HEARTS

## Sarah Harrison

This title first published 2011
in Great Britain and in the USA by
SEVERN HOUSE PUBLISHERS LTD of
9–15 High Street, Sutton, Surrey, England, SM1 1DF.
First published 1991 in Great Britain by Little, Brown and Company
under the title *The Forests of the Night*.

British Library Cataloguing in Publication Data

Harrison, Sarah, 1946-
  Secrets of our hearts.
  1. Social classes--Great Britain--Fiction. 2. Singapore--
  History--Japanese occupation, 1942-1945--Fiction.
  3. World War, 1939-1945--Prisoners and prisons, Japanese--
  Fiction. 4. Prisoners of war--Great Britain--Fiction.
  5. Prisoners of war--Singapore--Changi--Fiction.
  6. Changi POW Camp (Changi, Singapore)--Fiction.
  7. Burma-Siam Railroad--Fiction. 8. Revenge--Fiction.
  I. Title
  823.9'14-dc22

ISBN-13: 978-0-7278-8011-6   (cased)

*All Severn House titles are printed on acid-free paper.*

Severn House Publishers support The Forest Stewardship Council [FSC],
the leading international forest certification organisation. All our titles that
are printed on Greenpeace-approved FSC-certified paper carry the FSC logo.

FSC
www.fsc.org

MIX
Paper from
responsible sources
FSC® C018575

Printed and bound in Great Britain by the
MPG Books Group, Bodmin, Cornwall.

My special thanks go to Clifford Beck, Allison Mark and Edward McNeil for their invaluable help.

Material concerning Changi and the Thai-Burma railway has been verified to the best of my ability from diaries, memoirs and interviews with former POWs. I should like to express both my admiration and respect for those who were there, and the hope that I have recreated, as far as possible, the authentic spirit of that terrible time.

For Nick

## Author's Note

As an army child in Singapore in the fifties one of my most vivid memories was of going by car with my mother to do shopping in Changi Village. On our way out of the city we passed a forbidding building with high, blind walls. When I asked about it my mother told me it was a prison, the infamous Changi Jail and that 'bad things had happened there during the war'. Her words made me shiver, even though I didn't yet know that we had a family connection with the place – my uncle had been imprisoned in Changi, and subsequently on the Burma Railway.

The imaginative seed had been sown, and when some forty years later I embarked on a story about friendship, jealousy and social divisions among a group of men who had known each other at public school, I set it in the Japanese internment camps of World War Two, particularly the notorious Sonkurai camp on the Thai-Burma border. I wanted to place my characters in a setting so brutal and unforgiving that normal rules, checks and balances would not apply. Sadly my uncle in Malaya had died with his tale untold by the time I did my research, but many other former POWs were extraordinarily generous in describing – and so re-living – their horrific experiences. And going back to the Far East, retracing the prisoners' footsteps, was a powerfully moving experience

This is the first truly dark novel I wrote and curiously it seemed to spring ready-armed from the imagination. Once I'd completed a fairly lengthy period of harrowing research, I completed it in three months. Perhaps because of this, I still feel fiercely connected to it. SECRETS OF OUR HEARTS is a story I felt compelled to write.

# CHAPTER ONE

## 1989

I was standing on the Mount of Olives in the broiling sun, trying to ignore a pack of Arab hawkers, when I saw John Oliphant for the first time in forty-five years. Because of the distractions, the coincidence of encountering him when I was just concluding my peculiar pilgrimage (and he, presumably, was engaged in one of his own) didn't surprise me. The world gets smaller as you get older, I find. What I did discover was that my memories were so alarmingly vivid that it might all have happened yesterday.

He was trudging up the Mount, taking the more southerly track out of the Kedron Valley. He must have been out to mortify the flesh as a good pilgrim should, for the heat was punishing and I put him at a couple of years older than I and now in his late seventies. Even if he'd taken a breather at the Dominus Flevit along the way, it confirmed me in my view that religious people are dangerous zealots at bottom.

While he was still toiling up towards me a coach arrived and disgorged its load of English God-botherers on to the pavement. At once the hawkers, who'd long since given up on me, went into action: a moth-eaten camel was prodded and hauled to its feet and the air rang with the passwords 'Princess Di', 'fish and chips', 'Kodak' and 'change money'.

I'm not, nor ever have been, a believer but this still offended me, especially because I was sure the tourists would fall for it. They so hate to be rude. And they're such mugs. There was a Coke can lying in the lee of the low wall and I trod on it, feeling it buckle and fold under my shoe. Two of the old dears from the coach, wearing the obligatory sunhats and trainers, bustled in my direction. They leaned over the wall and one of them said: 'Look, there he is! He's done it. Rather him than me.'

Her friend agreed, and then put a hand alongside her mouth. 'John!' she called. 'John, we're up here!' Oliphant stopped and looked up, shading his eyes.

'Hallo-o!' called the ladies, waving merrily. He beamed and lifted both hands, clapping, as though they, too, had walked all the way from the Garden of Gethsemane. Then he lowered his head and pressed on. So he was a member of the coach party, where first names and cheery fellowship were clearly the order of the day. I noticed that the old dears, who were now being pestered by a boy with Holy Land keyrings, were wearing badges saying 'Christian Travel Inc.'. They were in a party of twenty or so, led by a bossy young vicar in an 'I pitch for Jesus' baseball cap.

'If you'd like to gather round, my team,' he called out in a Bristolean accent, 'I'll explain the view.'

They grumbled happily about there being no peace for the wicked, and pottered off in the direction of their leader.

'John's just coming,' said the one who'd yoo-hooed. 'He's on his way.'

As the vicar began his peroration I sat down on the wall and watched Oliphant. I'd known him at once by his big, pear-shaped figure, and by that walk, which was still lolloping and eager even beneath the burdens of age, heat, and a steep gradient. He was sensibly dressed for

2

sightseeing in the unforgiving climate of Israel in August, but his clothes were unmistakably those of a tourist: a loose short-sleeved shirt worn outside cotton drill trousers with turn-ups; towelling socks and yachting shoes; a cream hat with a floppy brim. Beneath the hem of the shirt there showed a glimpse of black canvas money belt. He did not, however, have a camera; an omission which I mentally applauded.

I still couldn't help wondering why he'd chosen to walk up at his age when he could have travelled in the comfort of an air-conditioned coach. And what had he made of Gethsemane? I'd have given a lot to have been kneeling next to him at the rail which encircled the Rock of the Agony. But I knew that to see his face, and to hear his whispered private prayer, would not have been enough for me: I'd have wanted to read his thoughts. Perhaps it was those very thoughts which had prompted him to toil up the gritty path, through the desiccated scrub and the sun-whitened rock, to where I stood.

I've never cared for the idea of visits to the past. It's been my stated opinion that they're unhealthy and result, as night follows day, in disappointment. You see it time and again, people trying to relive glory days, or to find in certain places whatever they saw in those places decades before. Fatal. Change and decay in all around they see (I detest organised sport, but the Cup Final has always made me cry), and then they feel cheated. Cary, ever the supportive friend and pragmatic New Yorker, wasted no time in reminding me of what I'd always maintained.

'And now,' he said, 'you're going to the Far East in the monsoon season to pick up some vile disease, and for what? So you can wallow in old miseries.'

'That's not true,' I said. 'I'm not going to wallow in them. I'm going to exorcise them. There have been too many books about the railway, most of them dreadful. I might

3

even be tempted to put the record straight.'

'Oh my God! Not memoirs!'

'They can't be ruled out.'

I only said this to annoy Cary. Though I intended to defray my costs by writing a couple of magazine pieces, I had no intention of adding to the ranks of turgid, self-important military autobiographies. I was no career soldier; I wasn't even an enthusiastic conscript. I was just one of the thousands of bits of human flotsam which the tide of war, quite by chance, brought back. The advance in my army career which put me, so to speak, in the front line, and made me of some use, came about more through my horror of boredom than any urge to serve King and Country. And when I came out of it alive, I thanked a God I've had little time for before or since, and left for the States. I only bothered to retain the outward show of Englishness – the accent, the speech patterns – because it was of some help in finding work as a freelance journalist. Now I've made my three-score years and ten and have no need to earn a living I regard myself as an American. On the rare occasions I come over to Britain I'm dismayed by it all – the drabness, the overcrowding, the ghastly, scruffy amateurism, the attitude everyone still has that the world owes them a living but hasn't paid up yet. I wouldn't go back. And yet I did go back to Thailand, and on my own. I invited Cary, pointing out that the Thai tourist operation is second to none these days, but he wanted no part of it. He told me he had better things to do than catch his death in a jungle, and would I mind if he took a lodger for the month I would be away? I said of course not. We understand each other.

Flying long distances cattle-class is not my idea of fun, but since I was planning to put a girdle round about the earth and am not made of money there was no alternative. And then it seemed only sensible to go via London and visit my married niece and her family. She is always touchingly pleased to see me. Through no agency of mine

4

she seems to regard me as some sort of war hero, and this more than makes up for my other eccentricities. Even if this were not so I should make time for Milly, because of all I owe her mother, my dear sister Hilda.

Milly and her eldest boy met me at Heathrow off the eight p.m. flight. Bernard rarely does these taxi-fatigues. The story is always that he works such long hours and must not have additional stress heaped upon him. He never seems in the least stressed to me. He is a dull, ursine fellow with that peculiar mix of boisterousness and timidity so typical of middle-class Englishmen. Ageless – was Bernard ever young? – and sexless. Whereas poor Milly . . . within that harassed, rumpled, breathless, hardworking wife and mother there is a warm, sensuous being clamouring for release. Where are all the unscrupulous Lotharios who used to prey on innocent girls and married women?

The boy Nathan was learning to drive, alas.

'Do you mind if he drives us back?' asked Milly with the grimace she uses to indicate a *fait accompli* for which she nonetheless takes responsibility and apologises.

Nathan said: 'I've got the test in two weeks, if I'm not safe now I never will be.'

I failed to see the logic of this, and insisted on sitting in the back of the Cortina, not out of politeness but from some rare memory of this being the safest position if you actually went into something.

Milly talked, while keeping her eyes on the road.

'It's so lovely to see you, we're all dying to know what prompted you to take this trip when you've always said – signal before you brake . . . fine. I do hope you can come on the way back so we can hear all about it. Otherwise you're going to have to send us a full report. Signal earlier, darling – how's Cary? You know Laura's planning to do coast-to-coast America next summer, so she may well turn

5

up on your doorstep, you won't mind if I give her your number? . . . second right off the roundabout . . . '

I tried to picture Cary in his black happy-coat opening the door of the apartment to find a strapping, pink-cheeked, frizzy-haired English girl standing there, bursting with the arrogant innocence that only a British single-sex education can buy. I told Milly she could give our address and number to anyone, ours was liberty hall. Serve Bernard right.

We got back to the house in Thurlow Road, NW3 in quite good order, barring a few filial flurries of temper occasioned by stalling in front of one's great-uncle.

Bernard was back from the commercial war zone he inhabited from nine till five.

'Marvellous,' he said, drawing me into the sitting room. 'Have a drink. How many meals did they give you on the plane? Because you realise she's killed the fatted calf.'

That was not all she'd done. As I sipped my gin and tonic (they never keep vodka) and listened to Bernard's panegyric on Thatcherism, I saw that the house had been washed and brushed up for my arrival. It presented the subdued, tidy appearance calculated to soothe an elderly relation after a long journey. Though I knew perfectly well that by this time tomorrow it would have reverted to its customary rumpled look, I was touched by Milly's efforts. In them, and in the fatted calf whose aroma floated up the stairs from the basement kitchen, I discerned a true daughter of Hilda, to whom the cherishing of 'family' was sacrosanct.

Laura was attending a University Film Club meeting, and Nathan went out not long after we returned, so it was just the three of us who sat down to a rack of lamb and mint sauce at ten o'clock. Bernard, of course, was tired and had lost interest in eating, but Millie and I did justice to our dinner.

'Are you going to write a book?' she wanted to know.

'No.' She was a person with whom you could never be

6

other than straightforward, just as with Cary straightforwardness was out of the question. 'No. I simply want to see how everything's changed, if at all. I shan't be disappointed if I find no trace of the past.'

'Trust you, uncle, to be contrary,' remarked Bernard, inserting my title to counterbalance the implied criticism.

'As long as you're not going to find it distressing,' said Milly.

'I don't think I shall, because I don't expect it to be. It was all so very long ago. It'll be partly a holiday and partly a way of wiping the slate clean. The whole period was in parenthesies to the rest of my life. I hope this trip is going to close the brackets.'

'What a good way of putting it,' said Milly, though I could see Bernard laboriously thinking through the analogy and eventually dismissing it.

'That film was on the box again the other week,' he said. '*Bridge on the River Kwai.*'

'Oh, yes?' I never knew how I was supposed to react to this, the movie that was most people's only idea of what life might have been like on the railway.

'We watched – well, we'd seen it before, but we looked again. It's terrific stuff. Guinness is immaculate.'

'Yes.'

'What do you think – forgive me if I've asked this before – about the authenticity? Of that film?'

I didn't want to have this conversation, especially with Bernard. I suddenly wished that I had never mentioned my destination, nor the purpose of my trip. I had confirmed them in their opinion that my war experiences were the most important and influential area of my life. Whereas in fact, as I had tried to explain, they had been downgraded in every successive prioritisation, and my intention now was to expunge their memory once and for all. There was one tiny area which still nagged like an old injury, but it had absolutely nothing to do with my experience of captivity as they would understand it.

'. . . be interested to hear it from the horse's mouth,' Bernard was saying. 'I mean it struck me as a pretty convincing picture of the conditions and so on, but one is constantly reading about books and films and whatnot which have enraged the people concerned with their lack of accuracy.'

'The film's fine,' I said. 'After all, it's drama, and works perfectly well as such.'

'That's a weasel answer if ever I heard one,' boomed Bernard. His voice had become very loud and jovial, as it did when I was annoying him. 'I want to know whether it was truthful, accurate. For instance, that Guinness character: a complete headcase, just courting trouble. I mean, did you ever meet anyone like that?'

This at least I could answer honestly. 'Oh yes,' I said. 'I knew someone exactly like that.'


Bernard went up to bed first, and Milly and I had a last cup of tea in the kitchen. Tea at all times, a throwback to our north country origins. I suspect Milly liked having me there to share this pot with her. I was sure Bernard only drank tea at four in the afternoon. What I most wanted to hear from Milly was why she had married Bernard. But I was never going to ask, partly because it would have seemed rude and partly because she would have lied anyway, out of loyalty, and I didn't want to see her lie.

'Is there anything you specially want to do while you're with us?' she asked. 'Three days is such a short time. I didn't want to organise anything because that can be so exhausting, other people's friends and so on.'

'Quite right,' I said. 'And you mustn't worry about me. I shall very probably take myself off to an exhibition or two, and it would be nice if I could treat you and Bernard to a show.'

'Oh, we couldn't – you mustn't feel you have to – it's so lovely to see you.'

'Please, I'd like to. I don't see you often, and I'm always staying here. It's the least I can do.'

She blushed. She was forty-four and could still blush. She said: 'You mustn't take this amiss, but I feel I know you well enough to tell you – Bernard is not good at the theatre these days.'

I remembered when we'd been to see *42nd Street* on my last visit. The endless fidgeting, the pulling at the collar, the high colour. Of course I remembered.

'And he works so late,' she went on. 'But if it's all right with you – I'd love to come.'

'I don't like to exclude Bernard,' I said, knowing I was now quite safe. 'Perhaps we could make it dinner somewhere nice instead?'

She shook her head. 'I really think,' she said in her honest, earnest way, 'that he'd prefer to be counted out during the week. He won't be in the least offended.'

I believed her. As it turned out he was going to be in Birmingham on my second night, the night of our planned excursion, so no possible taint of offence could cling to our going without him.

It was Nathan's night to wait on tables at a place called American Pie on Haverstock Hill. He suggested we might care to eat there before going into the West End, pointing out that it would be 'right up my street', but I knew too well about English representations of all-American food and declined politely. He wasn't a bad boy under the Gothic hair and musty-smelling black clothing. I detected the beginnings of an open mind.

Laura said that as we were going to be out we wouldn't mind her having some friends in. By the look on Milly's face I was sure Laura didn't usually ask – everyone had been put on stand-by for my benefit.

'Clear up after yourselves if you eat and drink,' said Milly, 'so we don't get back to World War Three.'

We took a taxi, though Milly deprecated the extravagance. I told her she was worth it just to see her blush again. She was looking very pretty, made up and wearing a bright blue Indian kind of dress with a quilted, beaded bodice and red and blue flat shoes. She didn't have Hilda's big, raw-boned figure, she was short and inclined to cushiony curves, but I could see Hilda's look around the eyes, and Hilda, too, in the slightly nervous way she settled her shoulders and clasped her hands as we sat in the back of the taxi.

'This is wonderful,' she said. 'What fun.' And then: 'What a shame Bernard couldn't come with us.'

I wanted to grab her and tell her it wasn't a shame at all but a blessing for which we should both be profoundly grateful. Instead of which I said never mind, there was always another time.

We saw *Lettice and Lovage* – her choice – and enjoyed it. The performances of the two Margarets proved once again that the British are being truthful, not conceited, when they say they have the best actors. The evening rose above its attendant discomforts – cramped seats, stuffy atmosphere, shortage of lavatories and inadequate bar facilities. Not to mention the exorbitant price of tickets in the stalls, which I made light of for Milly's sake but which nonetheless make the contest between live theatre and a good evening on TV an extremely close-run thing.

Feeling I'd been dismissive of Nathan's invitation, we looked in on American Pie on the way back – it was only a couple of hundred yards from Thurlow Road – but there was no bar there and Nathan told us it was more than his job was worth to serve us coffee or drinks only at a table, so we paid the cabbie and walked home.

The chitter and bump of modern pop music and the squawk of girls' voices came from the direction of the sitting room. I don't understand the protocol of living with grown-up children, but Milly simply opened the door and said, 'Hallo girls, we're back.'

The room was full of smoke and there were wine bottles, ashtrays, coffee mugs and glasses all over the place. This was *after* clearing up? It looked a mess to me, but Milly didn't comment on it. She presumably knew that there was a sink full of dirty crockery down in the kitchen.

She introduced me, and they chorused 'Hallo', without getting up. Except for Laura, who bounced to her feet – a big, heavy-set girl like her father – and turned down the music.

'Let me introduce,' she said, pointing at each of the four girls as she spoke. 'This is Tara, Jan, Sandy and Lou, who are in my year at Bedford . . . '

I took in a healthy-looking blonde, two indeterminate frizzy heads and a small brunette. I shook hands with them, which they seemed to find quaint but not too terrible. Milly went off to make tea.

'Good play?' asked Laura.

'Very good. Wonderful performance. Makes it worth-while – just – going to the theatre.'

'Well it's very sweet of you. Mum will have enjoyed it,' said Laura comfortably, as though she were the parent. Knowing I was *de trop* I lifted a hand and made to leave, but Laura said: 'I told them where you were off to. Jan's grandfather was on the railway, actually.'

'Really, is that so?' I turned back and prepared to exchange notes on a topic which could be of no possible interest to the girl concerned and of which I'd had enough from Bernard. But she was a polite child. 'I hear you're a writer, too,' she said. 'That's something I'd like to do.'

The kettle couldn't boil soon enough for me.


Milly had driven me to the airport for the second leg of my journey. It was a late evening flight, Nathan was once again on duty at American Pie and Bernard had paperwork. So it was just the two of us, which was nice.

'*Au revoir,*' Bernard had said. '*Non illegitimi!*' And they say the English are no good at languages . . .

But I was genuinely sorry to say goodbye to Milly. We both had tears in our eyes as we hugged each other.

'You will try and come and see us on your way back as well?' she asked. 'We'd all love you to.' She was touchingly anxious to include the whole, largely indifferent tribe in the expression of her own warm feelings.

'We'll see,' I said, not wanting to be too brutal but picturing Cary with the lodger. 'You never know.'

I was travelling Singapore Airlines. The sight of the slender hostesses in their long batik gowns and the orchid blossom pinned to the back of every seat, yea, even in cattle-class, set off a ripple of anticipation in me. I resented and resisted it, but it would not be stifled. It wasn't only the excitement of travel, of going on vacation. It was also fear. In the anonymity of my non-smoking seat I could afford finally to confront the fact: I was going back.

I was still shaken by my conversation with Laura's friend. Having been pushed unwillingly into the limelight, she had been delightful, as I might have expected. But her grandfather, for Christ's sake . . . How old that made him sound. 'They shall not grow old as we that are left grow old'. Well, no, but I'd never been a grandfather and that somehow made me younger. The POW Association, with which I had no truck, was full of grandfathers, even great-grandfathers. Their succeeding generations made them cling to the past because that was their identity. I'd never had to do that.

He died of cholera, she told me earnestly. A terrible death, she added, as if I didn't know.

Her name was Janice Dimitos, her father was Greek but her parents were divorced, she told me. She lived with her mother in Camden Town. She was really interested in the railway. It wasn't her fault. What could she possibly know? What could she even guess at?

*

Now it was the end of the trip, and here was John
Oliphant arriving, red-faced and sweating profusely, at
my vantage point overlooking the Kedron Valley and the
Golden Gate.

He was at once set upon by two young men with packs
of bookmarks. He shuffled sideways like a crab, waving
both his hands palm outwards. But he made the mistake
of smiling. They smiled back, copying his sideways walk
and brandishing the bookmarks. The backs of his legs
struck the low wall and he staggered and would very
probably have fallen over if one of the young men hadn't
grabbed his arm. He laughed. They laughed. They again
waved the bookmarks. He bought two packs, one from
each of them, and then sat down heavily, fanning himself
with his hat.

The rest of the group were still listening to the Holy
Man of Bristol.

I had the opportunity. I sure as hell had the motive. And
– who knows? – the means might present itself.

I walked over to him, cool in the heat.

'John Oliphant?' I asked. He looked up in that open,
naive way of his, face like country ham, eyes of cornflower
blue. He can't have worn the hat all the time: the top of his
head was peeling.

'Remember me?' I asked.

# CHAPTER TWO

# *1929*

'Please, Butler . . . ' Tillotson's voice was winsomely beseeching. 'Please may I not have quite so much?'

Butler paused, a plate in one hand, a ladleful of mutton stew in the other, and fastened a cool stare on Tillotson. Both were conscious of the Dickensian flavour of the exchange. The smaller boys along the table smirked openly. The older ones affected a lofty boredom but all were paying close attention. These were the confrontations that made school life worthwhile.

Butler lowered the ladle. 'Not quite so much? Not quite so much as what?'

Tillotson's eyes grew rounder and more limpid. 'Not quite so much as the others, Butler. Please.'

Someone let out a laugh between compressed lips, with a farting sound. Butler did not blink.

'Aren't you well, Tillotson?'

'Yes, Butler.'

'Yes, you're not well, or yes you are well?'

'I'm well, thank you.'

'In that case you should eat.'

'*Please*, Butler.'

This drew a hiss of scandalised delight from the listeners. Tillotson was actually, openly tarting. Serving spoons prodded blindly at the parsnips and mashed potatoes as eyes flicked from one end of the table to the other.

In the babel of Hall this confrontation had created its own island of hush.

Butler picked up the ladle once more, dolloped stew onto the plate, sent it on its way and helped himself. Then, taking potato from the fifth-former on his left, he remarked, almost casually, 'You eat that, Tillotson. Or you eat nothing, and go to Matron's room.'

He did not look at the younger boy, but took some parsnips and lifted his knife and fork, the cue for everyone else to do the same. Amid the squeak and scrape of cutlery Tillotson sat quite still, staring up the table at Butler. Butler did not appear to notice the stare, and even began a conversation with the fifth-former.

The stew was eaten: tension mounted. Except for Butler, no one at the table was talking. Tillotson's face had assumed an expression of tremulous hauteur, unique to him. His audience expected and enjoyed it. Butler was an adversary worthy of Tillotson's steel: a monitor, rugger captain, a lyrical tenor the memory of whose Macheath still sent shivers down the spine. More flamboyant than Tillotson and less subtle: a leader of men, not an *agent provocateur*. This was the sweep of the broadsword against the glitter of the flick knife.

Now Tillotson's cheeks were brushed with pink and his eyes glistened. He glanced down at the greyish meat, the congealing gravy patterned with glaucous blobs of fat and barley. The audience held its collective breath while squashing down potato with forks. Butler continued to converse, but it was clear from his over-deliberate manner that he was aware of what was going on.

Moving his chair back carefully Tillotson stood up. Butler looked at him, eyebrows raised.

'If you'll excuse me, Butler, I think I will go and see Matron.'

Butler nodded and looked away. Tillotson left Hall,

15

weaving between the noisy tables with the merest suggestion of fetching (and entirely bogus) martyrdom in his erect carriage and gracefully uptilted chin.

Butler said: 'Would anyone like Tillotson's helping before it gets cold?'

From the head of his less auspiciously placed table in the far corner of Hall, Jumbo caught Tillotson's departure from the corner of his eye and then, by twisting round and pretending to check the clock above the platform, he saw too the expression of well-being on Butler's face.

He turned back, pulling at his jacket, hoping none of the younger boys had guessed what he was looking at. But they were talking amongst themselves, not in the least interested in him. Or so he thought.

'Excuse me, Oliphant.'

'Yes, Carter?'

'What d'you think's the matter with Tillotson?'

'Um – nothing. That is, I've no idea. Get on with your lunch.'

When lunch was finished, Jumbo found Butler out in the crowded corridor regaling a couple of cronies with the Tillotson incident.

' . . . called his bluff! He needs bringing into line. He's become completely shameless.'

Birch and Carradine laughed loudly, heads thrown back, hands in pockets – like roosters crowing triumphantly, thought Jumbo as he approached. Butler acknowledged his arrival with a glance. Though Jumbo was the taller, he always felt dwarfed by Butler's more powerful physical presence.

'And speaking of shamelessness,' said Carradine, 'there she is. The ice maiden of the trolley.'

All three laughed again, this time a libidinous chuckle at

16

the back of the throat. Jumbo didn't join in, though he did look in the same direction.

The girl was inside Hall with her back to them, stacking the white china bowls from which date puddings had been eaten. Jumbo found something touching and vulnerable in her uniformed back view as she went about her tasks: collecting up the spoons in one hand, scraping the leftover bits of hard date and custard skin into a metal serving dish, bending to put the pyrex custard jugs on the lowest tier of the wooden trolley.

'Oh yes,' said Butler on a long exhalation of breath, *sotto voce* but not *sotto* enough in Jumbo's opinion. 'I do like her, most awfully . . .'

If the girl had heard she showed no sign of it. She moved to the end of the trolley in order to push it further along the table. She seemed older than any of them but then girls of that class often did, Jumbo noticed, just as their mothers seemed old women next to one's own mother. She had a full, short-waisted figure, the antithesis of the languid androgynous pageboy of high fashion. In middle age she would become a cottage loaf but now even in a shapeless linen overall she was almost indecently alluring. Her face, beneath the kitchen maid's cap that squashed her dark curly bob over her heavy eyebrows, was olive-skinned and round-chinned. There was the merest hint of dark down on her top lip and, to the right of the central indentation a mole.

She seemed not to notice them. Her eyes moved uninterestedly from table to trolley and back as she did her work.

So when, quite unexpectedly, she did glance up and caught Jumbo's eye he blushed hotly. Glancing round he was dismayed to discover that he was standing there on his own, the others having moved off along the corridor. As he began to hurry after them he distinctly saw a small, knowing smile appear on the girl's face.

Birch had gone, but Carradine and Butler were still in

17

animated discussion as he joined them. They paused at the side door where they would part company to change for games: Butler and Jumbo were in Summerville House, across the court, Carradine in Hartfield, between Big School and the town.

'I bet you couldn't,' said Carradine.

'I take exception to that!'

'Wouldn't, then. No, couldn't! I'm sorry – nothing personal, you understand, but there's things like where and when to consider. And what if she won't play ball?'

'She will. That sort always do.'

Carradine looked supercilious. 'The voice of experience?'

'Observation.'

Jumbo looked from one to the other. 'What are we talking about?'

Butler wagged a finger in his face. 'Nothing to trouble your innocent little head about.'

'Butler's going to have his wicked way with yon serving wench,' said Carradine sarcastically.

Butler grinned and unexpectedly put an arm across Jumbo's shoulders, so that he felt himself to be implicated. He was both flattered and embarrassed.

'She has got a name, you know,' said Butler. 'She's called Phyllis. I heard the Harpy shouting at her the other day.'

'Phyllis . . . ' breathed Carradine in mock rapture. 'Phyllis, be mine . . .!'

Jumbo was acutely uncomfortable. 'You're not actually – going to – are you?' he asked, knowing at once he had laid himself wide open to ridicule.

'Going to?' said Butler, removing the arm from across Jumbo's shoulders and standing off a little. 'Going to what?'

'Well – you know. With that girl.'

'What girl?'

'Come off it!' Jumbo squirmed. He jerked his head backwards. 'That one.'

18

'Oh,' said Carradine, 'he means Phyllis.'

'But what can the rest of it mean?' asked Butler, with a puzzled expression. 'Sorry old chap, no understandee question.'

'Never mind,' mumbled Jumbo.

The gardener's boy, Mick, who was puttiing bulbs in the round border, watched Butler and Oliphant crossing the court in the early autumn sunshine. Crouched on the grass in green overalls, with a cap shading his eyes and hands brown with earth, he was as good as invisible to them as they strode by, their tall figures framed by the elegant façade of Big School with its honey-coloured stone and mullioned windows.

Mick didn't care about being invisible. He saw it as an advantage that he could observe unnoticed. He didn't imagine they were bad blokes, just different. But he was curious. He himself was going on sixteen and had been earning his living for three years. Even before that, when he'd been suffering at the hands of Mr Plumtree at the local Mixed Junior, he'd been doing a paper round, cleaning boots and shoes and delivering groceries in the evenings and at weekends. And yet here were these two who must be what, seventeen? eighteen? – he could tell by their coloured waistcoats – and they were still at school! You could hardly credit it. What did they do all day, for crying out loud? And it wasn't as if they were runty or backward. They were great well set-up blokes with booming voices and confident manners. How they must hate it, being cooped up here with a bunch of crackpot schoolteachers and not a girl in sight. Mick shook his head and pressed another bulb into the soil with his thumb. He grinned to himself. Almost no girl in sight.

As it happened Mick was wrong about being invisible.

19

Jumbo Oliphant was often conscious of the gardener's boy watching them. Like Butler, he was someone you noticed. What was more he had a tattoo on his neck, a pair of slanting yellow eyes. So he seemed to be watching you twice.

Phyllis was surprised when one of the senior boys, the one with the black hair and funny dark eyes, came up to her as she was leaving after tea. The boys had two teas, one of bread and jam and occasionally cake at four o'clock, the other of meat, veg and pudding at seven o'clock. Between the two Phyllis and the other kitchen staff had their own single tea, which could be taken in the school kitchen or at home. Mostly she opted for staying at school where the food – especially the puddings – appealed to her. But about once a week she went home so she could look at the shops on the way, buy a few sweets. She didn't always choose the same day: the boy must have been looking out for her.

He ran up from behind and began walking alongside her as she headed down the side path that ran between the school's tradesmen's entrance and the main road where she caught her bus to the high street. To begin with he kept his hands in his pockets. They were supposed to be gentlemen but they didn't have gentlemen's manners.

'Phyllis – I hope you don't mind if I call you that.'

'It's my name.'

'Yes.' He walked a few more paces in silence. She was not discomfited by him. She knew what he was after, what they were all after. She could feel their eyes, hot and greedy, resting on her as she filled water jugs and scraped plates. She also knew they could be caned for what they were thinking, and expelled if they ever tried it. This boy was breaking the rules just by being here, so she didn't encourage him. But she didn't send him packing either. He was good-looking and she admired his cheek in a way.

She'd heard some peculiar things about the boys in these big posh schools, so it was nice to know some of them were quite normal.

'My name's Alan, by the way,' he said. Now he took his hands from his pockets and held out the right one. She didn't take it.

'Hallo.'

He didn't seem put out. 'I wondered,' he went on, 'if perhaps we could meet some time. One evening.'

'I don't mind,' she said. 'But you're not allowed to.'

'Don't worry, I'll see to that.' If she'd hoped to crush him by the reference to school rules, she hadn't succeeded. On the contrary he seemed proud of this opportunity to show his disdain for them.

'What would be a good time for you?' he asked.

They'd reached the gate to the main road, the dividing line between two worlds. There was a big gate for motor traffic, kept closed most of the time, and a little side gate for pedestrians. She went through the small gate and shut it so that it separated them.

'I'm free when we've washed up in the evenings,' she said, 'about eight-thirty.'

'Fine.' He'd been watching her mouth as she spoke. 'How about tomorrow?'

'All right.'

'Where?'

She shrugged. 'You say. You're the one who doesn't want to get caught.'

'It wouldn't be so wonderful for you, either, Phyllis. You'd get the sack.'

There was something in the use of her name, and his choice of words, which deliberately pointed up the differences between them. She wasn't having that. She began to walk away, not hurrying. What he'd said was true, but they both knew that the disgrace would be far worse for him. It was always the man's fault, in the end. Even if she lost her job she knew she could describe the reason to her

21

advantage to any prospective employer.

'Phyllis!' She glanced round and saw him vault the little gate. He ran up to her and caught her arm. 'Phyllis, come on. I just meant we both have to be careful. I don't want to get you into trouble.'

She allowed herself the slightest Giaconda smile; he seemed blissfully unaware of any double meaning. 'I'm glad to hear it.'

'So where?' he asked impatiently.

'What about the woods down behind the greenhouses?'

'Yes, I know where you mean. So it's there at eight-thirty tomorrow.'

'I'll do my best.'

' 'Night, Phyllis.'

By the time Phyllis joined the queue at the bus stop she had relegated this exchange to no more than a possible diversion after the tedium of washing up. Only possible, because she didn't think the boy would stick to the arrangement when it came down to it. She took a chocolate-covered caramel from her bag and popped it in her mouth.


Butler, having scarcely broken sweat on his sprint up the side path, collected his books and arrived only ten minutes late outside the third form classroom where he was due to supervise prep. A cheerful hubbub came from the other side of the door. He wiped the delighted grin from his face, assumed an expression of lofty severity and entered.

'Will you stop this infernal racket?' he thundered, and was rewarded by a swift hush followed by the scraping of chairs and creak of desk lids as books were taken out.

He kept them subdued with a threatening glare for a minute or two, then opened his copy of Cicero's *In Verrem* and his notebook. He studied the Latin text briefly, his eye alighting on the sentence: 'The scars on his back were not those of battle, but of women's nails.'

22

In his notebook, Butler wrote: 'Four weeks from now, Carradine will owe me five quid.'

Mick saw Phyllis in the bus queue as he raked up broken branches at a point where the school wall was quite low. He leaned the rake on the wheelbarrow and removed his cap, wiping his hands and face on it before throwing it on top of the pile of twigs. He leaned over the wall.

'Hey!'

She glanced round, her expression of surprise changing to one of amusement and delight. 'Hallo!'

'Come over here!'

She bridled. 'I don't want to lose my place, do I?'

'Which is more important, a bus or a kiss?'

She wasn't a blusher but her sallow skin darkened slightly. The four other people in the queue maintained a stony impassivity. She drew her thick black brows together and shook her head, but she was smiling.

'Come on,' he wheedled. 'Or I'll come over there.'

'Oh – you . . . '

She left the queue and came over to the wall. At once he grabbed the back of her neck and planted a kiss on her big, soft mouth which opened obligingly. She tasted of toffee and chocolate. Round the side of her head he caught the eye of one of the women at the bus stop, who was watching with fascinated disapproval. He winked.

'Cheeky young blighter!' The woman looked at the others for the endorsement they were too craven to give. 'Did you see that? I'll report you!'

'Bus is coming,' said a man with obvious relief.

Phyllis broke away from Mick. 'I must go.'

'See you soon, cutie-pie!' he called.

'Not if I see you first!'

She joined the queue and he watched her choice back view disappear up the stairs to the top deck as the bus moved away.

Mick went back to the wheelbarrow, put on his cap and continued raking, whistling as he did so.

Butler and Jumbo were making cocoa in the kitchen of Summerville. It was eleven o'clock at night and both boys were in their dressing gowns. The house – a Victorian villa purchased by the school some ten years before, shortly after the Armistice – was quiet except for the rustles and squeaks of after-lights-out conversation and a distant rumble as Stanhope, the house master, ran himself a bath.

'It's only a bit of fun,' said Butler. 'But I'd like to wipe the fatuous smile off Carradine's face.'

'Yes.' Jumbo agreed that was a good idea. 'But it's frightfully risky, isn't it?'

'It's damned risky, but where would be the fun if it wasn't?'

'I suppose so.'

Jumbo frowned as he moved the cocoa skin to the side of the cup with his finger. There was something he was dying to ask Butler, but he couldn't conceive of the conversational opening that would allow such a question.

He licked his finger.

'How will Carradine know you've done it? I mean, what proof will there be?'

Butler chuckled. 'In mediaeval times, Oliphant, you'd have been one of the family elders waiting outside the bedchamber to see the bloodstained sheet. Isn't a gentleman's word good enough?'

'Well, it would be for me, of course, but I don't know . . . '

'About Carradine? You're right.' Butler put his cup on the floor and swung his legs, ankles crossed, on to the kitchen table. 'I'll tell you one thing, though: there won't be any blood. We're neither of us novices. So perhaps we will need some objective proof . . . '

He placed his fingers together and tapped them against

his chin, his expression thoughtful. Jumbo supposed he'd been given the answer to his unspoken question. Or was it just bravado? His own world was so utterly divorced from the one where men and women met, and made assignations and got up to things, that he had no yardstick by which to judge the truth of Butler's statement. Certainly Butler was good-looking, bold and accomplished. He was a chap who drew the eye and inspired confidence and admiration. And these were, presumably, qualities which attracted the opposite sex. So it was probably true.

If Jumbo detected a streak of unsound judgement in his friend he did not condemn it. It was, in all probability, he reflected ruefully, this one small weakness which enabled the friendship between him and Butler to continue. Butler needed a trusting, trustworthy acolyte, and he, Jumbo Oliphant, was it.

'Tell you what,' said Butler now. 'You could provide the proof.'

'Me?'

'Yes.' Butler looked at him speculatively. 'You're the very man for the job. Impeccable integrity and that kind of thing. Father a man of the cloth, ambitions in that direction yourself, unsullied school record – anyone would believe you!'

'Believe me?' Jumbo experienced a horrid sinking feeling.

'If you said the deed was done.'

'Well – but how – how would I know?'

Butler swung his legs off the table and leaned forward keenly. 'You could act as my witness.'

Jumbo was aghast. 'You mean – watch?'

'There's no need to make it sound so disgusting. Not watch exactly, but observe. At a respectable distance.'

Jumbo closed his eyes. Gulped at the dry blockage in his throat. 'I couldn't. I honestly couldn't.'

From upstairs came the guttural snarl of water running

away as Stanhope emerged from the bathroom. Butler stood up, retrieved his cup from the floor and took the other from Jumbo. Standing over him, he said: 'Nonsense! Of course you could. Just a small favour for a friend. It won't be for a few weeks anyway. She'll need a bit of warming up.'

'No,' said Jumbo. 'I couldn't.'


Phyllis didn't get to the woods until twenty to nine. This was because she didn't take the tryst with the schoolboy (she'd forgotten his name) very seriously, and had no intention of hanging about. If he wasn't there waiting for her she would go straight home.

As it was he outflanked her by running up as she was walking past the big greenhouse and falling into step beside her as he'd done the day before.

'Hallo, Phyllis.'

'Hallo.'

'Do you know this place? Where shall we go?'

'Through here.'

She led the way in amongst the trees. There were some wild rhododendrons growing here which had reached a terrific size in their struggle to reach the light. In the dark their leaves gleamed slightly, but they made a good screen.

She turned to face him. 'Well, here we are then.'

'Come here, Phyllis.'

She allowed him nothing. Her elbows, knees and lips might have been on steel springs for all the access they permitted. She let him kiss and squeeze her, that was it.

But she wasn't unmoved by him, either. He was taller and stronger than what she was used to, when he crushed her against him her back and neck arched slightly, it made her think of Valentino in *The Sheikh*. And he was keen, really keen and eager. You could tell he hadn't been near a girl in weeks, his breath came short and shallow and he bulged against her stomach as though he'd burst. She felt a little ashamed of having led him on, but then who had started it? Phyllis wasn't 'easy', but her life was dull, and this was something different. It gave her a sense of power.

'Oh, Phyllis . . . ' he groaned into her neck (she was backed up against a beech tree at this moment), 'you're so wonderful . . . 6'

After about a quarter of an hour she pushed him away and straightened her coat and hat.

'I've got to go.'

'Oh, must you?'

'And you, or we'll both be in trouble.'

He glanced at his watch. 'I suppose you're right.'

They left the wood. There was a moon and the greenhouse reflected its still, white eye.

'Can we meet again soon?' he asked.

Without really knowing why, she said, 'Yes.'


Like a disaffected wife, Jumbo pretended to be busy when he heard Butler's footsteps approaching the study. He bent over his essay on the Romantic Poets, one hand thrust into his hair, the other tapping his pen on the page. There was no one else in the room. The other two, Pinker and Chatwin, had gone to choir practice. Their fag had been in earlier to make up the fire but it had burned down and was now almost out, just a heap of grey lumps and flakes veined with red.

The door opened and closed and Butler walked over and sat down on the floor near the fender. Rather to Jumbo's surprise he didn't say anything, but sat with his arms wrapped round his legs and his cheek resting on his knees, face averted.

Feeling that his silence might appear churlish, Jumbo put down his pen and said: 'So how did it go?'

Butler's voice was muffled. 'You make it sound like a visit to the dentist.'

27

'I didn't mean to.' Jumbo rephrased his enquiry: 'What was she like?'

Butler heaved a sigh. 'Marvellous. Wonderful. Out of this world.'

Jumbo was debating whether or not this was the reply of a sexual sophisticate when Butler suddenly unrolled like a length of a carpet and lay flat on his back, a broad grin wreathing his lips.

'Look at me!' he said. 'I'm bloody huge!'

October drew on and the half-term holiday loomed. Carradine became more than usually sarcastic.

'No joy as yet?' he enquired as they walked from chapel to Big School one cold, wet morning.

'Plenty of joy,' replied Butler. 'Any day now you'll owe me a fiver.'

'Hm,' said Carradine. 'I very much doubt it. For one thing it's getting a bit chilly for larking about in the woods with your nethers uncovered, and for another if you disappear to London for a week the girl's going to lose interest.'

Butler laughed. 'Nonsense. Haven't you heard of absence making the heart grow fonder?'

'Yes,' said Carradine sardonically. 'And out of sight is out of mind.'

'Fine. Before half term, then.'

'And how exactly will I know?'

'Oliphant will tell you.'

Carradine looked at Jumbo in his usual way, as though he'd only just noticed him. He asked the question Jumbo most dreaded.

'And how will he know?'

At this stage Jumbo would have liked the stone flags to open and swallow him up. He was tongue-tied, but Butler spoke for him. 'He will act as an impartial witness.'

Carradine let out a gasp of cruelly incredulous laughter.

'Will he, by Jove!'

'Yes, I jolly well will!' said Jumbo, blushing fiercely.

'I can't think of anyone,' said Butler, 'of more spotless reputation.'

'That's true,' said Carradine witheringly. 'Very well. But I shall want chapter and verse, mind, Oliphant. Where, when, for how long, and satisfaction on both sides.' Jumbo nodded wretchedly. Carradine put his mouth close to Jumbo's ear and added in a stage whisper: 'After all, there are places in London where people pay good money to watch that sort of thing.'

'Toad,' remarked Butler carelessly, wandering off.


Phyllis was annoyed to find that she was waiting for Alan (as she'd begun reluctantly to call him) on the Friday before half term. It was the second time it had happened, and she was afraid it betrayed her keenness.

What had begun as mere condescension on her part had turned into an addiction. She couldn't wait for their twice-weekly meetings. Though she wouldn't have used the exact words, he was so handsome and ardent, and besought her so passionately to give him what he wanted – she felt queenly and powerful. And she thought she might very well . . . perhaps tonight. Why not?

'Phyl! Oi, Phyl!'

She turned, smiling, in the direction of Mick's thick, urgent whisper. 'What are you doing here?'

'I was going to ask you that.' He put his arms round her and kissed her hard and expertly. His body against hers was small and taut, different from Alan's languid, limber strength. But as always there wasn't a thing she could do. With Mick, it was him that had the power.

She pulled back, gasping and laughing. 'I'm waiting for somebody.'

'Two-timing me, are you?' His teeth flashed white in the dark. He didn't give a damn.

'Yes,' she said.

'With that schoolboy?' He liked being able to call them that, even though they were bigger and richer than him.

'Yes.'

'Where is he then?'

'I don't know.'

'Maybe he's two-timing you.'

Now it was her turn to laugh. 'Go on! Who with?'

'You'd be surprised. Ways and means.'

He was referring to those things she'd heard about. It made her shudder to think of it. 'That's disgusting!'

'Mmm . . . ' He moved in on her and she could feel his right hand hitching up her skirt, strong fingers clawing at her knickers, while his left hand unbuttoned his fly. There was always a brief – very brief – moment when she heard her mother's voice invoking the hideous fate which awaited Bad Girls, but it was always too little too late and then she'd be carried away and forget.


'What if she gets fed up and goes home?' asked Jumbo anxiously, consulting his watch. 'It's a quarter to nine already.'

'She won't,' replied Butler. 'It'll do her good to wait. It'll make her worry.'

In truth it was Butler's own worry that flittered in the dark air of the gym corridor like an invisible bat. Its presence disturbed Jumbo even more than the prospect of bearing witness to whatever was to take place.

'No funking now,' Butler had warned. 'No looking away and hoping for the best. I've won this money fair and square.'

Jumbo noted the past tense. Butler's arrogance took his breath away, but he admired it because it would carry Butler through and win him his five pounds. By fair means –

'Come on,' said Butler. 'Let's go.'

30

*

It was a blustery, wet night rather than a cold one, the sky boiling with clouds and the wind thudding and hissing around the old buildings making the creeper ripple like an animal's pelt. Quite a few lights were still on in Big School – music rooms, the senior prep room, the library. The headmaster's study. Jumbo had a sudden horrifying vision of being summoned before the head to answer for this night's activities, and finding his father there wearing his most effective expression of wounded bafflement . . . For the hundredth time he asked himself what on earth he was doing here. But he knew the answer: it was exciting.

As they walked across the wet grass, away from the school buildings and towards the kitchen garden and the glimmering greenhouses, they appeared to be moving from one dimension into another. The sounds of the wind and the rain changed, and seemed to carry a message not audible in the world of lights and books and voices.

They crunched down the mossy gravel path beside the greenhouses. The trees loomed up, their tops switching and lashing against the sky, their trunks forming a dense black mass which gradually became a palisade as they got nearer. Butler's expression was sharp and watchful, like the face of a hunting fox.

They stepped into the wood. The trees closed behind them. The noise of the wind became more distant. It was like being at the bottom of a deep lake, the surface of which was choppy and turbulent. Down here it was damp, dark and still. The rhododendrons glinted in the wind-snatched moonlight. Butler put out his hand, palm backwards, to halt Jumbo, who was only too glad to comply. He would rather have been almost anywhere but here.

'I don't see anyone,' he whispered.

'Ssh.' Butler took a couple of long, stalking strides and peered forward. 'I'm pretty sure she's there.'

'What shall I do?'

31

'Give me – give me five minutes.' Jumbo caught the note of self-satisfaction. 'Then move in closer.'

Jumbo would like to have asked how long the whole exercise would take, but did not know how this would be received. Instead he simply nodded.

'Good man,' said Butler.


Butler saw Phyllis's face, a pale smudge in the dark, and was already smiling when he realised what was happening. The persistent, rhythmic sound like a record stuck on a gramophone . . . the solid black shape that obscured Phyllis's fawn belted overcoat . . . her little moaning exhalations . . . And then he could actually make out the strip of white flesh between the man's slightly sagging trousers and his jacket, and the black loops of his braces . . .

He stood quite still, unable to believe his eyes. He was shocked and outraged. He could go neither back nor forward. After what must have been a full minute he gasped: 'Phyllis!'

Equally shocked she let out a cry, and struggled to disengage herself from the man.

'Phyllis . . . ' said Butler again. Having surprised her he had a curious urge to apologise, and yet he knew he was the wronged party. The man calmly kept his back turned as he buttoned his trousers and hoisted his braces over his shoulders.

'I'm sorry, Alan,' said Phyllis in a plaintive but not particularly contrite voice. 'I thought you'd stood me up.'

Anger ballooned in him. 'You bitch!'

The man, whom Butler had so far ignored, now turned to face him. Butler saw that he wasn't a man at all but some youth or other from the town, vaguely familiar. There were some strange marks on his neck, which Butler supposed had something to do with Phyllis.

'Bitch!' he said again.

'No need for that,' said the youth. He took a cap from the pocket of his jacket and settled it on his head. His manner was insultingly complacent. 'It's what you were going to do, wasn't it?' Butler goggled, unable to reply. The youth grinned, his teeth white in his sharp little face. 'Or it's what you'd like to do. Eh?'

'How dare – ' began Butler.

The youth's face was suddenly no longer mocking but cold and menacing. He pushed it into Butler's, and Butler could smell Phyllis on his breath.

'Why don't you go back to school,' he whispered fiercely, sending small drops of spit on to Butler's cheeks, 'and put your flabby cock in some little boy's bum?'

Butler hit him then. But it was an inelegant, badly timed blow and the youth was already stepping back and managed to ride it quite easily. He chuckled and sauntered off, to be lost among the trees.

'Alan?' said Phyllis. But he couldn't bear to be there a moment longer and blundered back in the direction he had come.


The moment Butler went, Jumbo had withdrawn to a safe distance. He had no intention of watching anything. He didn't consider that his course of action was dishonourable since the whole set-up was dishonourable anyway. He had no doubt whatever that Butler would achieve his objective and win his fiver off Carradine. His job was a sinecure.

When he heard a series of gasps and angry whispers it suggested to him that things were reaching fruition. Tentatively he crept forward in time to see a figure in a light-coloured coat – Phyllis, he presumed – making off in the opposite direction. Within seconds he almost bumped into Butler who was crashing towards him. He was impressed. The whole thing had taken barely the allotted five minutes.

'Well done!' he said.

Butler stopped and peered at him. Jumbo thought he seemed confused, as if he hadn't heard him properly. He repeated his congratulations.

'Five pounds up. Carradine'll be livid.'

Butler snapped, 'Shut up, Oliphant!', and stormed off in the direction of Big School.


'Put it away. I don't want the damn money,' said Butler to Carradine next day after chapel. Jumbo was aghast.

'But Butler — '

Carradine's eyes narrowed. 'You did have her, I take it.'

'Of course he did!' exclaimed Jumbo. He looked at Butler who wore an angry, remote expression. He seemed uninterested in the whole conversation. The folded fiver protruded like a cigarette from between Carradine's fingers.

'Take the money then. I'm suitably impressed.'

'I don't want it!' Butler exploded, rounding on him. 'Can't you get it through your thick skull, Carradine? I don't want your poxy five pounds!'

He strode away. For the first and only time Carradine and Jumbo experienced mutuality of feeling.

'I can't understand it,' said Jumbo. 'He did do it.'

'Well,' said Carradine, replacing the money in his waistcoat pocket. 'Maybe he's fallen for the girl. Or maybe she wasn't happy with his performance. Better not to intrude upon private grief, hmm, Oliphant?'


Butler called along the dark dormitory: 'Tillotson! Tillotson, you're wanted.'

At the far end of the row of beds a figure sat up, fair hair on end. 'Yes, Butler?'

'Matron wants you in her room, quick sharp.'

'Yes, Butler.' Tillotson trailed down the central aisle,

34

yawning as he tied his dressing gown cord.

'Come along,' said Butler, one hand lightly on Tillotson's shoulder. 'Get a move on.'

'Yes, Butler,' said Tillotson.

# CHAPTER THREE

# 1989

It was as a wide-eyed stranger that I'd come to Singapore the first time, and I was still wide-eyed when I returned some three weeks before my chance encounter with John Oliphant on the Mount of Olives.

It was eleven o'clock at night as we banked steeply over the harbour and the pilot pointed out to us, as though we were children, the constellations of lights down below.

'Still one of the busiest harbours in the world,' he remarked. 'But we're heading for Changi Airport at the eastern tip of the island . . . ' He said this in case we might seriously have supposed we were to land, like a flying boat, on the water. But the word 'Changi' gave me a jolt. I looked round at my fellow passengers. Apart from a few children, almost all wore expressions of weary indifference. Changi had no resonance for them.

In accordance with precedent my bag was among the last to come through. I could see the Chinaman from the tour company standing thirty yards away in the crowded concourse holding a strip of card with my name on it. When I waved he averted his head as if he hadn't seen me.

When I eventually got through, and identified myself, he was civil and distant. He relieved me of my bag (though I could have given him six inches and a stone and a half), and led me down the escalator to the main entrance.

Outside the glass doors the tropical heat flopped on to us like a warm, damp towel and I began to sweat as though I'd been switched on.

We waited with a crumpled and unhappy-looking young couple for the company minibus. On the other side of the slip road was the usual vast, segmented airport car park, full to capacity. It was hard to believe that only a mile or two from where I stood now was the jungle peninsula where we'd been herded together, tens of thousands of us, the embarrassingly extensive spoils of the IJA's victory in Singapore.

We climbed aboard the bus and the tour representative gave our names, and those of our destinations, to the driver. The young couple, who were British, were staying at a very much smarter establishment than I could afford, courtesy of a Singapore Airlines stopover.

'Oh, my God,' said the young woman, fanning herself with her passport, 'I hope they'll have efficient air conditioning.'

'Of course they will,' replied her partner, a tad pettishly, aware of me sitting in the back. 'This is the tropics.'

We drove along a broad boulevard, bordered with neatly spaced palms garlanded with lights. Could this be the East Coast Road, along which we had marched, staggered or been carried according to our condition? It was unrecognisable. Far off to the left, beyond a wide strip of beach, also palm-dotted, I could just make out the gleam of the ocean, pushed back and kept at a distance by a brisk bout of land reclamation which (my inflight magazine had enthused) had given the island greatly increased leisure facilities and Changi airport itself. If I had hoped for a pang of perverted nostalgia, I was so far disappointed.

'It's like Florida,' commented the young man.

Our Chinese driver nodded enthusiastically. 'All government money,' he assured us. 'Millions of dollars to make a tourist paradise.'

'You've never been to Florida,' said the girl.

'I have,' I said, and they both glanced round, startled, as though I'd invited them to admire my member. 'And it is.'

'Soon everywhere will be the same,' said the young man comfortably.

We drove on. My companions were dropped off at a hotel near the city centre, the front of which was pagoda shaped. We entered the drive and circumnavigated an elaborate fountain consisting of a huge, pop-eyed, blubber-lipped fish with ornate fins, balancing on its chin and contriving at the same time to spout water upwards in a perpendicular column. At either side of the shallow flight of steps which fanned out from the glass acreage of the hotel's main entrance stood a guard of honour of equally hypothyroid stone dogs.

'Oh!' cried the young woman. 'How gorgeous!'

Her husband caught my eye, man to man. 'As long as you're happy.'

'The best hotel on the island,' declared the driver.

A slender, liquorice-eyed young Malay in green and gold livery skimmed down the steps as though these were the first guests he'd seen all day. Our driver jumped out and went to the back to fetch cases. The English couple were about to follow suit – in fact he was already stooped awkwardly in the doorway of the bus – when they realised I was not accompanying them and therefore presented no further social threat.

'Are you not staying here then?' he asked.

I replied that I wasn't.

'Not a stopover – I mean,' he added playfully, 'we could never rise to this.'

I confirmed that I was not a guest of Singapore Airlines.

'On holiday?'

Not exactly, I said.

'Combining business with pleasure . . . ?'

I allowed 'you could describe it like that,' and ignored his naively collusive smirk.

'Come on, darling.' His wife ushered him down the steps. 'Well, bye bye, then,' she said to me, 'and have a super stay.'

He ducked his head back in. 'Yes. All the best.'

I thanked them, and watched as the Malay porter carried their bags up the steps and they followed with quite a spring in their stride as they headed for a night of gilded, air-conditioned luxury.

The driver jumped back in, gunned smartly round the spouting fish and headed north up the main road. My hotel was in Bukit Timah Road. But for that I'd have had no idea of our whereabouts. Bukit Timah had been a village, I seemed to remember, but I could not believe there were any villages left in this 'tourist paradise'.

The driver, glancing at me in his rear-view mirror, said something.

'I beg your pardon?'

'Family hotel, your hotel. Better than that fancy place. You relax and be comfortable.'

'I'm sure I shall.'

He grinned. It didn't seem to bother him that I now knew he was two-faced and had no cause to believe a word he said. I stared out of the window. We were on a broad, two-lane highway on either side of which hotels alternated with cubist office blocks and flats. We drew up at traffic lights and suddenly I spotted, standing back from the road as if holding itself aloof from its *arriviste* neighbours, a big old colonial-style house with a pillared verandah and a first-floor drawing room with rattan blinds. I could see the blades of the ceiling fan slowly turning in the soft yellow light . . .

Then the lights changed and we moved off with a lurch. But I was experiencing a rush as powerful as anything I'd had from the occasional snort of recreational substances on the Upper West Side. That house had shown me the Singapore of my memory: that other country, waiting its moment in the shadows.

That night in my sparse, hermetically sealed cell of a room in the hotel for which 'family' was the charitable description, I found it hard to sleep. Jet-lagged, disoriented, dehydrated and a little homesick, I tossed and turned and consumed all the water in the carafe and the courtesy papaya. I sat cross-legged on the rough madras cotton bedspread and thought of ringing Cary. But I resisted the temptation. Let him miss me too. Lodger, forsooth.

# CHAPTER FOUR

# 1942

Jumbo read the adjutant's message in the garden on Rochester Avenue. It was couched in the usual debonair language.

'Small party of Japs landed in NW. Objective: send them packing. Useful exercise with live ammo.'

On reading this, Jumbo experienced the same profound unhappiness he had known when attending pantomimes as a child. It was scarcely credible that otherwise sensible adults could make such fools of themselves, and a source of dread that he himself might be called upon to join in. At the same time he was not bold enough – either then or now – to voice his objections.

Jumbo knew that as a soldier he was a plodder, dutiful and unimaginative. He often caught the men looking at him with a wry sympathy that said, 'Poor sod. Who'd have his job?' He would like to have replied, to have conceded that he was no great shakes and could only do his best, but naturally that was out of the question. The charade of officers and men had to be maintained, and as he stared at the adjutant's message he could have blushed for shame.

Of course there were those like Butler who managed to transcend the muddle and make-do by force of personality: soldiers of genius, or lunatics, depending on one's point of view. Jumbo knew he could never aspire to their ranks. He often thought he should have opted out altogether. Too late now, though.

Mind you, one would have had to be completely blinded by patriotism not to feel a growing unease over the past couple of weeks. The Fen Tigers had disembarked in torrential rain, the only thing which had stood between them and annihilation by Japanese bombers as they entered Singapore harbour. In what now seemed quite unaccountably high spirits they'd marched from the docks to the barracks, with the locals cheering them to the echo. But even amid the general euphoria a Chinese woman had run alongside Jumbo, waving her hands and shouting, 'Don't need troops! Need aeroplanes!'

Overcome by the noise, and the steam heat, and his first sight and smell of the tropics, Jumbo had favoured her with a polite, nervous smile. But on several occasions since then her remark had come back to him with a ghastly aptness. The crowd that thronged the pavements to greet them had obscured their view of wrecked buildings and unburied corpses. The ensuing week had demonstrated unequivocally that the enemy to whom popular mythology ascribed poor eyesight, dwarfish physique and laughably outmoded aircraft were in fact well-equipped and ruthlessly competent.

From the barracks they had made a slow and painful journey to the north coast of the island, stopping and starting beneath the ceaseless Japanese barrage, and gazing with dismay at the tide of refugees from the mainland coming in the opposite direction. Babies, chickens, grandmothers, goats and everything including the kitchen sink headed south. The faces of these people wore the look of helpless yet stolid dependency common to all refugees. Jumbo thought with dismay of what awaited them in Singapore City. The island was filling up.

They spent the next couple of days in a position overlooking the Straits of Johore. They dug trenches and set up barbed wire entanglements. At night they were bitten to pieces by mosquitoes. The sea lapped the sand with oily calm, leaving ragged bands of black weed and flotsam. Of the enemy there was no sign. Even the planes had gone quiet. Someone said the Japs were moving down through Malaya on bicycles and they laughed heartily at that. What sort of enemy launched an offensive on push-bikes? A dwarfish, myopic, poorly equipped enemy like the one that had flattened Singapore City, thought Jumbo fearfully, but he said nothing.

On the third day Jumbo's party got orders to withdraw. With their mortar, ammunition and few remaining supplies loaded on a lorry they joined the trekkers south. Jumbo sat next to the driver. Occasionally the lorry's blaring horn split the column and they got up into second gear. Then the refugees closed round them again. There was no question, Jumbo noticed, of letting the saviours of the free world have right of way . . .

Their destination was a requisitioned house, one of three of similar design situated on some rising ground on the west side of Rochester Avenue in the posh northern suburbs of the city. The Orders of Evacuation were stuck to one of the gateposts. Oliphant already had a fistful of house and car keys that had been pressed on him by agitated civilians queueing to leave at the docks, but he had no idea whose they were. In any event, this house stood open. Abandoned.

The men, fallen out, collapsed on the lawn, swearing and groaning from the heat. The lorry hissed to a juddering halt in the drive. There were trees, shade, quiet. They had the treacherous sensation of having come home.

Jumbo and the NCO, Copley, took a look round. They surveyed with silent misgivings the cycle lying on its side on the grass and the maroon doll's pram, its occupant unseasonably dressed in a knitted layette, her chubby plastic hands sticking out in front of her as if begging to be picked up. From the open garage door a hosepipe emerged, most of its coils still lying beneath their hook on the wall. The outside tap, hastily turned off, dribbled onto the concrete. Four striped swimming towels hung over the side of the first floor verandah.

'Got away in a hurry, sir,' observed Copley. 'You can't blame them.'

Inside it was the same. The place was like a giant's doll's house from which the dolls had been snatched away. Upstairs in the sitting room which gave on to the verandah the fan was still turning. An Agatha Christie lay discarded by one of the rose-patterned armchairs. Two tall glasses containing the dregs of Pimm's stood on the tiled coffee table. Ants swarmed over the sticky fruit and cucumber slices.

The bedrooms set the time of the owners' departure. The two children's beds were rumpled, drawers were half-open, the mosquito nets were down but drawn back. A stuffed toy animal, sludge-coloured, one-eared and eye-less, loved well past identification, lay on the floor between the beds and the door. Jumbo pictured a wailing child, a frantic adult, a smack. He picked up the toy and put it on a chair.

In the main bedroom the bed was undisturbed beneath its white cotton lace counterpane. The wardrobe was open. One or two garments hung drunkenly from their hangers by one shoulder, or had slipped to the floor among the ranks of shoes.

In the kitchen, the cupboards and fridge were full. They'd had instructions to leave everything strictly alone, but feeling the weight of abandoned keys in his tunic pocket Jumbo thought that was pointless. These people were not coming back.

'I think we should go ahead and use this stuff,' he said to Copley. He meant it to be a firm declaration, but could detect in his own voice his wish for Copley's endorsement.

'Quite right, sir,' said Copley kindly. 'No one else is going to.'

44

They were crossing the shady, pillared area beneath the verandah when the planes came over again.

'Bloody hell — !'

'Where did they spring from?'

The men scrambled up like picnickers surprised by thunder. But instead of the expected whine and crash of bombs, there was only paper, sheets and sheets of it, a bizarre tropical snowstorm. As the planes droned away the men picked the sheets off the grass and laughed raucously at the contents. Corporal Willard, always a big joker, slitted his eyes and drew back his top lip in a vaudeville imitation of an oriental: 'Oh Tommy, I am so lonely without you . . .!'

'That'll do,' said Jumbo. 'Right you are, men, let's get ourselves organised here.'

He and Copley detailed them off, and he picked up one of the leaflets and glanced at it. A scantily clad girl – blonde, but almond eyed – bemoaned her loneliness. A winsome urchin asked, 'When will I see my Daddy again?' A spherical Churchill mourned, 'So many brave men! All lost!'

Jumbo screwed up the piece of paper and stuffed it in his pocket. Not for the first time, he found himself unable to join in the general mirth.

The gun crew set up their mortar on the lawn between the drive and the green metal swing. Sleeping quarters were assigned. They ate a supper of tinned stew and pineapple chunks. There was a tin of forty Player's on the sideboard in the dining room and these Copley distributed, keeping some back for the next day.

Jumbo wasn't hungry. Those not on stand-to were still eating when he lit a cigarette and wandered down the drive. The broad flank of the lorry radiated the day's heat along with a faint smell of petrol and rubber. In the branches overhead birds chirruped and fluttered. Since the leaflet raid there had been no further enemy aircraft, and no more news of the Japanese advance. It was almost possible to believe that this was an ordinary evening in an affluent suburb of a cosmopolitan but essentially British city. The sound of the men's voices disguised the ominous quiet of the empty houses. Jumbo was lulled by the leafy peace. Between the gateposts he stopped and looked either way. To his right the road sloped down towards Singapore City. About a hundred yards away there was a crossroads, with traffic lights still functioning, directing non-existent traffic. To the left, the road moved gently uphill and widened, heading towards the Johore causeway. Tall, elegant coconut palms were outlined against the sky. It was like a comic-book representation of a desert island.

Theirs was the second to last house on this side of the road. Opposite the gateway where Jumbo stood was a stretch of mown grass dotted with trees, which gave way to a valley filled with lush green scrub and banana palms. On the far side of the valley the rising ground was crowned with a one-storey wooden building like a cricket pavilion, with some satellite attap huts. Not a soul was in sight, but as Jumbo gazed there was the sudden screech and crash of a monkey in the branches opposite. The sound made him jump violently.

'Tea, sir?'

Jumbo saw Copley looking round the lorry at him.

'Thanks. I'll be there in a minute, sergeant.'

'Right you are, sir.'

Jumbo turned back to the road. His heart was still stumbling and tripping. Now his cigarette, down to the stub, burned him and he dropped it.

'Damn!'

He removed his cap and wiped his forehead and hair, first with one forearm, then the other. He was running with sweat. He tried not to think of cold showers and swimming pools and ice clinking in tall glasses. But

46

instead came the image of his father's parish church at home in Tripstowe: cool and dark, the tranquillity of centuries protected by ancient grey stones; the sun just managing to poke long dusty fingers through the windows so that the stained-glass saints made a rainbow on the threadbare red carpet of the sanctuary, the silence inside intensified by the clunk and trundle of a lawn mower laboriously pushed over the tussocky grass of the churchyard . . .

What was that sound? Jumbo plunged back into the here and now. It was an engine, getting closer. And now a motorcycle appeared from the south, turning right into Rochester Avenue against a red light. Jumbo stiffened. Was this to be his nemesis – taken by Japs while daydreaming in the driveway?

But the bike was unaccompanied, and as it drew closer he saw the rider was a British officer.

'Hallo there!'

'Butler!'

The motorbike snarled and spluttered to a halt. Butler remained astride it, looking at Oliver with those queer, opaque eyes.

Jumbo beamed. 'Butler, what the devil are you doing here?'

'Came to see how the other half lives.' Butler, arms folded, peered up the driveway with exaggerated curiosity. 'Every comfort and convenience, I see.'

Jumbo felt in his tunic pocket and took out a cigarette. 'Here, have one. We found a stash of them.'

'No, thanks. Plenty back at BHQ.'

Jumbo replaced the cigarette. He was enormously pleased to see Butler. The person who had seemed so dangerous in peacetime had a curiously calming influence in war.

'So what's the score?' he asked, recognising immediately his assumption that Butler would know.

'Nips nine hundred declared, rest of the world face the

47

follow-on.'

'What makes you say that?'

Butler leaned his folded arms on the handlebars. 'I've been on a recce. Did you realise that you and your little lot are the front line?'

'No – no, I hadn't realised that.' Jumbo's stomach rolled over. 'Are you sure?'

Butler nodded. 'There are some Suffolks down the road, off to the left —' He indicated the direction from which he'd come. 'But this way —' He pointed ahead. 'After you, nothing but the Japs.'

'Well,' said Jumbo doubtfully, 'we did have a message from the adjutant — '

Butler laughed harshly. 'Didn't we all?'

'To the effect,' Jumbo ploughed on, 'that it would be nothing we couldn't cope with.' He knew how utterly ridiculous this sounded. He didn't even believe it himself. Butler bore out this view by carrying on as if he hadn't heard him.

'I imagine,' he said, 'that we shall all have to rely on the bulldog spirit to see us through. I mean, why break the habit of a lifetime?'

Jumbo remembered the reference to a 'small party'. 'How many do you think there are?'

Butler gave a deprecating shrug. 'Thousands of the bastards. Flushed with success.'

'Where are they then?'

'Search me.' Butler kick-started the bike, raising his voice to speak above it. 'Too close for comfort is my guess!' He lifted a hand and moved off, north away from the houses. And as he did so darkness enveloped him with a soft, swift hand, like a footpad.


Later, as Jumbo sat in a wicker chair on the verandah fighting off sleep and mosquitoes, he wondered where Butler had obtained the authority to go running round the roads on a civilian motorbike, doing a private recce beyond the lines and subverting messages from GHQ. He decided, with wistful admiration, that no such authority had been obtained. It was simply Butler's natural cheek. He hoped, without much expectation of fulfilment, that Butler would take reasonable care.

Butler came back just before dawn. The stuttering whine of the motorbike got the lookouts' hackles up and woke the rest of them. Jumbo stumbled out into the garden, once again sure he had missed some vital message and that his men were about to be bayoneted as they yawned and scratched. When they saw who it was their salutes were sluggish with relief. One man – Jumbo could guess which one – said quite audibly: 'Bugger me, it's an ossifer out for a bike ride, and there's us thinking we were done for.' Jumbo pretended not to have heard. Butler drank a cup of strong black tea in the kitchen. He was taut and lit up with adrenalin, putting the rest of them to shame. He looked, thought Jumbo wistfully, as though he could have fought off an invasion single-handed.

'So what did you find?'

'I take no pleasure in being proved right,' said Butler. 'There's a big contingent, about four hundred or so, no more than a couple of miles up the road. And there's thousands of them over at the reservoir, it's like a Jap holiday camp.'

'You went to the reservoir?'

'No, but I came across half a dozen Malay Volunteers who did. They've got us bottled up in a few square miles. They can afford to swim and relax. Where the hell could we go?'

Jumbo realised what he was being told: that there was no hope. He made himself face it, then gathered up his fear and rammed it back as far down his gullet as he could. He couldn't quite swallow it; it sat there in a hard lump, but at least it wasn't crawling over his face.

He ordered a general stand-to, taking control and doing his best to instil a sense of urgency without panic. The men sloughed off their heat-sodden lethargy and became tense and focused. Was it his imagination, or were they more of a unit with Butler there?'

Around mid-morning, with still no sign of the enemy, he asked: 'How long, do you reckon?'

'Depends what they've got in mind.' Butler seemed almost gleeful. Jumbo had read in novels about the pale eyes of crazed killers. Butler's eyes were very dark, with scarcely any white showing, like the eyes of a bird, or a shark.

He suppressed a shiver. 'Shouldn't you be back at BHQ?'

'Don't you think I tried? Status impossible, chum. The whole place is snarled up with danert wire. They've created a new front line, and we're in front of it.'

Butler laughed, noisily and long.


It was dawn the following day when the long-awaited attack came. By then their nerves were fraying fibre by fibre, and their eye sockets seemed to be lined with sandpaper. Jumbo had prickly heat all over his body. Hot, tired, hungry and feeling as though a colony of red ants had requisitioned his shirt, he did not think it possible to be more miserable.

The first they knew of the enemy's proximity was a volley of small arms fire from the trees on the hill opposite. It appeared they had been outflanked under cover of darkness, and were now to be toyed with. Bluffing, to disguise their isolation, they retaliated in kind, keeping the mortar quiet for the time being. Butler, perched in a fork of the tall tree between the lawn and the road, fired in occasional rapid bursts like a boy potting rabbits in a field. As far as they knew they hit no one. Each side was firing blind at the other. Butler presented the most obvious target, but his reckless approach seemed to encourage the men so Jumbo made no comment. Besides, Butler was a fellow officer.

That evening, food was carefully rationed. They eked out a couple of tins of ham and some canned peaches, and Copley dished out the remaining cigarettes. Water was still on tap, but Jumbo rationed it to a pint and a half per man per day. The grim warnings of his RSM in training rang in his ears.

'Can I ask why?' asked Butler, running the kitchen tap and slapping cold water on his face.

'Well . . . ' Jumbo began to wonder why. 'To acclimatise them for possible future deprivation.'

'Ah, I see.' Butler's face was expressionless, but Jumbo could not escape the impression he was being laughed at.


For thirty-six hours they survived without casualties, not counting one man fallen from a tree, another slightly grazed by a bullet ricocheting off the side of the lorry and a third cut on the lid of a tin. But towards the end of the second day the enemy fire intensified. Perhaps they realised they were dealing with an isolated group. One man was shot dead and a second, Staynes, wounded in the arm severely enough to warrant his removal to the Regimental Aid Post. The RAP, as Butler pointed out, was in Gregory Road about half a mile to the south-east of them, though it might as well have been five hundred miles, separated as it was by ramparts of wire, God knew how many enemy units and their own front line staring back at them with rifles cocked and nerves on edge.

'On the other hand,' he added, 'we have the lorry. They're built like tanks, these things. I'll give it a go tonight.'

'In my opinion you'd be very unwise to try it,' said Jumbo.

Butler gave him a sidelong black glance. 'Opinion noted.'

They buried the dead man, Private Eric Carter, in a sheltered plot near the amah's quarters at the back of the house. Jumbo read a couple of passages from the funeral service out of the prayer book his father had given him. It was one of two religious books in his possession. They had all been issued with a Bible, inscribed with a message from the King to the effect that they were fighting on the side of Right. As he intoned the valedictory sentences over the rough, reddish oblong of newly turned earth he hoped Private Carter's mother in Royston, Hertfordshire, would be able to take comfort from this fact.

Before they'd finished there was the earsplitting chatter and whine of small arms fire from the trees across the road and they scattered. For the first time Jumbo gave the gun crew orders to train the mortar on the enemy position and fire at will. Perhaps a little of Butler's dash had rubbed off on him. He sensed the men's need for more positive action (he tried not to think of it as revenge) and since he didn't give much for their chances it seemed only fair to give them their heads. His fear was now aggravated by a helpless, dull anger.

Staynes was not a stoic. His wound was not that bad, but without medical attention, principally drugs, it would fester in the heat, something which already appeared to be happening to the victim's morale. He was thoroughly spooked, quivering and jerking every time he heard gunfire and giving Willard, who was attending him, a hard time.

'Look, you bastard,' Jumbo heard Willard say, 'I don't care what happens to you so keep a civil tongue in your head or I'll choke you with it.'

Jumbo did not look forward to Butler's departure. He felt his authority, such as it was, had been enhanced by Butler's presence. He dreaded the resumption of sole responsibility – dreaded it more than a Japanese bullet or even ultimate defeat.

For the first time during their occupancy, the house

seemed to assert itself and exercise a warning influence. Its original identity seeped through the sweat-stained khaki, and the kit bags and rifles reminded Jumbo of the owners, and the terrible haste with which they had abandoned their intimate domestic things and fled.

Butler squatted down next to the wounded man, without touching him. He stared keenly into his face. Willard looked with a sceptical expression.

'Chin up, soldier,' said Butler, 'we're going to get you out of this.' His turn of phrase embarrassed Jumbo, who knew it was an act, and a cynical one at that. And yet it worked. Staynes quietened and even said, 'Thank you, sir,' though all he'd been given were a few standard words of encouragement which came without a guarantee.

Demoralisation stalked the garden, making little darts and dashes at them when the rifles sounded from the hill opposite. When things were quiet it was worse. Sometimes they could even hear the enemy talking, strange cadences and inflections that meant nothing to them. The occasional laugh.

At one a.m., after it had been quiet for an hour and a half, a couple of the men carried their wounded companion through from the downstairs study on a desk-top covered with blankets, a rolled jungle hat between his teeth to stop him making a noise. Everything was brutally flooded with moonlight.

'That's good, I shan't be using lights,' said Butler.

Grunting, sweating, clumsy with tension, they slid the makeshift stretcher into the back of the lorry. Then Butler got behind the wheel, with another man riding shotgun in the passenger seat and Willard in the back with the patient.

'Good luck,' whispered Jumbo.

'Don't worry,' said Butler. 'We'll be back.'

*

53

They didn't come back. Jumbo waited as the lorry coasted in neutral down the drive and into the road, then started up with a tremendous coughing roar and droned away, the rising note of each successive gear tearing the thick air like a bread knife going through cardboard.

It could only have been a couple of seconds before the first shot rang out accompanied by a shout, and then a whole volley of shots. Had it not been a matter of life and death there might have been something comical about the infinitesimally delayed reaction and the angry peppering of rifle fire. As it was they sent a couple of mortar rounds across the road and listened, teeth clenched, for the boom and flare of the lorry going up. It didn't happen. After this passage of arms, which lasted only a few minutes, everything relapsed into silence and they could hear the rumble of the lorry's engine drawing further away. Jumbo said a perfunctory self-interested prayer like those he had said as a child:

'Dear God. Please let them be safe. Please let us be safe. Please make all this go away, and I'll be good. Yours, John.'


The whole of the next day passed in silence. No shots, no vehicles, no voices. Because of the quiet and their own tense watchfulness, the heat was irksome. Jumbo's rash was no better, though Copley had provided him with some special soap purchased in the city a week ago. A week which seemed to hang like some fragile, unsteady jungle bridge between one world and another. They stood-to in shifts. There was now nothing to eat but Bourbon biscuits and cream crackers. When the first of the men went for their water ration at dawn the tap retched up a couple of gouts of tea-coloured liquid, and nothing else.

'Didn't Captain Butler say the Nips were at the reservoir, sir?' enquired Copley. Jumbo agreed that he had.

By nightfall they were beginning to feel dazed with the heat and the heavy silence. They were also thirsty. Copley pointed out that there was an anti-malarial drain on the far side of the road which was bound to contain water, even if they had to boil it.

Copley himself and another man volunteered to take over a couple of large Thermos flasks from the kitchen, and a jerry can from the garage, and collect what they could. It was decided they should make the attempt at about five o'clock in the morning when it would be darkest and the Japs at their least alert. If they were still there. A small hysterical note of hope had crept in amongst them – perhaps the Japs had moved on and forgotten about them. The fact that the sky was lurid from the sack of Singapore City only a few miles to the south did not stifle this hope. Their world had shrunk to this moment, in the house on Rochester Avenue.

Copley and his companion slipped across the road just before five. They ran crouching, legs bent, like apes.

When, at seven o'clock, Jumbo crawled down over the lawn and between the overgrown trunks of the trees which lined the road, he was confronted by the unwelcome sight of a pair of gleaming riding boots like those of some home counties MFH. Beyond them, the bodies of Copley and Daniels lay on this side of the anti-malarial ditch, dirty, wet and with the thermoses and jerry can ranged alongside them. They had been bayoneted in the back.

# CHAPTER FIVE

# *1942*

As Jumbo came face to face with the enemy for the first time he experienced a curious blend of shock and recognition, and saw that his Japanese opposite number did too.

But before that, one of the highly polished boots shot forward and cracked him beneath the chin. He bit his tongue, instinctively put up a hand to mop the blood and was cracked again, this time on the wrist. Both blows were accompanied by a monosyllabic shout. The toe of the shiny boot jerked upwards several times only inches from his face. One did not have to understand Japanese to get the message.

Hunched over he rose cautiously to his feet, blood dripping from his mouth. Behind him he heard other fierce, sharp cries. They were surrounded. Too stunned, at that moment, to feel fear, he looked into his captor's face. Looked down into it, for he was by some inches the taller of the two.

Here, then, was the reality behind the propaganda and the cartoons and the disparaging rumours: and it was the same, but different. In a microsecond the two men took in all they needed to know.

Jumbo, being tall and inclined to portliness, was

ashamed to be cringing and dripping blood and saliva in front of this trim, wiry representative of the enemy. The man's uniform was immaculate. He had a pencil-fine Basil Rathbone moustache.

He stepped back, barking something over his shoulder and two men came forward. Jumbo was roughly and peremptorily relieved of his revolver. To his astonishment he was then struck again, this time on the side of the head with a rifle butt. He had no idea why and drew himself up to protest, only to receive another thwack. Infinitely worse than the pain was the humiliation. He had never felt so helpless.

There were more shouts, and he was directed, with much superfluous arm-waving and brandishing of rifles, the short distance along the road to the end of the drive. Here he found the rest of the men lined up. He saw in their eyes a reflection of his own frustrated outrage – and something else. It was like the expression on the faces of the Malay refugees, a desperate and demanding dependency. So here we are, it said: do something.

The officer strode to the centre of the road and stood there, legs apart, one hand on the hilt of his sword. He seemed to Oliphant, accustomed to noticing such traits in others, the very acme of braggadocio.

Jumbo pulled his shoulders back and began, rather over-loudly, to speak.

'May I ask what you plan to do with us? Where, for instance – '

He was cut short by a blow on the back of the head and he pitched forward, nearly blacking out, bile mixing with the blood and spit in his mouth. There was another fusillade of screamed commands and his collar was pulled. Shuffling and staggering he got back to his feet. He wanted to stand up straight, for the men, but couldn't. He knew what a poor figure he must cut from their point of view. The Japanese officer began to speak in perfect but curiously accented English.

'The Imperial Japanese Army has taken Singapore. Complete surrender is a mere formality. Your superiors have sacrificed you in a useless game. You cannot say you were not warned. You are our prisoners and we shall of course be merciful.' Jumbo heard a snort of derision closely followed by a thud which made him wince.

'If you conduct yourselves in an appropriate manner,' went on the officer, 'no harm will come to you. You will now join other prisoners. Take with you only what you can carry. March!'

They were taken to the Regimental Aid Post in Gregory Road. It was another requisitioned house, bigger and newer than the one they'd just left, and with few remaining signs of its original owner. This house was set in a large, rather bare garden on the side of a steep hill, so that the upper storey was on ground level at the back. There were no swings, prams and soft toys here. Japanese soldiers stood on either side of the gate and dozens more milled about on the grass and near the front door. A couple of lorries were parked in the road outside: one of them was that in which Butler had set off the previous night. It was unmarked, but seeing it there made Jumbo afraid.

He and his group were left standing under guard in the driveway while the officer conferred noisily and long with a colleague about their disposition. It was made clear to those who showed signs of standing easy that they were to remain at attention.

The uncertainty was hard to bear. Finally the officers disappeared altogether and the guards relaxed and began to chat to each other, only breaking off to bawl incomprehensible invective at any prisoner who moved so much as a muscle.

It appeared they'd been forgotten. Jumbo wondered if they were to be left here indefinitely. The extended hiatus had allowed his injuries to come back to life. His head seemed to be in the process of imploding agonisingly with each beat of his heart, and his tongue was swollen and sore. Should he make some kind of move? But the officers had not returned, and he suspected that the guards would take a dim view. He decided against it. They stood, and it grew hotter.

When they had been there for more than an hour Jumbo heard a sound like a sigh. A man had fainted. The attempts of his neighbour to revive him were greeted with screams of rage and a brisk battering in the ribs with a rifle butt. Jumbo realised he was out of his depth. There had been no training that covered this kind of thing.

They continued to stand.

From his position he could see the whole of the front of the house, and he was sure that the sick and wounded occupants of the RAP were still inside. Once he saw a man with a grubby, reddened bandage around his upper chest looking out from one of the upstairs windows.

There was also an undertow of many voices from some source he could not identify. Something about the timbre and frequency of these voices made him think that they were not Japanese.

As their wait dragged into its third hour his response to the voices fluctuated between a rather foolish relief they were not alone, and despair that so many had been captured.

By early afternoon they were still standing in the drive, and had had nothing to eat, though the Japanese had consumed rations of some sort. He was afraid he too might faint, something he had done with some regularity in assembly and corps parade at school. It was partly to divert himself from this awful possibility that he took a couple of steps forward and addressed the nearest guard.

'I wish to speak to your commanding officer.'

The guard glared at him, bayonet poised and eyes narrowed. Jumbo braced himself for more summary chastisement, but then the officer referred to emerged from the house and strode smartly down to where they stood.

'You have a request?'

'Yes.' Jumbo cleared his throat. 'We have been standing here for some hours without food or water. One man has already fainted. May we please have food and water and some rest before others do the same?'

To his astonishment, he was neither struck nor shouted at. The officer replied quite civilly in his circuitous way: 'It was not time before for prisoners to eat. Now it is time. Please sit.'

He indicated they should sit where they were. They did so, heavy with exhaustion. There followed an exchange in Japanese between the officer and the guards, and two men were despatched in the direction of the house.

'Food is coming,' said the officer.

When it arrived it was apparent that the RAP cupboard was nearly as bare as the one they'd left behind at Rochester Avenue. They were each given a slice of luncheon meat and a couple of spoonfuls of rice, some in tumblers, some in china cups. When they'd finished that the cups and tumblers were quarter-filled with water. It wasn't much, but it went a little way towards reviving their strength and spirits. Then they were ordered to their feet again.

They were marched round to the back of the house. Now Jumbo could see the source of the mysterious voices. Something like four hundred allied soldiers were herded together in a tennis court cut out of the side of the hill. Outside the wire netting were a couple of dozen Japanese with rifles pointing inward. The tennis net had been extended upwards and on either side with camouflage netting to form a partition. There were considerably fewer men on one side than the other. As Jumbo's group appeared one of the guards, covered by his comrades, opened the door, which was in the more populous half, and motioned them to enter. There was a lot of greeting and commiseration and asking after people. Jumbo was pushed and prodded through the crush, and made to scramble under the net into the emptier half. He had no idea why, and entertained a fleeting, panic-stricken idea that he'd been earmarked for instant execution.

'Welcome,' said Butler, 'to the Officers' Mess.'

Jumbo was inordinately pleased to see him. In spite of all the evidence to the contrary, it made him feel that they were not quite such helpless victims.

'What happened to Staynes?' asked Jumbo.

'We got him here. He's upstairs.' Butler tilted his head in the direction of the house.

'Is he all right?'

'He will be, but they're running out of medical stuff. The ones who are worse off don't stand a chance. They moved in just after we got here.'

'What do you think will happen?'

'God knows,' said Butler. 'And let's hope He comes down on our side.'

In the early evening some bully beef and biscuits were brought out of the house by a couple of Japanese soldiers and thrown over the wire netting. The scrum on the ORs' side was terrible.

'We can't have this,' muttered Butler. He pushed his portion under the net, then went to the wire and yelled: 'I want to talk to whoever's in charge! We need more to eat.'

One of the guards came over and banged at Butler's fingers with his rifle butt. Butler withdrew his hands, pressed them together prayerfully, bowed like something out of the *Mikado* and said, smiling: 'Look, you arrogant little bastard, we need more food, and we need this bloody partition taking down.' He mimed eating, and the removal of the net. Bowed again.

Jumbo watched the Jap with held breath. Butler was gambling on him not having understood a word. There was a lot at stake. The guard stared suspiciously for a few

61

seconds. Butler repeated the mime, and the bow. The guard nodded approval. Two minutes later some more chunks of bully were lobbed over, to loud applause. The net, however, remained in place.

They sat down in a corner of the court with two young lieutenants of the Suffolks to eat and review their situation.

'This set-up is ridiculous,' said one of the Suffolks. 'A dozen more at the other end and they won't even be able to sit down.'

'There's been no news of a surrender,' said Jumbo. 'We mustn't rule out the possibility of being freed.'

'Oh, yes,' said Butler. His eyes were like slits in a mask. 'I think we must.'


After dark a contingent of about a dozen prisoners arrived, half of them injured men. Three of the injured, on stretchers, were taken not to the house but to the tennis court. The men who were already packed as tight as cigarettes in a tin down the other end were yelled at and pushed to make room. In the slanting yellow light from the house Jumbo saw that one of the men had been shot through the throat, and the other was burnt: his left forearm was covered by a gigantic inflated blister that wobbled like a jelly, and his face was swollen and cracked.

'Surely they should be in the house,' said Jumbo to the orderly who accompanied them.

The man shook his head. 'Japs say there's no more room.'

Butler went to the wire again and shouted: 'If wounded men are to be put in here we must make more space!'

This time the guards took no notice of him. 'Right,' he said, turning back, 'let's do it.'

He began pulling at the camouflage netting. Within seconds the rest of them were at it. When they'd disposed of the netting they threw it over the wire and wound the tennis net down to the ground. The men poured through on to the officers' side, bringing their smell with them. One or two of the Japs ran up and screamed abuse, and one of them even fired his gun into the air, but they seemed nervous and no further action was taken. Jumbo was apprehensive. When this independent measure was seen by the officer in the light of day there could be hell to pay. But, whether to save face or from compassion, he made no comment.

During the night the man with the bullet hole in his throat had died. The other whimpered incessantly. Conditions in the tennis court were becoming squalid, and since they were drinking water from an anti-malarial drain which contained a couple of dead Malays, it seemed only a matter of time before the squalor increased as a result of diarrhoea.

It was on this day that they were told the British had surrendered. They were now, officially, the lowest form of life, unlikely to see England or their families again, servants of his Imperial Highness the Emperor of Japan who would reward loyalty and hard work.

'In that case,' said Butler, 'we might as well dig latrines.'

They used their hands, belt buckles, penknives and nailfiles, overlooked by the Japanese, and dug three reasonably sized holes near the perimeter netting on the house side.

During the afternoon, as the holes filled up, the guards moved back taking their machine guns with them.

'Aha,' said Butler. 'The time-honoured deterrent.'


They were five days in the tennis court. The stinking, tattered mass of prisoners began to assume separate identities for Jumbo. The officers tried to maintain order and morale, but conditions were against them.

Jumbo did his best not to think of home, or the past, or the terrible, uncharted future. On the whole, he succeeded. He divided each day into periods of talking – he tried to strike up a conversation with somebody new each time – and movement, which meant shuffling to the other end of the court and back. He tried to concentrate on those small things which could be done rather than dwell on those for which there was no possible remedy.

His dreams, unfortunately, were beyond his control. The sleep he craved, and which came in such miserably small doses, brought with it the recurring vision of the church in Tripstowe – his father at the altar preparing the communion with the same slow deliberation with which he washed the dishes, and his mother, soberly hatted in her usual seat near the back, conquering her natural reserve in the interests of lending moral support.

Sometimes there'd be a bird flying around under the roof, which made Jumbo nervous. These invaders would leave the odd dropping on the carpet and even on the parish Bible where it lay open on the lectern. But his father liked a bird in the church and would make references to it in his sermon. Then he and the church wardens and Jumbo's mother would remain behind afterwards with brooms and ladders and all the doors open trying to shoo the terrified creature out into the light and freedom it so passionately sought. In the dream this bird was always just out of sight, fluttering and swooping near Jumbo's head so that he twitched and grunted in his sleep. And always, when he woke up, in the murmurous darkness of their cage, the fear of the bird became his present fear, so there was no relief.

In an attempt to calm himself he would reflect on his parents. He would like to have inherited his mother's quiet competence with his father's verbal assurance and spiritual certainty. Instead of which he was fettered by his mother's shyness and his father's physical clumsiness. Letting them both down, it seemed to him.

Early one night when the lights were still on in the house he got out his prayer book and riffled the tissue-fine pages close to his face, sniffing in the scent of the paper and leather and some other smell which he always thought of as the odour of sanctity itself: the smell of his father. He peered at his father's message, written on the flyleaf in spidery handwriting: 'Dear old Jack. Take good care of yourself, body and soul, but remember it's the first which is dispensable. Our thoughts are with you always. Father.'

The last word brought home to Jumbo an essential awkwardness in his dealings with his father. Once he had stopped, out of sheer self-consciousness, calling his parent 'Daddy', he had not found a suitable replacement. 'Dad' was too blokey and familiar, and 'Father' he associated irreversibly with God. So for the past fifteen years he had used no form of address. It bothered him terribly now, as did the notion that their thoughts were with him. Because how could they be? They would be incapable of imagining his present circumstances. And as to whatever lay ahead – he hoped they wouldn't even try.

'Excuse me.'

Jumbo found himself hurrying to replace the prayer book in his shirt pocket. The voice came from close by, and was also neutral, carrying no overtones of rank.

'Yes?'

'Excuse me, only I saw you trying to read. A kindred spirit, I thought.'

'Oh!' Jumbo nodded vigorously.

'The name's Steward.'

'Oliphant.'

'Captain Oliphant, yes, I know.'

Jumbo was at a grave disadvantage. 'I'm afraid I don't –'

'Well, this isn't exactly the Café Royale.'

'No.'

'I simply saw that you were reading.'

'It's a prayer book my father gave me,' explained Jumbo.

'Ah.' Jumbo thought he sensed the tiniest withdrawal in

ths man's manner. He squinted at his face, and made out a small, thin person, bespectacled and with receding hair. He, too, held a book.

With increased confidence, Jumbo asked: 'What's yours?'

'Metaphysical poets.'

Now it was Jumbo's turn to say, 'Ah'. His father had not approved of the metaphysicals and this disapproval had affected his own attitude to them, though he had secretly enjoyed reading Donne and Marvell at school.

To cover his awkwardness, he added: 'They didn't take it, then.'

Steward shrugged. 'Silly, isn't it? Nothing's more seditious than the written word, and yet they overlook it.'

His voice was dry and detached with a faint regional accent. Now he obviated the need for further conversation by saying simply, 'Good night, then,' and curling up on the ground with his eyes closed. What was more, Jumbo noticed enviously, he gave every appearance of going to sleep.

Jumbo eventually dozed. When he woke again it was still dark, but the man Steward had gone.


On the fifth day the door of the cage was opened and they were told to come out and line up. They were a sorry sight, filthy and in poor condition, but the Japanese kept rifles trained on them at all times. The sick and wounded were brought from the house, accompanied by the MO and orderlies, and first the officers, then the men, were told to fall in behind them. Jumbo observed that his companion of the night before was in the last group. Staynes, arm bandaged, raised a thumb at Jumbo. Some of the fit men were ordered forward to help carry stretcher cases.

'Wonder how far we've got to go,' mused Butler. 'If it's further than the end of the road half that lot won't make it.'

Their captors must have thought the same, for after the

usual period of hanging about the stretcher cases and the worst among the walking wounded were loaded into lorries.

When they had moved off, the Japanese CO took up a position at the front of the column, and guards fell in on either side and at the rear.

'Prisoners! March!' screamed the officer. He turned on his heel and swaggered off, toes pointing slightly outward, the tip of his sword almost brushing the ground. The rest of them, chivvied and prodded by their escort, followed with rather less panache. They marched down into Singapore City, through a landscape that reeked of defeat. Insects buzzed over the hundreds of unburied bodies and the air stank of sewage and putrefaction. There were burnt-out vehicles everywhere. Smoke rose from many of the bombed buildings. The road was clogged with debris – mattresses, bicycles, telephone wires, furniture, building rubble. Malays and Chinese lined their route, as once before, but this time waving Japanese flags. Jumbo couldn't blame them. What else could they do? And they received precious little gratitude – when one cheering man got in the way he was knocked aside with a rifle butt.

When they reached the Cricket Club *padang* they were allowed a rest. For some reason the *padang*, with its smooth, lovingly tended green turf, the inviting verandah of the pavilion, the white spire of St Andrew's Cathedral and the view of the open sea, brought home to Jumbo the absolute finality of their capture. Here was the epitome of the expatriot dream, and the gracious, parochial pastimes of the English *tuan*. Jumbo saw his own filthy and bedraggled figure beside the ghosts of those cricketers in their immaculate whites. Cricketers with nothing more challenging on the horizon than the possibility of a few quick runs and a cold Tiger beer or gin sling in the clubhouse afterwards.

'March!' came the order.

Lynch, one of the Suffolks, fell in next to Oliphant and said: 'We found out where we're going.'

'Where?'

'East, to Changi. Everyone's there, apparently.'

They set off again. It was twelve-thirty, and the temperature was still climbing. Behind them on the smooth greensward of the cricket pitch, positioned at mid-on, they left the body of a man who had died.

# CHAPTER SIX

# *1989*

'So how's it going?' asked Cary. 'I mean I have no idea why you're there, but whatever the itch is, is it being scratched?'

'You know I'm not sure,' I replied. 'It's all so different.'

'You must be insanely disappointed not to find the place overrun with sadistic Orientals,' he said.

I ignored this. 'For one thing the geography's different. They've actually made the island bigger. At the same time it's more crowded, and a lot of the old buildings have gone — '

'I swear to God,' said Cary, 'anyone would think you were visiting the flower-filled meadows of your childhood instead of the scene of one of the most brutal and ignominious defeats of recent history.'

He was impossible in this mood. 'Let's leave it, shall we? You're clearly not interested. I'm sorry I called.'

'Nonsense — '

I hung up.

Five minutes later he called back. 'Look, I'm sorry. I miss you.'

This cut no ice with me. 'You could have come along.'

'Thanks, but no thanks.' I didn't help him out. He sighed heavily, making a little pa-pa-pa sound with his lips. 'It's hot as hell here.'

'And here.'

'But wet, huh? Doesn't it rain every day? I've read the books.'

'We've had some rain, yes.'

Pa-pa-pa . . . 'So tell me what you've been doing.'

'I went out to Changi.'


'Changi village?' asked the driver.

'Yes, partly. I want to take a look at the whole area. Go for a drive around.'

'Fine, okay. Start with airport – great shopping!' He grinned at me in the mirror. 'Only a joke,' he added, in deference to my mood but quite uncowed.

'Changi village is fine.'

It was late afternoon as we zoomed along the four-lane highway by which I'd travelled from the airport a couple of days before. We had gone beyond the landscaped picnic and recreational area, and the road was now separated from any sight of the sea by a forest of high-rise flats in greyish-white concrete, every other window sprouting a drying rod hung with washing like bunting. Whether the clothes would dry was doubtful – the sky was piled with a sullen mass of navy blue clouds.

'Very good government accommodation,' remarked the cabbie, as if trying to sell me some of it. It was certainly different from the raffish, overcrowded streets of Chinatown where I'd stood like a good tourist that morning and taken pictures with which to appall Cary. 'Jesus Christ!' I could hear him exclaim. 'A sideshow, and you fell for it!'

The cabbie leaned across and drew my attention to the other side of the road. This involved taking his eyes off the road for a less than judicious interval, and guiding the steering wheel with the forefinger and thumb of one hand while gesturing expansively with the other. 'Along here, factories.'

70

'So I see.'

You certainly wouldn't have likened this to Florida. It could have been any industrial suburb with its servicing council estates. Only the clammy heat and the drying poles marked it as different from such an area in Paris, New York or Sydney. And, I suppose, the driver's pride in it. I felt sure his view of Chinatown would have corresponded exactly to Cary's.


Changi village, well . . . Yet again, I was thwarted in my blind, hopeful nosings around after what Dylan would have called Memory and Fate. The past remained hidden. This was the present and then some, roaring heedlessly into the future.

When the cabbie first mentioned Changi village it had immediately conjured up a picture of one of the Malay *kampong* outside the camp perimeter. A cluster of stork-legged wooden houses . . . a ribbon of woodsmoke . . . the smell of cooking . . . a brown child tapping a dawdling cow with a twig . . . pretty, glossy girls preparing food and giggling gently . . . To us those *kampong*, foreign though they were, had embodied the very essence of 'home', with its peaceful, ordered domestic patterns. More so than our own distant and beleaguered homes because these were still complete and undisrupted, the headman in his place and the wife going about her duties.

I had yet to see such a *kampong* in the Singapore of 1989, and now I was disappointed once more. Changi village was a brick-built Chinese shopping centre with all the usual worldwide commodities from Coke to suntan lotion, a liberal scattering of non-biodegradable litter and a car park stiff with American and Japanese cars.

'I wait while you shop. No extra charge,' offered the cabbie. In any other country in the world I'd have laughed in his face and negotiated the price there and then, but the last forty-eight hours had shown me that he probably meant what he said. Everything here was straight, sanitised, hassle-free.

'I shan't be long,' I said. By the time I'd closed the door he was deep in a copy of *Playboy*.

I had no intention of shopping. I wasn't even sure what I sought, but I knew it couldn't be had for Singapore dollars. I wandered along the brick and concrete walkways for about ten minutes and then went down some steps and over a bridge in the direction of Changi Creek, helpfully signposted in both Chinese and English.

The creek was different. Sure, there were hideous low-rise modern buildings on the far bank, echoing those I'd just left. But the waterfront itself was scattered with ramshackle boats and barges, and on a patch of bare earth beneath a tree were a gaggle of skinny-legged men in shorts and vests, some holding bicycles, all talking up a storm. A monkey was tethered to a horizontal pole. It ran along the pole, upended, then swung by one hand, jumped down, ran back and climbed up again to repeat the process. Run, swing, jump, climb, over and over, its eyes world-weary. Near the foot of the bridge was parked a rusty white 1960s Merc. A huge tawny chicken roosted in the dust beneath the car's trunk. I smiled to myself. I remembered something like this. I was getting my thumbnail under the scab.


When I got back to the car the driver expressed himself amazed that I had (a) done no shopping and (b) torn myself so swiftly away from the many enchantments of the village. I explained – again – that I was only looking around.

He took me on a circuit of the Changi peninsula, but there was nothing to interest me. The road hummed over flat, reclaimed land, with the airport and runways always in view. There was nothing of the undulating, half-wooded country that I remembered, the spaces laboriously carved out between beach and bamboo. Only the occasional view of islands floating in the near distance was the same. We used to stand on the beach and strain our eyes looking at those islands and that calm sea which we had no means or hope of crossing.

'You want to stop, walk around?' The cabbie looked in the mirror at me.

'No, thank you.'

'You want to go to prison?'

The irony of this question made me laugh and say, 'No!' I'd not gone back to Changi prison itself, but the place was still a curiosity. 'Sure,' I added.

'Fine! Okay!' He raised both hands off the wheel and returned them with a force which made the car jink. 'We go Changi Prison!'

With a definite objective in view he put his foot down. He slowed only once to jerk a thumb to the right and say laconically: 'Selarang Barracks.' I glanced over briefly. Smooth green lawns, a freshly painted guard room and regiments of bedding plants couldn't quite disguise the notorious three-storey blocks into which we'd been crammed: a useful exercise, it turned out, in what might be termed squalor-survival; something in which we were to become *summa cum laude* graduates . . .

It was beginning to rain as we pulled up at the gate of Changi Prison. The guard told me that these days a special pass was needed to tour the prison itself, but that there was a museum and a replica of a POW chapel which I might find interesting and which were always open.

'Some people hold a service in the chapel this evening,' he added in a tone which implied there was no accounting for taste.

'You can go!' said the cabbie indulgently – after all he did have the rest of *Playboy* to read – 'I wait in car park.'

Rather against my better judgement my curiosity was piqued. I got out and followed the signs to the chapel. I wondered who these people were who bothered to come and hold a service in a mock chapel in the grounds of a prison. Prison staff? Missionaries? Ex-POWs, even? I had no intention of either joining in or introducing myself, I simply wanted to see.

The rain had now set in with drilling insistence, and I was soaked. There was the chapel, an exact, carefully tended replica of the real thing: an attap hut open on three sides, a steep pitched roof covering the altar and rows of wooden benches outside. A big black and yellow bird rose from under one of the benches as I approached but a couple of little sparrows continued to cheep and rustle around the altar under the sheltering leaves.

I stopped, far too wet to care about getting wetter. Up to the right, overlooking the chapel, was the blind white wall and domed entrance of the prison. In sharp relief against it the figure of an Asian woman in a bright sari moved along the road. She was carrying a black umbrella and a bag. Her presence reminded me of the prisoners, silent and invisible behind the wall.

I walked up to the altar, disturbing the sparrows, and found a noticeboard where previous visitors had pinned notes and messages in memory of loved ones. The sentiments were honest but corny. I felt a bit ashamed of my own detachment when I read things like: 'Though the road of life is long/Our love for you is ever strong/You are now beyond all pain/God willing, we shall meet again.' And: 'To dearest Uncle Bobby who died for his country in a foreign land – from Judy, Reg, Michelle, Lorraine and Carl back home in Adelaide.' These after all were private thoughts, and indubitably sincere – only sincerity could have been that mawkish.

I read on, fascinated by the tone of the messages. I wondered what need or appetite it was in otherwise well-adjusted people that made them equate suffering with heroism. These sons and daughters and nieces and nephews seemed to believe that because their lost relative had borne much he had done so with fortitude. They truly thought that his tribulations had ennobled him. It was depressing to bear the knowledge of how wrong they were.

I was so deep in all this that I didn't realise I was no longer alone until a voice behind me said: 'Welcome, brother.'

They were neither prison staff nor ex-POWs. They were young Malays and some Chinese, and they were Born Again. They had with them a couple of electric guitars, service sheets and prayer books in a plastic carrier bag, and a refrigerated box containing refreshments. They were so astonished and delighted to find they had attracted passing trade in spite of the weather that they opened the box at once and plied me with lemon squash and fishpaste sandwiches. It seemed not to cross their minds that I might be anything but a *bona fide* worshipper in search of spiritual sustenance.

'What brings you here?' asked the young man in charge.

I began to explain, guardedly, that I had lived in Singapore years ago, and was returning to some old haunts.

No, no, no, they laughed kindly. What had brought me *here*, to them, to this chapel?

I decided to take honesty out for a walk. 'Curiosity,' I said.

'Bless the Lord!' cried the leader. 'For He moves in mysterious ways and has brought our brother here across land and sea to worship with us!'

'Bless the Lord!' The others agreed, lifting their eyes and hands to the lowering skies. With Him on their side they were obviously able to turn anything to their advantage. I could see this had a heck of a lot going for it, but not enough for them to get their hooks in me.

Miserable sinner that I was, they sat me down on one of the wooden benches upon which polythene bags had been laid as protection against the wet. A beaming

Chinese matron shared her umbrella with me and we sang 'Praise my soul the King of Heaven'. I could just about stumble through the tune but was the only person there whose eyes never rose from the book. After the hymn attention was again drawn to the fact that the good Lord had guided me hither and that nothing He did was without purpose. It seemed pointless to tell them that on this occasion He'd picked the wrong man. The whole thing was so deliciously bizarre.

Our leader told us that his own week had not been without incident. He had been constipated, but the Lord had directed his hand to the correct bottle on the chemist's shelf. The congregation applauded warmly. One or two others stood up and proffered instances of divine intervention both at home and at work. I remained silent, but the Lord had subtle ways of punishing the unworthy. I was ushered to the front and the congregation, numbering about a dozen, gathered round me and laying their hands on me prayed loudly for the success of my trip, the increase of my tribe and the preservation of my eternal soul.

I closed my eyes, and besought whoever was listening to grant me endurance. In my mind's eye I could see Cary's astonished face, and his lips framing the words: 'How in the world did you wind up with this bunch of fruitcakes?'


'You did what?' he asked. His incredulity smacked over the line so that I moved the receiver slightly away from my ear. 'But you wouldn't even come along to humour me on Christmas!'

'This was different.'

'I'm having difficulty picturing this.' He paused theatrically and I could imagine him massaging his temples with fingers and thumb. 'What the hell is going on out there?'

'Nothing,' I said calmly. It was good to be unsettling him a bit. 'Just a few new experiences.'

'Listen,' he said, 'I take it all back. Really. I think I preferred the old ones.'

'Ah,' I said, 'but now I've got God on my side.'

# CHAPTER SEVEN

# 1942

It was funny, thought Jumbo. Here they both were, he and Butler, attending chapel, and he was pretty sure that of the two of them he was the more devout. Well, he believed in God. And yet it was Butler whose head was bowed and whose eyes were closed, and he himself who couldn't seem to concentrate.

The padre was a man in his early thirties with a high-candlepower manner. Jumbo found this a bit hard to take. It went against his sense of order to hear some chap, donkey's years younger than his own father, droning and intoning like an archbishop. He knew that his faith should outweigh these considerations, that he was confusing the Almighty with the Reverend Roderick Oliphant. But this was why his mind kept wandering.

They were kneeling on the ground. As they mumbled and growled through the General Confession he let his eyes roam along the row in front. Out of eight men, about half had something identifiable as a shirt; the rest wore vests. There were a few pairs of roughly patched boots and many pairs of sandals made from wood or rubber tyres. All the backs were thin and knobby and the skin scabrous with rashes and bites. One man had a sore on his leg and the dirty bandage was damp with pus. One or two of the shorts didn't look too good either: dysentery was no respecter of persons. 'Speedy benjo!' was the first phrase of Nippon-go they'd learnt.

The padre was now embarking on the Absolution: 'Wherefore let us beseech Him to grant us true repentance, and His Holy Spirit, that those things may please Him, which we do at this present; and that the rest of our life hereafter may be pure and holy . . . '

In the parish church of Tripstowe these pious hopes had seemed likely to be fulfilled. At least there was no fear of any major spanner being thrown in the works. Everyone was in their best clothes and on their best behaviour, looking forward to an uplifting sermon, a glass or two of sherry and a succulent roast . . . followed perhaps by blackberry and apple crumble, with cream. Jumbo's mouth watered.

Here, those things which they did at this present were exclusively directed towards self-preservation. And as for the rest of their lives being pure and holy – if cleanliness were next to Godliness they were a lost cause. And the rest of their lives might not amount to much, either. Jumbo's eyes strayed once more to the suppurating sore. They had already extended the cemetery twice.

'O Lord, open Thou our lips,' demanded the padre.

'And our mouths shall shew forth Thy praise,' they replied.

'O God, make speed to save us.'

'O Lord, make haste to help us,' they agreed fervently.

Jumbo turned the page of his prayer book and wondered how long it would be before he gave in and sold it, or used it himself, for cigarette papers. The cock, he felt sure, was simply waiting to crow.

They struggled to their feet to sing a hymn. Jumbo felt deeply ashamed and sang in a voice loud and tuneless with emotion: 'My richest gain I count but loss/ And pour contempt on all my pride . . . '

Butler liked coming to chapel for the same reason he had once enjoyed driving his car. Not that there was any thrill or exhilaration to be had here. No, it was the sense of doing something constructive while doing nothing at all. Buzzing from A to B in the Alvis had provided a sense of purpose without any appreciable effort. It was the same with chapel. You turned up, you sat down, off you went. Doing the Right Thing.

Hymn-singing was all right, too. Butler knew he had a good singing voice. Pity about poor old Jumbo, whose religious credentials were impeccable but who had the voice and musicality of a rogue elephant.

'Forbid it, Lord, that I should boast,' they sang. 'Save in the death of Christ my God . . . '

Butler reflected on a recent stroke of luck. He had made the acquaintance of an Australian corporal who had lost his teeth in a riding accident but who was prepared to remove his dentures to perform fellatio in exchange for tobacco.

He closed his hymn book and fixed his eyes on the face of that prat, the padre. The human spirit was indomitable.


When they had shaken hands with the padre, Derek Tidy, Jumbo said: 'Are you going to the concert party tonight?'

'I don't know.' Butler managed to make it sound as though there were dozens of tempting alternatives. 'I hadn't thought about it.'

'I think I might go.' Jumbo said diffidently. He was dying to do so. 'They need the support.'

'Amateur dramatics,' said Butler waspishly, 'is generally more diverting for those on the stage than those in the audience.'

'Well . . . ' Jumbo hoped he wasn't blushing. 'Just the same . . . '

They were walking near the perimeter fence. To their right, about twenty yards from the fence, was a rudimentary shower house, an attap shelter with a perforated hosepipe caught up to the ceiling. Two skinny men were sharing a dribble of water in full view of the road which ran parallel to the fence and about the same distance from it.

'Christ, I'd rather be dirty,' said Butler.

'I've got a small piece of soap at the moment.'

'You'll enjoy that.'

'Do borrow it if you want to,' said Jumbo, and then looked away before Butler's amused stare. He was an old woman. He was sure that was how Butler, and most probably others too, referred to him behind his back. But what could he do? These foolish remarks had always slipped out before he'd had time to think. Glancing covertly at Butler he wondered how it was that he appeared cleaner, or at any rate more wholesome, than the rest of them. He seemed to thrive on the exigencies of life in camp. He was thin – who wasn't – but had not yet succumbed to dysentery and managed somehow to extract nourishment from the wretched diet of badly cooked polished rice with threads of greyish 'yak' meat. Jumbo sighed.

A Sikh guard stood on the other side of the fence. Butler stopped and took from his shorts pocket a tin containing makings – wisps of black 'Sikh's beard' tobacco and a few sheets of Deuteronomy. With calm deliberation he began to construct a cigarette. Jumbo knew it was simple provocation, for matches were like gold dust and the nearest homemade lighter was back in the sleeping hut. He sweated. What did Butler hope to achieve by this?

Now Butler turned towards the guard, the cigarette held lightly between the fingers of his right hand. 'I say, got a light?'

He darted back just in time – having, as Jumbo saw, planned the whole thing – to avoid the rifle barrel as it shot through the wire like a striking snake.

They walked on, Jumbo rather faster than Butler.

'Treacherous scum,' said Butler.

Scum. Jumbo couldn't even think the word without crippling self-consciousness. You had to be a particular kind of person to get away with language like that.

Their pace steadied. They began to move in the general direction of the sleeping hut. There was nothing to do. The tedium made them maniacally resourceful. Bartering, evasion, invention and self-improvement helped to fight the wastes of time which were otherwise populated with fear, homesickness and raging hunger. Oh, the hunger! Jumbo dreamed regularly of mashed potato and gravy. It was the closest to a wet dream he'd had in thirteen years. To wake up and confront another day of rice with grass soup or yak meat had often brought tears to his eyes.

They circumnavigated the rising ground where the latrine boreholes were. Crouching figures dotted the area like Halma men, some huddled quite close together and deep in conversation – 'borehole' was camp argot for 'rumour' – others with the hunched loneliness of the desperate.

Beyond the boreholes they encountered Murdoch, a Cambridgeshire man who was a bit of a gardener. He carried two pails suspended from a pole across his shoulders and was accompanied by an armada of flies.

'Morning, sergeant,' said Butler. 'Garden fatigues?'

'Yes, sir. Sakito's allotment.'

'Let me know when he's got a few of those stick beans.'

'You bet I will, sir.'

Murdoch carried on, knees bent, his emaciated frame trembling under the weight of the slopping pails.

Jumbo grimaced. 'What a job.'

'It's shit that makes the garden grow. Our shit to be precise, so we might as well reap a few of the fruits.'

Dysentery Dick, Sakito was known as. His vegetable plot was a kick in the arse of every man – and that was most of them – who had squatted over the boreholes with his guts in uproar. Jumbo could not have forced down one mouthful of Sakito's vegetables, not if it was the last food on earth. But Butler took pride in creaming off one or two of the best ones, through Murdoch's good offices, and distributing them amongst his inner circle.

'I shall look forward to that,' said Butler, smacking his lips. 'Pity we can't tempt you, old man.'

Jumbo shook his head. The trouble, he thought, is that I can't hate them enough. It was hate, pure and simple, that fuelled Butler and set him apart. You could see it in some of the others, too, officers and men. It was a useful source of energy hate, and one not available to Jumbo.


That evening they went to the show. The set-up was pretty much the same as the chapel, the stage area under cover, the audience out in the open. There were only a few benches, and these were mostly reserved for Japs who would laugh and applaud immoderately throughout. They'd learned to mistrust this display of bonhomie: a streak of sentimentality ran through the Japanese character, as soft and treacherous as quicksand. Such seats as remained were intended for officers, but only a few took up the offer, and Butler and Jumbo were not among them. The rest of them sat where they could: on the ground, which sloped slightly upward around the stage in a natural amphitheatre, on each other's shoulders, and in the branches of nearby trees.

Waiting for the show to begin Jumbo fell to examining himself. It was quite a pastime, this running of the fingers over the depredations of the regime. He had developed a chimpanzee-like fascination with his body and how much it could take. At the moment he was displaying the early symptoms of beriberi, and was sorely in need of an egg. Idly he pressed his forefinger into his shin and felt the bone give spongily. His feet were puffy and purplish, reminding him of the hands of a master at school who was said to be an alcoholic. His balls were scabby and itched painfully. He was only glad he couldn't see his face. Butler (of course) had a triangle of mirror glass that he used for shaving, but Jumbo avoided looking in it. He kept in his mind's eye a picture of his old face – round, fresh, pink and smooth – and was not too naive to recognise that the shock of the new one would be terrible.

Someone struck up the overture on an upright piano, its tone severely impaired by the humidity. The tune was 'A Pretty Girl Is Like a Melody', and was greeted with cheers and hoots by the audience. Jumbo experienced a thrill of excitement. There was no risk here that he'd be expected to participate, like those fearful childhood pantomimes. The jokes and the cruelty would be at the expense of the Japs – there were numerous coded ways of delivering insults – and he could sit here, one sick, ragged, smelly man amongst hundreds, and be perfectly anonymous and safe.


Butler was impressed. It could have been a real girl up there. Especially now the man had abandoned burlesque. He was kitted out in a diaphanous gown made from pieces of mosquito netting, with a long scarf of the same around his neck, and was dancing to the pianist's plucky rendition of 'Night and Day'. The audience had gone quiet. The Japs sat there enraptured, arms folded and silly smiles on their faces. They continually impressed upon the 'purisonas' that they were the lowest of the low, subhuman and degraded, yet they were passionately addicted to the frivolous ingenuity of these makeshift shows. Not for the first time Butler idly contemplated leading the entire audience in a coup, overwhelming the Japs and making a break for it. But it was just a daydream. If they got out of the camp, what then? The whole bloody island was a prison, and the Japs knew it. Their complacency enraged him. He focused once more on the twirling, swaying figure on the stage. He was really awfully good. Trying to work out why this chap had got everyone in the palm of his hand, Butler concluded it was because he was playing it straight. He was in a world of his own, and that cast a spell over the rest of them. In this outlandish context Butler was able to appreciate skills which in another time and place he would have despised, at least publicly. Here such skills were acceptable, part of a general currency of bluff, counter-bluff and survival. As the applause swelled round about him he promised himself a little trip backstage afterwards.

Jumbo was entranced. Artistic talent, like coolness under fire and organisational ability, was strange and wonderful to him. This, in its way, had been every bit as inspiring as Butler's lone stand in the tree top at Rochester Avenue. He clapped until his palms were sore.

They began to drift away from the theatre. The Japs left first, chuckling and slapping each other on the shoulder. Jumbo caught sight of Butler looking at them, his face bleak. But when, with that sixth sense which tells us we are being watched, he turned and caught Jumbo's eye, his expression relaxed and he came over.

'A pretty good show, I thought.'

'Marvellous! How do they do it?'

'That little bloke in the Jessie Matthews outfit was quite something.'

'Yes. I don't know him, do you?'

Butler shook his head. 'Thought I might go round and find him, though. Say well done.'

'I'll come.'

The short tropical dusk was setting in. Away from the theatre among the huts and shelters one or two fires gleamed, ready to heat up stuff brought back by the men who were clearing bomb damage in Singapore City. Those who had been detailed to the docks were especially adept at siphoning flour and sugar out of bags, and filching odd tins of cigarettes and food. Very occasionally a man was caught red-handed and would be beaten senseless, and then there might be a period of crack-downs when everyone had to be careful. But generally speaking, with so many prisoners to be contained, and the administration of Changi left to the inmates, pilfering and black marketeering thrived unchecked.

In theory the officers 'earned' slightly more than the men, but there was precious little on offer. Jumbo, wearily dragging himself up to the stage in Butler's wake, reminded himself of the necessity of getting hold of an egg.

Four stage hands were hefting the few bits of scenery to the back of the platform and covering the piano with a tarpaulin. One of them was Willard. Another Jumbo recognised as the man who had lain next to him at the tennis court, who had asked what he was reading. As Jumbo approached there was a burst of laughter.

'Hallo there,' he said. 'Congratulations on a very good show.'

'Glad you enjoyed it.'

'Enormously. I can't think how you chaps manage it.'

Steward shrugged. 'Helps to keep us sane.'

'You've got a star in that Jessie Matthews.'

'You're not wrong. Excuse me.'

Jumbo felt rather *de trop*, standing there watching them work, and besides he could see Butler making off round to the back of the stage. He lifted his hand.

'Cheerio. Good luck with the next one.'


The cast was getting changed in a canvas and bamboo lean-to. A hurricane lamp was suspended from the roof bar, its roar punctuated by the spit of burning insects. A wasted Tarzan was pulling on his shorts near the entrance.

'Very good,' said Butler. 'Wonderful stuff.'

'Glad you liked it.'

'Who organised it?'

'Gilbert Rowntree. Captain Rowntree — ' Tarzan craned around, and then pointed. 'Over there.'

'Thanks. I must shake him by the hand.'

Butler began making his way through the steaming crush, beaming and crunching shoulders as he went. Jumbo hung back. He knew it was foolish to feel awkward here, when he had crouched miserably flank-to-flank with most of these men at the boreholes at one time or another. But there you were all victims of nature. These men were exhibitionists even if their ribs did stick out and their skins were crusty with jiggers and ringworm. He averted his eyes and withdrew from the tent.

On the edge of the aura of light cast by the hurricane lamp Steward squatted, his forearms resting on his upbent knees, his long hands dangling skeleton-like in front of him. Jumbo was startled to find him there. He looked like a beggar, patient and fatalistic. Waiting.


'Here he is,' said Rowntree to Butler. 'Our star.'

The small figure turned to face them, his confident grin a gash in his death's head face. Around his mouth there remained a reddish smear of lipstick. His eyes glittered with self-satisfaction. Two smaller, yellowish eyes were tattoed on his neck above where his collar bones stuck out like coathangers.

'Like it, then?' he asked.

It cost Butler much to find the breath to answer. 'I most certainly did,' he said. 'Terrific stuff. You were – you were extraordinary.'

He was glad of the dim light, and the crush. He was in pain.

'Don't get the wrong idea,' said the little man. 'I'm choosy.'

'Yes,' said Butler. 'I can believe that.'

*

Butler brushed past Jumbo as though he couldn't see him. As he stumbled past, Steward rose stiffly and went to stand in the doorway.

Jumbo had the strange feeling that he had been here before. But that was impossible. He turned and followed Butler into the dark.

# CHAPTER EIGHT

# 1942

It was early September and they'd been prisoners for over six months when their captors ordered them to sign forms promising not to attempt to escape. They refused and the message was carried back to the Japanese by the commanding officers. Silly really, when anyone with an ounce of realism knew that the chances of a successful escape were virtually nil. But as Butler put it, 'Why should we give the buggers the right to shoot us the moment we have a go?'

The Japanese response to this was swift and draconian. The prisoners were ordered to collect their kit and convene in Selarang Barracks. This turned out to be an area about two hundred by two-fifty yards bordered on three sides by blocks designed to accommodate between eight and nine hundred men. The two roads into Selarang were clogged solid with nearly twenty times that number of prisoners. They'd arrived at Changi with little enough, and whatever possessions they'd managed to scrounge, swap, snitch or construct since they were determined to hang on to. Cooking utensils, bedding, musical instruments, ducks, chickens, boots, hats, mosquito nets and rudimentary items of furniture were lugged the three miles to Selarang in the intense heat by whatever means was possible – on heads, backs, suspended coolie-style from poles or balanced precariously on homemade barrows. Trucks from which the Japanese had circumspectly removed the engines were loaded with supplies, homemade ovens and even the concert party's piano and pushed by teams of men. The mood was bloody-minded.

A small group of them – Butler, Jumbo, Rowntree, the two young Suffolks Lynch and MacMahon, and Derek Tidy – had decided that exposure to the elements was preferable to the stifling human anthill inside, and made for the roof of the central block on the north side of the square. It took them over half an hour to get up there, by which time the afternoon downpour had set in. The roof was already occupied by the remnants of three other battalions, some of whom had had the foresight to bring tarpaulins and had managed to rig up shelters. These were crammed to capacity, so there was nothing for Jumbo's group to do but sit it out. When the rain stopped as suddenly as it had begun, the buildings and verandahs emptied and the square teemed with people, moving through the steam like figures from the Inferno. It was rumoured that there was a functioning water tap somewhere in the building, but it took so long to get down the rope ladder and through the crush that those on the roof opted to remain where they were for the time being and share the small amount of water they had with them.

That evening they dismantled doors and cupboards to make fires for the cooks. It was rice as usual, with whatever flavouring could be gleaned from the supplies they'd brought. Helpings were meagre even by Changi standards: by the time they were back on the roof they were hungry again. After supper the CO came round, and they sent MacMahon down the rope ladder to bring back information.

He looked glum as he relayed the message. 'They're keeping us here till we sign the no-escape forms. There won't be any rations issued, and anyone going anywhere near the perimeter wire will be shot. They've got armed guards right round and a machine gun in place by the clock tower.'

Tidy asked: 'What about water?'

'A pint per man per day. For everything.'

'It's blackmail, pure and simple,' said Rowntree.

'And it'll probably work,' said Butler, 'if they don't kill us first.'


Jumbo thought he might well die from queueing. Each block had six toilets which the Japs had rendered unusable, so men were put to digging boreholes in the asphalt parade ground. Teams of five or six pushed a crossbar round and round, like donkeys, until the central auger had created a hole over twenty feet deep. When they'd made dozens of these holes the officers haggled for truckloads of timber to make thunderboxes to put over them. From these a more or less permanent queue snaked away amongst the crowds and makeshift shelters of the square, and squadrons of gluttonous flies poured in and out each time a box was vacated.

It was the same with food. For half a cup of wet rice you could wait for anything up to three quarters of an hour, twice a day. And since there was only one water tap in use, the queue for that began at first light and continued into the night. It was in this queue that Jumbo suddenly heard himself addressed.

'Excuse me, sir. I think we know each other.'

The voice had come from behind him. Jumbo turned and looked down on a small man, who in spite of his thinness looked trim and wiry. Jumbo at once recognised a physical presence which, though not as gently reared or well maintained as Butler's, was equally impressive. He was a bit younger than Jumbo, with dark hair brushed straight back and receding slightly at the peak. He wore a grubby bandana round his neck. He did seem familiar, though Jumbo couldn't have said why.

'I'm sorry. I don't think I – er — '

Even as he mumbled he thought how peculiar it was that these forms and observances should still matter – that he should mind being caught at a minor social disadvantage when only yards away a row of men relieved themselves in full public view.

'No reason why you should remember, sir,' said the small man. 'It was a long time ago.'

Jumbo frowned and smiled at the same time, communicating an earnest keenness to be reminded. 'I'm afraid you've got me . . . '

'When you were at school, sir.'

This was even more baffling. To cover his confusion Jumbo shuffled forward a few paces to fill the gap their brief conversation had created in the queue. In his mind's eye there rose a tottering pile of bricks waiting to be dropped. Had he been – could it be – that they had been at school together? But this chap was an OR. He spoke – well – he was a bit of a rough diamond. What, thought Jumbo wretchedly, was the correct response?

He resorted to heartiness. 'School? Now that really was a long time ago! You're going to have to give me a few clues.'

'I spoke to Captain Butler. He remembered all right.'

'Did he?' He would, thought Jumbo.

'I worked in the garden. For old Jack Rowley. You remember him, sir?'

At last, a name Jumbo recognised, and the information necessary to provide a secure footing in this hitherto slippery conversation. He beamed. In response to a scathing look from a man further back in the queue he took another few steps forward. There were still twenty-odd men between him and the erratic trickle of water from the tap.

'Mr Rowley, of course. Great character. Splendid old chap. So you worked for him, did you?'

'That's right, sir. I used to see you most days, going about the place.'

'Good Lord! What an incredibly small world it is.'

92

'And getting a bloody sight smaller by the minute, eh sir?' said the man confidentially. Jumbo felt he had been included in a private joke. He felt absurdly flattered.

They shuffled forward. It was now nearly Jumbo's turn. As the man in front of him filled his mess tin, he asked: 'I'm sorry, I never asked your name.'

'Maitland, sir. Mick.'

As Jumbo carried his precious bottle of water back across the barrack square he suddenly realised why Maitland had seemed familiar. It had nothing to do with school. Private Maitland had been the graceful and alluring star of the variety show. How strange that Butler had not mentioned such an extraordinary and, Jumbo thought, pleasing coincidence.

'Yes,' said Butler when he commented on it. 'Yes, as a matter of fact I did realise who he was.'

'Rather a nice chap,' said Jumbo. 'And surprisingly chipper.'

'These theatrical johnnies are often like that,' said Butler acidly, and then added: 'You're right, though. A tough little beggar, not a bad sort. But the sad fact is,' he sighed, 'he probably won't make it.'

'The same goes for most of us, surely,' suggested Jumbo.

Butler shook his head. 'The odds have to be shorter on a small man like that. Especially one from his kind of background – poor diet, been working his socks off since he was a lad. He won't have any reserves to fall back on.'

'Nevertheless,' said Jumbo stoutly, 'he has plenty of spirit.'

'He's going to need it,' said Butler. 'We all are.'

He was right. Disease took hold. It hadn't seemed possible for the Selarang Square to become worse; now it became apparent how much room there had been for deterioration. Such space as there was between the ever-shuffling queues of weakening men was now crammed with makeshift 'hospital' accommodation – lean-tos, tents, shambling structures of corrugated iron, planks and cardboard, anything to keep the merciless sun off the sick and dying. There were no drugs; there was virtually no water; there was no means of keeping them, their dressings or their miserably inadequate bedding clean. To the stench of unwashed men, insanitary buildings and excreta was now added the smell of death. Jumbo, sitting listlessly on the roof and looking down at the scene below, considered the phrase 'dying like flies'. Here they died and the flies flourished.

For the first time Butler was also listless. Conditions in Selarang were claustrophobic. There were no outlets for his restless energy. Any kind of normal movement around the barracks was impossible. Life here was at a standstill. Neither were there any opportunities for wheeling and dealing. They were like rats in a trap.

His mood became black and he noticed, as he had not done before, his own poor state of health. It unnerved him. The thought of dying cooped up in this hellhole was intolerable. He had been against signing the no-escape forms, but even that seemed preferable to this squalid inertia.

On the second night he slept a sleep that was like a mad, whitewater rush through his past. When he awoke before dawn, certain images filled his head and wouldn't let him be. The meeting with Maitland had shocked him. Not, he told himself, because of what had happened all those years ago – God knows, one's attitude to such things had been pretty unbalanced. No, it was because Maitland represented now, as then, a world in which Butler himself was ill at ease. A world, in fact, that had much in common with

Butler's home.

Alan Butler was the only surviving child of Claud Butler and his wife Marguerite. Alan's elder brother, Roland, had died of pneumonia in the trenches of the Yprès salient. Butler hadn't really known him and accepted his death with equanimity, but the effect of the tragedy had been to make him the centre of his parents' attention.

Claud was a peppery, energetic man from a middle-class family, affluent through his own considerable efforts in the field of estate agency. His territory comprised the leafy, comfortable suburbs of Muswell Hill, Parliament Hill and the less expensive parts of Highgate. The Butler house was large, comfortable and well appointed, and during those years when the boys were growing up Claud was at the peak of his success. He was chauffeured each morning to his office in the Archway Road by Milne, an employee who conducted himself with the exaggerated deference of the working-class snob. By the time Roland had died and Alan was at public school, Claud, though only in his late fifties, had handed over the reins to his junior partner and assumed the role of elder statesman. Unfortunately for Butler this state of affairs meant that his father had more time to devote to his family, of which he had high expectations. He was a fantasist who wanted his son to be the sort of man he himself could never be, and whom he admired: a dashing blade. This would have been a heavy burden for Roland who was a thoughtful, bookish young man. It came as no particular hardship to Alan, who was by nature rash, strong-willed and unscrupulous. Given a sports car, Butler drove it too fast. Invited to a party, he was the making of it. Sent to a reputable if second division public school he quickly became a force to be reckoned with – a run-maker, a try-scorer, a humbler of masters and flutterer of hearts.

The problem for Butler was Claud himself. Butler despised him. Worse, he had seen the same scorn in the eyes of his mother, and even of Milne.

Marguerite was a very different proposition. Butler adored her. But he understood, being an instinctive rather than a cerebral boy, that she was incapable of real warmth. She was a tall, glamorous, dark-haired woman with an extravagant manner and a luscious magnolia skin. Her voice was husky and resonant and she affected a theatrical exuberance which made her a great asset at social gatherings. Claud openly doted on her. She was taller than Claud and liked to make a play on the fact, patting his cheek, pulling his flushed face to her bosom, putting her arm round his shoulders and so on. Claud would roar with laughter Butler, who was sexually precocious, was uneasy. He noticed a difference in his mother's manner towards certain other men. With these men she was in effect less coquettish and more restrained. And yet this restraint contained an unspoken invitation. Butler would often watch her in a roomful of people silently transmitting the invitation to a man some yards away in another group. It also did not escape Butler's attention that one of these men was Milne. A tacit dislike grew up between them.

Marguerite Butler was excessively demonstrative with her younger son. His dark looks and wayward charm, so much like her own, she found flattering. She only had to see him to cry out with delight, 'Alan, my darling, come and give me a kiss!', and then to embrace and caress him and chuckle over his tie or his hair. But he always knew that these attentions were only the means of drawing him into her spotlight, to enhance her performance, not to shed light upon him. He was her accessory and happy to be so. Just as well, perhaps, that her strokes and cuddles were self-centred, for Butler desired her ferociously. When he was quite small, and Roland was away at the school to which he himself would later go, she would rustle into his room, arms spread wide, and swoop down on him to bestow a warm, fragrant, good-night kiss that would leave him taut with lust for hours. He was plagued by the question: How could she bear his father?

By the time he went to Sandhurst – only missing the Sword of Honour because of a tendency to wildness – Marguerite had died of a massive cerebral haemorrhage, so ensuring that she remained enshrined in her son's memory as the epitome of the desirable woman instead of the fat, vulgar, overbearing old termagant she would undoubtedly have become.

Without her, Claud shrank and shrivelled and lost the Jack-the-laddishness that had carried him along. Butler felt sorry for him, and the pity made his scorn still greater. He never asked any of his friends, either from school or from Sandhurst, to stay at the house in Harpur Avenue after his mother's death.

It would have astonished Jumbo Oliphant to know how unsettled Butler had been following a weekend out from school at the rectory at Tripstowe. In the shambling, faded, gently self-assured atmosphere of the Oliphants' house he saw all too sharply the tensions and unevenness in his own. The Oliphants were not well off and lacked pretensions. But they had – Butler fished the word gingerly out of his lexicon like a small girl handling a snake – standards. The food was dull and indifferently cooked, the chair arms were threadbare and the carpets balding. But the rectory had the kind of calm that came from a sense of moral order. No such calm was to be found in Harpur Avenue. Here, everything was what it seemed. At home, nothing was. Butler dazzled them all weekend, and fled back to school vowing never to return. Nor did he.

The fact was Butler had no aptitude for intimacy. His self-knowledge extended to recognising how much he preferred the large stage and captive audience of school, Sandhurst and the army to the stifling and entangling world of close relationships. He loved and left girls because after the conquest they wanted to know more, and he did not wish to be known, or to know them. He fled from the girls as he'd once fled from the rectory. But no one knew this, and it only enhanced the reputation his father, now dying in a nursing home, had wanted for him.

He had never lost touch with Jumbo Oliphant, and had been quite pleased when they fetched up in the same battalion at the outset of the war. Jumbo was far too humble and awkward to expect to be more than a permanent audience.

Gradually, as Butler lay in the dark, his ribs, hips and shoulders fighting painfully with the concrete roof beneath him, the past receded. The faces of his parents were replaced by that of Maitland. Who as far as he knew had looked into his eyes only twice. And, on both occasions, seen his soul.

Another long day followed. Everyone was edgy. Scapegoats were found. The British, who had been appointed cooks, had no idea how to treat rice and the result was a gluey mess that could only have been palatable to the starving. The Australians were particularly scathing about this Pommie pap, and the food queue was enlivened by witticisms like: 'Who called the cook a bastard?' 'Who called the bastard a cook?'

That evening up on the roof they heard singing from one of the other blocks. Everyone had been trying to keep their spirits up with sing-songs and bad jokes, but this was different. It was a performance. A lone tenor warbled: 'What'll I do, when you are far away, and I am blue, what'll I do . . .?' On the second chorus it was joined by another voice, reedy and less confident. The effect was curiously touching. Jumbo, along with others on their roof, rewarded the effort with a brief burst of applause. Encouraged, the first voice began another song, 'You're the cream in my coffee, you're the salt in my stew . . . ' Jumbo salivated. In came the second voice on the lines, 'You will always be my necessity, I'd be lost without you.'

Jumbo peered at Butler, who was sitting with his back

into the corner of the shallow parapet, his cap pulled down over the upper part of his face. 'Butler, did you hear that?'

Butler nodded.

'That chap can sing a bit.'

'Mm. A bit. Practised in the local *palais*, I shouldn't wonder.'

Jumbo was taken aback. It wasn't like Butler to be openly snobbish.

He listened for a while longer, and then said, 'I think it may be that chap Maitland.'

Butler shrugged. He had not lifted his cap from his face. Jumbo decided to leave it at that. He huddled down, his stomach griping and complaining, and listened to the singing. He didn't attempt to sleep, for that was fatal. He gazed up towards the sky. Butler's loosely clasped hands intruded on his view of the stars. Bones and veins stood out on them like those on a medical lecturer's dummy. The fingers, Jumbo noticed, appeared oddly stubby. He squinted at them, and saw that the nails had been savagely bitten. He closed his eyes.

The first man – Jumbo was sure it was Maitland – was now singing, 'We're going to hang out the washing on the Siegfried Line/ Have you any dirty washing mother dear?' Jumbo wondered how long the singing would continue before someone put a stop to it. He also wondered whether he could face the long haul to the thunderboxes or risk a dismaying emergency.

He opened his eyes again and saw that Butler had turned on to his side, his hands buried in his armpits.

'Christ,' Jumbo heard him mutter, 'why won't some friendly Nip put a bullet in him?'

Jumbo's bowels spluttered warningly and he struggled to his feet and began the slow descent towards relief.


The following morning a group of senior officers left the camp in trucks under Japanese escort. No one knew where they'd gone. Restless anxiety settled over Selarang. Men wandered too close to the perimeter and were yelled at and threatened. The machine gun near the clock tower was trained on the thickest part of the crowd.

Living conditions were becoming more dangerously filthy by the minute in the flyblown squalor of the square. The numbers of sick soared in the torrid heat. Jumbo knew that anywhere but here he would have been accounted seriously ill. His skin burned with assorted excoriating rashes and eruptions; he was permanently weary and weak; the symptoms of beriberi which he had managed to contain outside were creeping back; and he was pretty sure he was getting dysentery. Nonetheless he was better than most. He dared not even entertain complaint. What Butler had implied was true: officers had a firmer hold on life.


Once during that uneasy day Jumbo saw Maitland. He was with Steward, helping reconstruct a couple of ragbag shelters which had collapsed on top of their more or less senseless occupants. He appeared pretty fit by the standards of the moment, and had that jaunty air which Jumbo found so appealing, because jauntiness was foreign to him. Steward, however, looked bad – white and weak as a ghost, his eyes filmy behind the spectacles which were tied at the back of his head with string. After months of living with men *in extremis* one learned to differentiate between degrees of desperation. Jumbo didn't like the look of Steward.


The officers returned during the afternoon, looking grim and drawn. They'd been taken to Changi beach to witness the summary execution of four POWs who'd been caught trying to escape. Meetings were called. The courage of the men executed was commended.

100

The object of the exercise had been clear, said the officers: to demonstrate the kind of treatment which would be meted out to any prisoner attempting to escape. In addition, the Japs were threatening to bring in the sick and wounded from the hospital. Tension and hostility rocketed on both sides of the wire. The number of armed guards on the perimeter road doubled.

The senior officer in charge, the Australian Colonel 'Black Jack' Galleghan, ordered them to sign the no escape forms. He would be responsible, he said: the order came directly from him and there'd be no stain on anyone's character. This would be an action carried out under duress.

The Fen Tigers' senior officer endorsed this. 'If we all die, either in this stinking hole or trying to get out of it, we'll be neither use nor ornament,' was how he put it. 'It's only a form of words, there's nothing to stop anyone trying to escape anyway. But we need to be alive to make things difficult for the Nips.'

It seemed like sense. There were mutinous rumblings, but nothing more. The forms were ready to hand and laid out in piles on a table in front of the clock tower, manned by two Japanese soldiers.

More queueing, thought Jumbo. Just as well the British were so good at it. He had never seen Butler so angry. Long after most objectors had accepted the wisdom of signing, he was haggard with rage, his eyes black slits in his white face. Sheepishly, for he himself was anxious to sign, Jumbo hung back for as long as he dared.

'Can't they see how wrong this is?' growled Butler. 'It goes against every bloody thing we've been taught as soldiers!'

Jumbo didn't know what to say.

In the end they found themselves picked up by the tide and washed into the queue. The general mood was lightening. The onus of responsibility was off the men; they were going to get out of this place and on with the job of trying to stay alive. They talked of their billets in Changi as one might talk of going home. All things were relative, thought Jumbo.

At the signing table this mood prevailed. The Australian two places ahead of Jumbo signed himself 'Ned Kelly', and the next man, straight-faced, wrote 'Shirley Temple'. Jumbo, never an exhibitionist, put: 'John Oliphant.'

He stole a quick look at Butler's signature. The writing was so fast and the pressure of the pen so great that it had almost torn the paper. He'd written: 'Butler Youbastards'.

When they'd signed they were allowed to leave the barracks. They passed between ranks of Sikh guards, down to a small valley where some of the open-air concerts were held. Though they smelt foul, the air seemed sweet and fresh here. They took great gulps of it and stretched their arms. The greenness was wonderful after the concrete confines of the barracks. Jumbo felt absurdly lighthearted. 'Thank God that's over,' he said.

# CHAPTER NINE

# 1989

I went all over and by and large I was a typical tourist, alone in the crowd. Whether I took cabs, rickshaws or buses, or rode the bustling, spotless subway, I remained solitary. I was conscious of being 'on my own' in the way people mean when you have embarked on a rash enterprise and they can't be bothered with you.

It must be said that after the Changi chapel incident I was even more disposed to keep myself to myself. Apart from breakfast, when I made a point of reading a book, I avoided the hotel restaurant like the plague and went out to eat. The food was better, and cheaper, and I could escape the irritation of people trying to befriend me. Mornings I looked round the island. After lunch I took a nap. Afternoons, more rubber-necking, then back for a shower and out for dinner. Then I'd walk back to the hotel, have a swim and go to my room to read or write. I read contemporary, witty, hard-edged stuff – Martin Amis and Malcolm Bradbury and Alison Lurie (though she made me homesick for the States) – and I wrote a continuing letter to Cary which I intended posting when I moved on.

I sent some postcards. I sent one to Milly and Bernard, and another to Nathan and Laura. I then tore them both up, deciding I was both ageist and sexist, and wrote only one, addressed to 'The Ramsey family'. This was so insufferably arch with its Bloomsbury overtones that I tore it up too, and did what I really wanted to do which was address a postcard to Milly alone, and include the rest in a 'best regards' at the end.

I went to Macritchie Reservoir and took in the oasthouse-like Shinto shrines which prisoners had helped to build. It was just a pretty park. In another park, the Botanical Gardens, there were Chinese wedding parties round every corner: dimpling brides in Di dresses and Fergie frocks, fondling orchids or gazing into lily ponds while their enchanting young grooms stood in attendance carrying the bouquet. A positive orgy of straightness. Those technicolour flowers, velvet lawns and saccharine smiles discomforted me more than anything I'd so far seen.

I walked down Outram Road but the infamous police station which had been the Kempei Tai HQ was no longer there. So many men had been tortured there. Stories had abounded then, and been corroborated since, of the depths to which cruelty and suffering can sink. They said a man had kept starvation at bay by eating the black beans he found in Japanese excrement. History did not recount how this prisoner had gained access to the executive washroom – oh, I deplored my own cynicism – but if even a fraction of the stories were true, if they had even a nodding acquaintance with the truth, it was terrible. And though I had not been in Outram Road, I knew what terrible was.

It was the endless mythologising that repelled me. I dreaded participating in it, even by association. When the cabbie slowed down reverentially outside the Kranji War Cemetery I told him to drive on with the lofty indifference of a milord. No one was going to catch me mooning over empty graves.

Unable, as ever, to resist a ride in a boat (I must have done the Circle Line Trip a hundred times, with or without the jaded Cary), I took a Chinese junk 'tour' of the Singapore river. It was not extensive. We covered no more than a mile, half of that between rows of unlovely godowns to the metal bridge which had burned during the Japanese bombing of the harbour. The walnut-faced boatman, an oriental Charon if ever I saw one, sat at the helm while a taped voice described, with advantages, what we could see for ourselves, threw in a few well-thumbed historical facts and made a pitch for modern Singapore, the tourist paradise.

But when we left the godowns and emerged from the river into the harbour proper, beneath the pop-eyed, fishtailed lion, I felt the ghost at my shoulder again for a moment. For there was the great Palladian frontage of the Post Office, and the stretch of beach where George Aspinall, the Changi photographer, had walked on the morning after the British surrender as the city burned. We'd been cooped up in the tennis court then, but that photograph of Aspinall's had served since as a metaphor for the pathetic, murderous chaos that had prevailed: soldiers of a vanquished army strolling on the beach like sightseers, while behind them smoke billowed up from the ruins of a colonial dream.

Back on the waterfront I bought some greasy food at one of the dozens of little Chinese cafés, and then walked back towards St Andrew's Cathedral. This was the best part of the city, where the elegant white colonial buildings were. There were two wedding groups on the steps of the town hall, in direct competition, with the photographers bobbing, weaving and ricocheting off one another like boxers to get the best angle.

And here was the Cricket Club *padang*, still gracious but no longer affording, as it once had, a view of the sea. A match was in progress on this sultry Wednesday, slow and concentrated beyond the urgent clamour of the traffic.

I wandered into the car park of St Andrew's. Inside,

some kind of *puja* was in progress, mothers with young children clapping their hands and singing beneath the slow-turning fans. One of the women caught sight of me staring in and flashed me a sisterly smile which sent me running for cover. The Almighty had had his pound of flesh and more.

I'd have liked to have sipped a Singapore Sling or a Stenga at Raffles (that, at least, Cary would have approved of), but it was closed for refurbishment till further notice. The famous porticoed frontage, boarded up by the builders, looked rather small and dismal with the gleaming skyscrapers of a new generation looming over it.

Skyscrapers are what I'm used to now, though. In a skyscraper, in my experience, you can get a proper drink with plenty of ice in an air-conditioned atmosphere. I was melting, and the afternoon was thickening in readiness for another downpour. I abandoned adventure and went in search of refreshment.

That evening was my last in Singapore. I finished my long letter to Cary. I wanted the letter to say the things that weren't so easily said over the telephone. I wanted to be truthful, with him and with myself, which was easier without his mocking voice down the line. I described my wanderings, and explained that every now and then I did catch a glimpse of the past. I told him I had high hopes of the next stage of my journey. But I didn't mention the girl I'd met in London.

In the middle of the night the air conditioning broke down. I awoke at about two a.m., damp with sweat, in a room which had become a sauna. The window, of course, was sealed. I rang the night housekeeper who apologised, said everyone was in the same boat and suggested I open my door.

I decided against taking this advice. Instead I sluiced myself down with cool water and lay on top of the bed, still wet. The ghost crept to my side and lay down next to me. So often I'd lain like this, on my strip of sleeping platform, deathly still, perspiring, staring into the dark. I remembered vividly a recurring sensation of those nights . . . My body was so wasted that it had no more substance than a dry leaf. I seemed to float above myself, tethered by the thinnest of cobweb-like threads. But when I looked back down, there were so many skeletal, shrunken figures lying motionless on the platform that I could not tell which one was me. How could I go back when I didn't know where to go back to? But then, just as I prepared to sever the thread and drift away altogether, I'd suddenly regain full consciousness, staring out of my skull like a rat in a trap.

I had ordered a cab for six a.m. to take me to the station. Down in the hotel lobby a couple of Malay cleaners were polishing the floor with slow, scything motions. An electric fan had been set up on the reception desk, and another on the ornamental table opposite the main door. Outside it was dim and pearly, the slightly threatening dawn common to places where sunrise brings punishing heat. I paid my bill and loitered near the fan, my bag at my feet. Dead on time the cab driver presented himself. *En route* he made conversation. 'Where you going?'

'Bangkok.'

He cackled with laughter. 'Bangkok? All the way by train?'

'That's right.'

'That take long time. Two three day.'

'Not quite. And I'm having a night in Penang.'

'Penang? Only one night?' His facetious incredulity was getting tiresome.

'That's right.'

'Penang holiday place. Very scenic. Very beautiful. You should stay for longer.'

'I dare say, but I want to get to Bangkok.'

'Uh-huh.' His tone changed. He was a man of the world.

'I see.'

I couldn't be bothered to correct the impression that I was desperate for cheap sex. At least it had shut him up.

At the station there was a queue snaking back from the barrier and out of the main door so we had to pull up on the corner. When I'd paid the smirking cabby I fell in (those expressions were beginning to come back to me) behind an Indian woman in a peacock blue sari. She had a baby on her back, a toddler in a stroller, and an enormous suitcase. I had just decided that when the queue began to move I would opt for assisting with the case rather than the kids, when the barrier was opened and she set off, case in one hand, stroller handle in the other, with an easy rolling gait. The queue surged forward with a noise like a parrot house at feeding time. I was in danger of being trampled underfoot. Tiny children were scooped up or urgently ushered forward; bags, baskets and bedrolls were carried or dragged. A couple of tiny bent old people were steered respectfully in the right direction. The old woman had bound feet like little hooves. A fat Malay in cut-off 501s carried a wicker cage containing some kind of rodent. A dim memory of Rikki Tikki Tavi led me to suppose that it might be a mongoose. While the cage rested on the platform the animal swung back and forth, back and forth with metronomic regularity. When its owner picked it up it crouched down, ears flattened and eyes glaring, a picture of terrified ferocity. I was glad I was travelling first class.

Not that it was exactly the Orient Express. The queue chattered, wailed, groused and squawked its way through passport control, though happily I was nodded through quickly and was able to take my seat. I guessed that what distinguished first class from the rest was the upholstery – vintage Railway Panscourer – and the in-carriage entertainment. High in the far corner a TV set was showing *Raiders of the Lost Ark* dubbed into Chinese. The picture was terrible, but it was nonetheless interesting to see how Harrison Ford's craggy features appeared to take on a more oriental cast to go with his new voice.

The train was half an hour late leaving, and then set off with all the urgency of a tortoise on dope. It trundled through the scattered suburbs and out over the Johore Causeway as though uncertain of its destination. As we had been, all those years ago. The ghost slid into the seat next to me and whispered in my ear, 'Better this time, huh . . .?'

There were diversions, not to say compensations. A continual stream of delightful Malay boys from the adjoining buffet car kept plying us with refreshments – huge polystyrene pint pots of tea, 'saucered and blown' as my sister would have said, heavily sugared and topped up with evaporated milk. To accompany this resistible beverage, breakfast: curry puffs and chicken rice, also in polystyrene caskets. I tucked in, just to see them smile, and found, to my surprise, that it was good.

We were beyond Johore, and beginning to chug, still at our sedate pace, up the Malay peninsula. Indiana Jones gave way to *Three Men and a Baby*. I gazed out of the window. Then, there had been more of the oily, bright green jungle and fewer of the red earth roads and shanty towns, but it was still familiar. We passed through, and sometimes even stopped at, village halts. They were affectionately tended, like the English country stations of pre-Beeching days. Rockeries and gardens were outlined with white-painted pebbles, and station masters in glistening white jackets and caps carried furled flags. But no one seemed to get on or off. Perhaps the stops were only to provide movement and colour in the lives of the railway officials. I didn't recall so many stations. But then most of us hadn't been able to see where we were going, anyway.

The boys came round again – different ones this time, in

the same fetching outfit of crisp white shirt, powder blue vest and dark trousers – and offered more food, more tea. They beamed and were pressing, without the least trace of impertinence. And they knew, of course, we all knew the game we played, but it was played with a gentleness and discretion that was utterly charming. I would tell Cary about them and make him eat his heart out.

Because of the boys' insistence about food I lost track of time and was surprised on looking at my watch to discover that it was two o'clock. We'd been travelling for five hours. I had no idea where we were, and I didn't care. The ghost was still there, but was silent and companionable. I was suspended between places and between times in a sensuous melancholy. I wondered, were I to try and tell the boy stewards what I was doing here, whether they would be impressed and treat me as a hero. But I stifled the idea at birth. A fine thing, to go capitalising on the past I was here to examine and exorcise. Nobly, I desisted.


We trundled through the afternoon. More and longer stretches of bright green jungle. Palms. The occasional startling red of a Chinese temple in a clearing. In a ramshackle *kampong* a group of immaculately turned out schoolchildren in white blouses and black shorts and pinafores, carrying umbrellas, threaded a path between chomping goats and piebald cows.

I fell asleep for a while, and woke up as we pulled into the Moorish splendour of Kuala Lumpur Station. I got out on to the platform and strolled up and down, stretching my legs. Ours was the only train in and on the opposite platform, near the main entrance, were all the usual offices – 'Women's Lavatories and Prayer Room', a snack shop and a money-changer.

The only other people to alight were a bespectacled student and an American couple, also travelling first class. Of the jabbering horde who had got on at Singapore there

110

was no sign, and yet no one, as far as I had been able to see, had got off at any intervening stop. I walked the length of the train and there they were, sitting tight, prevented from taking the air, perhaps, by some superstitious dread of being left behind. I went over the bridge, beyond which gilded minarets and elaborate white plasterwork glinted in the late afternoon sun, and went to the shop. I bought some chocolate and changed a few more dollars. The money-changer grinned. The old crone, crouched on a mat outside the women's lavatories, scowled.

The stop at KL dissipated my melancholy. I ate the chocolate, to the approval of the stewards who peeped down the aisle at me from the door of the buffet car.

Gradually, the landscape changed. To my left, westwards, the country opened out and was flat and swampy, with rivers and pools gleaming here and there. To the right there rose the first hills of the journey, which soon became mountains, the lush green mass of the Cameron Highlands.

They'd told us we were going there. Rest camps, they said, where we'd be able to grow plenty of good fresh food, and the climate would be healthy.

And it was as we crawled along the flank of these jungle-cloaked hills that we finally acknowledged what we'd secretly suspected all along. That they'd lied to us.

# CHAPTER TEN

# *1943*

'We're the dregs,' said Butler. 'Look at us.'

Jumbo looked, and then looked back at Butler. He wasn't sure how to take this assertion. The evidence supported it, and yet Butler's tone was almost boastful.

'If we are,' said Jumbo, 'it's not our fault.'

The first of sixteen trains carrying F Force north was making a *benjo* stop. It was the middle of the day – Jumbo's precious wristwatch was thickly beaded with condensation and nobody's was working reliably, so it was hard to be precise. The train had pulled up in the middle of nowhere. To the east, about a mile and a half from the line, the land rose in a range of thickly wooded hills. To the west it was flat and marshy, dotted with waist-high scrub. It was on this side that the prisoners had alighted, but since the sun was at its height neither hills nor train afforded any shade.

It was still a great deal better being off the train. Each steel box car measured seven by seventeen feet. The allocation was thirty prisoners, and sometimes a Korean guard, per car. The movement of the train provided some air for those lucky enough to be taking their turn near the door, but since it never travelled at more than twenty miles per hour, and the temperature inside rose to 120 degrees during the day, it was canned purgatory for most of them. When a man was ambushed by a loose bowel movement – which was often – he had first to struggle to the doorway, there to be suspended from it, his bare arse hanging over the side of the track as he relieved himself. It had occurred to Jumbo more than once that had the train been travelling any faster those sitting in the truck behind the afflicted person might have had an unpleasant shock. The stinking, flyblown mess spattered along the side of the track attested to the passage of earlier trainloads. Unfortunately many sufferers were physically unable to fight their way through the crush and the condition of the floor had become unspeakable. It was, perhaps, a blessing in disguise that there was no room to lie down. The best they could do was to perch on their kit.

The timing of this stop was a typically unpredictable decision by the Japs. There was no set pattern. The prisoners felt they were being toyed with. If they had not been clinging to the idea of the promised up-country rest camps, and severely weakened by four days and nights in the rice trucks, they might have been more rebellious.

It was now the hottest part of the day and there was very little cover. The wretched men with dysentery, of whom there were more each day, were crouched amongst the scrub – thin, stooped figures like a flock of scrawny storks, their faces pinched with pain and a desperate relief.

'Excuse me,' said Jumbo. He left Butler's side and walked as far as he could from the train before first peeing, then squatting. His gut was grumbling, but things weren't too bad yet. When he'd finished he straightened up and gazed about at the dense green landscape. They were virtually unsupervised. The Japanese officers from the HQ car, 'the Pullman', were clustered together at the front of the train. The Korean guards were mostly lounging close to the box cars. Jumbo or any of the other men now milling about aimlessly could simply have walked away. Except that both they and their captors knew it would be hopeless. They were sick and enfeebled and had no idea where they were.

He wandered back, the heat dragging at him. Back at the box car he sat down, very gingerly, in the doorway. The metal was scorching, but just bearable. Behind him in the semi-darkness several prisoners, past caring, had taken the opportunity to stretch out on the floor.

Butler returned, walking briskly from the direction of the front of the train. He'd been on the *qui vive*.

'I went to order us some supper in the compartment,' he said, 'but nothing doing.'

'Ah.' Butler's little ways were diverting as ever, but Jumbo had temporarily run out of the energy to respond. 'I tell you one thing,' Butler went on, 'we should have kept up with the evening classes. The interpreters are travelling Pullman.'

'Officers anyway, aren't they?'

'By no means. I saw that private, the bespectacled chap who's pally with Maitland – he's in there. He was swotting up the Nippon-go back in camp.'

Recalling the last time he'd seen Steward, Jumbo decided the fellow had taken a wise course of action.

'Maybe we should do the same,' he said, 'When we get there.'

They'd left Changi in high spirits. The new camp, they'd been told, was in the Cameron Highlands. Comfortable quarters, a healthy climate and the opportunity to grow plenty of good fresh food. And there was no option. Many thousands of men had already gone, and the numbers of those left behind were dwindling fast.

They loaded everything, all the precious stuff they'd hoarded against a rainy day – clothing, medicines and tinned food – and Jumbo saw Maitland and one or two others from the concert party shoving the piano into the back of a truck. They might have been going on holiday. Except that on the station platform it was chastening to compare themselves, the former lords of empire, with the

114

brightly clothed and healthy looking Asian and Malays around them. The officers looked a little better than the men – some of them had shirts – but by and large they were a tattered, verminous, disease-ridden rabble. Jumbo found it hard to feel anything but shame. It was all right in principle to talk about fighting back in captivity and giving the Nips a hard time, but the reality was that they had lost, and their circumstances were desperate beyond what had been imaginable eighteen months ago.

As they shuffled up the siding to get into the trucks he'd spotted Maitland – who had survived so far in spite of Butler's prognosis – with his usual bunch of cronies. Willard was entertaining them and they were laughing a good deal. As he hoisted himself up on to the train, Maitland flung out an arm and sang: 'Oh I do like to be beside the seaside . . .!' in his throaty tenor. Jumbo was much affected. Where did such resilience come from?

There were occasional erratic stops for rice and sometimes a drink. At one of the stations some of the prisoners had the bright idea of filling their water bottles from the tanks used to fill the engine boiler. They drank the stuff, and sloshed it over their heads and shoulders. Jumbo noticed both Butler and Maitland in this group, but wasn't tempted to join them. It might be a bit late to worry about what one fed into one's system, but the thought of that greasy, flyblown, tepid liquid . . . He shuddered.

Because of the inadequacy and infrequency of the food rations many men were saving their rice and eking it out. The MOs warned that this was courting disaster, and were proved right. The rice went bad, the men ate it anyway and spent half the journey with their backsides hanging out of the truck. Still, they told themselves, anything was bearable if it meant getting to a better place.

Climbing back on board after the *benjo* stop was dreadfully dispiriting. The air outside wasn't fresh, but it was better than the foetid darkness of the trucks. For a few minutes they'd been surrounded by green, empty space and the open sky. It was like escape, and recapture.

The train rattled forward, creeping like a thick snake round the long curves of the line. The hills to the east got higher, the vegetation more lush. These, surely, were the Cameron Highlands. Jumbo recalled the words of a psalm, and said them in his head: 'I will lift up mine eyes unto the hills, from whence cometh my help.'

They drew in at Ipoh. They'd heard this was to be the stop, the one where they would detrain for the new camp. For the first time in days Jumbo felt a buzz of adrenalin. They were going to get off!

But as the box cars crawled the length of the platform and jolted to a halt, there was no order to disembark. And outside, a wall of black faces: Indian coolies, waiting to get on.

When, half an hour later, they left Ipoh, the prisoners were silent. The unfortunate coolies, many of them ill, were crammed in wherever they'd fit. The stench of sweat, disease and ordure was overpowering. Urine and faeces sloshed liberally over the hot steel floors. Groans, grunts and ululations filled the air. The only tiny consolation was the greatest number had been shoved into the Pullman, where there was most room.

'Serve them right,' muttered Butler.

Jumbo didn't answer. Though he hadn't eaten for twenty-four hours, he felt that if he opened his mouth he might vomit, and he was at the furthest point from the door.

'What suckers we were,' went on Butler, to whoever could listen. 'We're slave labour.'

Not long after that a few notes of Jap-issued Malay currency floated like leaves from one of the box cars as the realisation dawned on some wretch that he would have little use for it where he was going.

At some point they crossed into Thailand. Thickly forested snaggle-tooth peaks pressed in on either side of the train as it wormed its way northwards. The weather began to change. Steamy days were offset by nights cold enough to make their teeth chatter. The light grew heavy and lurid and the sky was mountainous with monsoon clouds. Several of the coolies succumbed and were jettisoned. A woman in an adjoining car died giving birth. The screams of the starving infant ceased shortly thereafter. Both were thrown out into the jungle.

On the fifth day they were shunted into a siding. No one was allowed off, and the heat in the rice trucks rose. A Korean guard marched up and down outside the train enforcing the rule that the doors should only be open a few inches when they were near a station. They were effectively imprisoned while thousands of flies, attracted by the feast, swarmed in and out freely. For the second time, Jumbo thought: This is it. Things can't get any worse – and tried to take a grain of hope from knowing he had reached the nadir of misery and discomfort. One of the Indians had slumped on to his shoulder and was ululating softly. It didn't help.

'Your shift, Captain Oliphant.'

An arm waved near the door, indicating that it was Jumbo's turn to press his nose to the aperture.

The press was now so tight that when Jumbo moved the weeping Indian remained upright, still held at the vertical between those on either side of him, his pitifully bony legs sagging like those of a laboratory skeleton.

Jumbo reached the door and stood with his face to the chink. A guard passed and made a lunging motion with his rifle butt, telling him to get back. He did so, and then leaned forward again.

Now he could see that the guard had been walking along the sleepers of a second railway track running parallel to theirs and no more than a yard from it. Beyond the track there was some kind of goods yard, an assembly of broken-down sheds with a clearing of red earth on which were parked a couple of flat-bed trucks.

There was an interrupted background noise of voices, and the fierce hiss of a cooling engine; the jolt and clang of trucks coupling. Another train drew up alongside theirs. It was packed full of Thai soldiers but compared to their own it looked the height of luxury with its wooden seats and luggage racks.

Jumbo gazed out with his half face and one yearning eye at the men in their smart grey uniforms.

'What is it?' someone near him asked.

'Looks like Thai troops.'

He moved his face across to look out with the other eye. As he did so, an arm emerged from the open window of the carriage opposite. In the hand were the two halves of an enormous mango. The orange fruit gleamed like a lamp in the shadow between the trains, giving off moisture, fragrance, hope. The hand waggled slightly in invitation. A couple of drops of juice slid from the mango. Desperately Jumbo wriggled until he could push his own hand through the gap. He had no idea where the guard was. He forced the door back a couple of inches and reached for the mango. In his imagination his fingertips already touched the sweet, cool, glossy surface —

The rifle butt cut across his knuckles with a clatter, drawing blood instantly. Jumbo yelped and withdrew his hand, but he felt no pain. All his distress was for the mango halves which had been knocked from the soldier's grasp and were splattered in an orange mess on the ground between the coaches.

The guard, screaming angrily, slammed the door shut. Jumbo stood in the dark with his knuckles in his mouth,

118

tasting the salt of blood and tears.

In a few minutes they heard the Thai train pull away, heading south. Not long after they moved in the opposite direction.

Later that day they arrived at a station and stopped alongside a sign reading 'Banpong'. The boxcar doors were not closed, and the guards motioned them to get out. They stumbled on to the platform, stiff, hungry and clotted with dirt and sweat. The Indian coolie remained folded marionette-like on the floor of the truck. He had gone quiet: had either given up, or was dead. It would come to the same thing.

Butler came up to Jumbo's shoulder: 'Will you look at that?'

They were confronted by a row of Japanese soldiers in immaculate green uniforms and with fixed bayonets. Crisp white shirts showed above their jacket collars, and they wore the same soft leather knee-length boots that Jumbo remembered so vividly from the morning of his capture. Their long sword scabbards almost brushed the ground. The Koreans began rushing about, asserting their authority with much yelling and brandishing of rifles.

Butler shouted: 'To attention!' Adding, more quietly, 'Don't give them the satisfaction.' He himself took a step forward, shoulders back, chin lifted, in a parody of military smartness. A guard immediately thumped him in the chest and shouted at him to stand back. This he did, with much stamping of feet. He must have been winded by the blow, but if he was it didn't show. Jumbo noticed the ghosts of smiles on one or two faces. His admiration for Butler was matched by concern. A man could get killed for less.

The stuff from the baggage trucks was unloaded, and each man picked up as much as he could carry. Jumbo was shocked to find that a modest load comprising his own kit, a blanket, a few tins of food and a saucepan was almost more than he could manage. By the time they were outside the station he was sweating and trembling. The piano caused much merriment among the guards. The prisoners' last sight of it was on the end of the platform, as pathetic and out of place as a beached whale.

Mercifully they stopped, were lined up once more and shouted at by the Koreans. Then one of the Japanese officers stepped up to address them.

'You will march to the Prisoner Camp about one mile. You will march well, without talking to the civilian population. This is the beginning of an important time for all prisoners, the beginning of their time of service to his Imperial Majesty. March well. Work well. It is an honour to serve the Emperor. The spirit of Bushido will inspire and strengthen you in the task ahead . . . '

There was more, but Jumbo did not listen to it. He was nearly asleep on his feet like an old horse standing under a tree in the rain.

'Prisoner, march!'

He came to as he was shoved in the small of the back. The Koreans were displaying their loyalty to the Emperor. With a considerable effort, he walked forward.

They trudged through the town. The sky was black and purple, but the heat was intense. The road was flanked with wooden-fronted native shops. Scruffy and run down it might be, but this afternoon Banpong was *en fête* to welcome another trainload of sacrificial lambs for fleecing. The locals were enjoying a boom. There would be plenty of time to relieve this latest instalment of suckers of their possessions. This was just the softening up.

Butler grinned bleakly. 'They like us! They really like us!'

'I wish I could buy some food,' said Jumbo.

'Go ahead.'

'We can't stop. And we're not supposed to talk to them. I don't want to be pistol-whipped at the moment.'

120

'You don't have to stop. They'll run to keep up with you. Point at what you want. The Thais are among the most entrepreneurial nations on earth, you know.' It was true. The column of prisoners towed with it a flotilla of mobile stalls, baskets, rickshaw boys, and even chortling mamas offering fresh, plump young girls.

There was a dizzying array of food – fruit, sticks of roast meat, sticky cakes, sweets, bananas in batter, chunks of fresh coconut. Jumbo bought some meat and a piece of coconut and was astonished to have half his money waved away.

'They're generous people,' he remarked.

'You think so?' said Butler.

'They won't even accept full payment.'

'I hate to destroy your illusions, old man, but they don't need to. It will be given unto them a thousandfold.'

Jumbo stuffed the sticky red shreds of meat into his mouth. Even now his weakened digestive system was rebelling and he knew he wouldn't be able to finish it, but it was acting on him like a shot in the arm.

A fat woman with greasy hair and teeth blackened by betel-nut juice caught at Butler's sleeve.

'Officer! Want jig-a-jig? Good girl, fourteen years, good jig-a-jig.'

Jumbo was shocked. 'Butler . . . fourteen.'

'Forbidden fruits.' Butler slowed his pace and glanced at the girl, who was comely and giggling. 'I'm tempted.'

'Butler!'

Butler chuckled, shaking his head, and the woman and her daughter fell back to try their luck on the next group.

'You're a prig, Oliphant,' said Butler. His eyes were as black as a snake's.


The outskirts of Banpong were less colourful. The hangers-on didn't follow them that far, and there was nothing to conceal the drabness of the jerry-built shops

121

and shanties around which pigs and dogs rooted in drifts of malodorous refuse. Beyond the buildings there was no relief, none of the jungle-clad mountains they'd passed further south, but a landscape flat as a board, chequered with glinting paddy fields. It was, thought Jumbo, like an oriental variant on some setting for an M R James story. How had this lonely, scruffy town sprung up? Where did the people come from? And how did they live when they weren't propositioning prisoners?

Word came back down the line that the camp was in sight. Jumbo and Butler could see only a thick curtain of yellowish dust. As they got nearer it began to rain. The ground underfoot turned to sludge, and now they could see a square wooden gateway with a large notice nailed to the transom: Japanese characters and the translation 'Camp for Cattle, Coolies and Prisoners of War'.

'Mark the pecking order,' said Butler. Jumbo's heart sank. The rain quickened and soon they'd be soaked through. The meat growled and twisted in his gut.

Depressing details became visible. Beyond the gate a milling mass of prisoners was being herded about by guards brandishing sticks. Beyond them was a collection of long, low attap huts in a poor state of repair. Around the perimeter were a few dead trees on whose bare, arthritic limbs patient buzzards sat with hunched shoulders under the downpour.

'My God,' muttered Jumbo. 'My God!'

'Why have You forsaken us,' supplied Butler.

At the gate a tiny man stood waiting to meet them. He had a porcelain-smooth face and delicate womanish hands in one of which was a golf club (a five-iron, Jumbo noticed inconsequentially) with which he arbitrarily struck every sixth or seventh man. Jumbo trembled, sure it would be him. He wished he were not so large and lumbering and conspicuous. He stooped and dropped his head, the picture of crushed humility. Next to him he was conscious of Butler walking very upright.

They both passed through unscathed. Almost the minute they'd done so there was the hiss and crack of the five-iron making contact with flesh and bone. Apprehensively, Jumbo looked over his shoulder. To his surprise the victim was Maitland, whom he hadn't seen since KL. A savage gash had been opened high on the right side of his forehead, next to the widow's peak. He was staggering along, supported by the man next to him, blood trickling between the dirty fingers he had pressed to the wound.

Jumbo touched Butler's arm. 'That was Maitland.'

'Really?' said Butler, without turning. 'You don't surprise me.'

Jumbo might have commented, however mildly, on this callousness, but then something happened to distract him. Maitland looked over his shoulder in the direction of the *heiko* and with no attempt at concealment lifted two bloody fingers in a V. When he turned back, he was grinning all over his gruesomely daubed face. The *heiko*, intent on singling out his next victim, saw nothing.

When they were inside the camp they were herded together and ordered to form ranks and stand to attention. The rain was so hard that it spurted up from the ground, coating their legs with mud. This was not the first of the monsoon rains: there was abundant evidence that the latrine trenches had overflowed several times recently.

After about ten minutes a Japanese officer appeared, a greatcoat swinging from his shoulders, accompanied by a fat, scuttling Korean carrying a black umbrella. The officer stood on a box and told them they would soon be taken to their billets, but would only be here for a short while because a Great Task awaited them: the completion of the mighty overland railway which would carry the forces of the Emperor to victory in Asia. Insubordination, treachery or disobedience of any kind, he warned, would meet with swift and severe punishment. But honest toil, the privilege of working for the Chrysanthemum Throne, would bring its own reward.

123

They stood in the mud for a further twenty minutes, and were then herded furiously – as though it were the guards and not they who had been kept waiting – to a cluster of huts near the perimeter fence.

The hut in which Jumbo found himself made him recall Changi with the tenderest emotion. It was in a state of chronic disrepair, the sides in shreds and the roof sagging in several places. At the far end the bamboo sleeping platform had partially collapsed and was submerged in black, raw sewage a foot deep, on the surface of which floated banana skins, tins, excreta and other rubbish. The rain had eased off, but water still trickled through the roof.

Jumbo realised he was shivering with cold. From outside the hut came a voice singing, 'Be it never so humble, there's no place like home . . .'

It sounded like Maitland.

Butler had waded the length of the hut and had organised a couple of men to help resurrect the sleeping platform. Jumbo hauled his kit on to the platform next to him. Everything was slick with the same fluid that slopped about their legs. Involuntarily, he put his hand to his shirt pocket and felt the firm shape of his prayer book.

'Hey!' It was Butler, with an arm aloft. 'Dead man down here!'

They carried the poor fellow out, dripping and heavy with moisture, looking rather healthier in death than he must have done in life due to the bloating effect of the water. Jumbo and a couple of privates volunteered to bury the body while Butler pressed on with the salvaging of the hut. It would soon be dark.

'I wonder,' said Jumbo, 'where the cemetery is?'

'Padres are never here when you need them,' agreed one of the privates.

In the end they found the cemetery. They carried the body to a space near the fence, appropriated a couple of chunkels from an Australian and dug a grave. The only advantage of the rain was that it had made the ground soft. Jumbo felt a bit warmer after the exercise, and was perspiring as he stuck a length of bamboo at the end of the grave and read out a few lines from the prayer book to the embarrassment of his helpers.

Inside the hut they'd lit a couple of candle-ends, and Butler had managed to raise the sleeping platform out of the slough. The men lay, exhausted, down either side. This hut, and the many that came after it, were always to remind Jumbo of catacombs. As he paused in the doorway some-one joined him.

'Captain Oliphant?'

Jumbo saw it was the man Steward, the interpreter. His rather unprepossessing appearance was modified by better and marginally cleaner clothes than the rest of them wore.

'Yes?'

'I thought I'd better spread the word – one or two things I picked up.'

'Oh, yes?'

Steward took off his glasses and wiped them on his shorts. This gesture revealed small, weak eyes in pale sockets. It made him seem more vulnerable.

He replaced them. 'For one thing it seems likely the Kempei Tai will have a crack-down in the next couple of days, so it might be worth dumping any contraband. Some of the earlier blokes said there was a dry well in the camp. There's a lot of stuff there already.'

'Thanks,' said Jumbo. 'I'll pass the word.'

'Secondly, about the railway.'

Jumbo had the uneasy feeling that this man was eking out the bad news according to some sadistic private principle. He couldn't like him.

'What about it?'

'About two-thirds of it's completed. Our lot are the last to arrive, so we've got the last section to do. They intend marching us two hundred miles up country to the railhead.'

'I see.'

125

'I thought,' said Steward, 'you ought to know.'

'Thank you.'

'Forewarned is forearmed.'

'Quite.'

Steward peered into the hut. 'Is Corporal Maitland in here?'

'I don't believe so. No.' Jumbo remembered the singing. 'But I think he may be next door.' He experienced a sudden, uncharacteristic desire to tell this officious little man something he didn't know. 'He got a nasty crack from that Nip with the golf club.'

Steward was already walking away, but Jumbo thought he detected an increased urgency in his stride.

The latrines at Banpong consisted of a bamboo platform, into which had been cut a row of holes, balanced above a trench. There were no screens or partitions and the whole area was busy with white maggots below and glossy green blowflies above. It was a popular spot with the indefatigable Thai traders, who would emerge from the bushes at the rear, squat alongside, and open negotiations.

Butler went there often. Despite the squalor of this camp, he had a shrewd suspicion they would look back on it as a free trade paradise a couple of weeks from now. A lot of the men had parted with such valuables as remained to them, for knockdown prices, and had even sold things like mess tins and spare boots in order to take advantage of the shopping. Butler had not done so, and was in consequence a walking Aladdin's cave and in a strong negotiating position. He purchased mainly bananas – huge bunches of twenty for ten cents – eggs, aspirins and cigarettes. Eggs had taken on a special importance as a concentrated source of the vitamin B needed to counteract beriberi, so these were pooled and eaten by the day. The other stuff he was careful with, sharing some with

Oliphant and hoarding the rest. There were piles of stores and provisions left behind by previous train parties, rotting in the open and in trucks. Not a good sign, but it did mean that stuff was there for the taking. One of the MOs, Joliffe, gave him a tip: 'Get hold of a couple of jars of Marmite and don't touch them till you go down with a real dose of beriberi. Works like magic.'

Butler laid his hands on three jars and gave one to Jumbo, passing on the advice.

It wasn't only food that was on offer. The scrub behind the latrines rustled day and night with the movement of jig-a-jig. The rate was a pair of trousers for a young girl; shorts for a thirty year old; and socks (in good repair, mind) for a mama. Butler was one of the relatively few men whose libido had survived the rigours of captivity thus far. Since Selarang he had lost touch with the obliging sergeant with the loose dentures. The decision whether to take advantage of the Banpong ladies' offers exercised him considerably. Not because of any issue of conscience – the girls were obviously warm and willing – but because he did not wish to add a painful and embarrassing affliction of the private parts to the numerous others doing the rounds. He could live without that. On the other hand, this looked like being the last opportunity for some while.

One particular mama had singled him out for special attention. His looks, his demeanour, his status, all commended him to her. Time and again as he buttoned his fly she was there, placing a restraining hand over his, ushering forward her enchanting daughter of some thirteen summers, her body as plump and glossy as as plum. And time and again Butler affected indifference and moved away. But the temptation was strong. And thanks to some inspired scrounging around the derelict stores he had two pairs of brand new shorts which would fit the bill . . .

The girl was a virgin. 'Good girl, clean girl! Fresh!' the

127

mama was always saying, as though selling carrots. The mere thought of it made Butler burn. Here was a promise of sex with a girl so young, so untouched, so unsophisticated that it would require not even the most cursory social niceties. They didn't even speak each other's language.

He masturbated furiously for three nights. On the fourth day the rumour spread they'd be leaving to go up-country within twenty-four hours. Butler decided to have the girl.

He went to the latrines and then hung about near the scrub. There was no sign of the ingratiating old woman, although the agitation of the foliage indicated that business for somebody was brisk. Butler stood there, trying to appear unconcerned. Of all the locations for a rendezvous this had to be the least salubrious. The stench was sickening, the air abuzz with flies, men crouched on the bamboo platform not twenty yards away. And yet he had never been more excited. Now he had made his decision he could hardly contain himself. If only the old bag would show up!

'Thanks, sweetheart.'

Butler heard the voice at the same time as the mama arrived at his side.

'You take girl? Very nice, very fresh. Good jig-a-jig.'

Butler did not answer. His eyes were fixed on Maitland, who was running his thumbs round the sagging waistband of his shorts like an alderman after a good luncheon.

The girl appeared, bridling happily. There was a red mark on her neck. For the first time she spoke. With one hand on her breast she lowered her eyelids coquettishly and said: 'I good.'

Butler thrust the two pairs of rolled shorts at her mother. Ignoring her squawkings and protestations he walked away, just managing to get out of sight behind a hut before throwing up.

## CHAPTER ELEVEN

# *1943*

The tiger joined them ten miles out of Kanchanaburi. The first person to comment on the distinctive odour was jeered at: how the blazes could you tell, the state they were all in? And the man, professing to be an old India hand, was dismissed as a pompous windbag. What did it matter anyway? It was the least of their worries. The monsoon rains had now set in. They were soaked day and night, expected to march on almost empty stomachs and to sleep out in the open. They were dying off. If there was a tiger – and they were doubtful – it might be the means of a swift and merciful release.

Still the idea, once voiced, took root. They each began to sniff the air, to detect something different there, especially at night. The guards moved from the periphery to the middle of the column.

They'd already had to abandon more than a hundred men to certain death. Those continuing on the march were the nominally 'fit', one or two of whom gave up the ghost each day.

Jumbo assisted the padre, Tidy, in dealing with the corpses as decently as possible. They marched mainly at night, and carried the dead with them till they stopped at dawn. Then while the rest made some kind of makeshift camp – spreading sodden clothing to dry on bushes, and crawling beneath them to sleep – they would bury the bodies in shallow graves, mark them with rough crosses, and say a few words from the funeral service. Jumbo warmed to Tidy; he had a notebook in which he entered the names of the dead men, and the location, as far as he could deduce it, of their graves. At the other end the notebook contained scores from the bridge school at Changi. Both records were meticulously kept. Jumbo respected such diligence, under the circumstances. 'Essential,' said Tidy. 'You never know: someone may want to come and see where a chap's buried when this is over.'

Jumbo agreed, but it was hard to imagine the jungle politely standing aside to leave the graves exposed when it was engaged in constant furious growth. As the men of F Force stumbled through it in the dark it fought them with sodden, sinewy limbs. It pulled at and cut them. It sent out thousands of tiny envoys to bite, suck and sting them. It hissed and clattered round them. It swelled beneath the ceaseless battering rain.

Where there were proper tracks they were stony, and the stones were sharp, or slippery when wet. Deep runnels filled with water coursed over them, into which the debilitated men frequently fell. A pair of boots was now one's most valuable possession. Almost all the men had diarrhoea and were crusted with sores, and most were shivering with some form of *dengue* – tropical fever. Morale was desperately low. The officers did what they could to keep everyone going, but they too were at the point of collapse. The magic word now was *yasumi* – rest.

At one staging camp they were joined by a group of Highlanders. The march for the next twenty miles or so became characterised by the wistful song of the pipes winding back through the jungle, giving them a lead. When the Highlanders dropped out at the next camp their desolation was out of all proportion to their loss.

Jumbo clung to his responsibilities with Tidy like a drowning man to a plank. He wasn't especially fit and his lack of physical co-ordination put extra stress on his big, ponderous frame. But having a useful role to play sustained him.

It was inevitable, under these conditions, that a host of unlikely relationships should spring up. A couple of men pooling their resources could manage to be more than the sum of their parts. Loads could be shared, possessions more easily protected, a weakened or injured man could be spurred or helped on by a fitter partner. Jumbo was interested to see such a partnership developing between Butler and Maitland. They didn't seem to talk much, but as often as not they were to be found trudging along together as if they had some private understanding. This was surprising on two counts. Officers generally marched separately from the men, but then Butler was a law unto himself. And also it appeared that Jumbo had misunderstood something.

'I don't know why,' he said during a brief, and rain-free *yasumi*. 'But I thought you'd taken an instant dislike to that chap.'

'Who, Maitland?' Butler's eyes were closed, but he smiled. 'Not at all. He's a good man. Tough. Sense of humour.'

'You didn't think he'd last,' Jumbo reminded him.

'I've amended my judgement.'

Jumbo was obliged to accept this. Besides, it was unwise to jeopardise, even by implication, an alliance that was of mutual benefit to those involved.


Butler's judgement of Maitland had not been amended, on any front. The fact that Maitland had forgotten, or was choosing to ignore, the humiliating incident with Phyllis was particularly galling. Was the whole thing so unimportant to Maitland, then? Butler was hypnotised.

He watched obsessively, and his obsession gave him the strength simply to ignore exhaustion, pain, and near starvation. With only a tiny store of energy at his disposal, and most of that required simply to endure, he used what remained to scrutinise his rival.

If Maitland was aware of this scrutiny, he didn't show it. He remained determinedly ebullient. Either, Butler reckoned, he thought he had a reputation to maintain or it was simply the only way he knew how to behave. His curious pal Steward had swung a lift, as interpreter, in the HQ truck, and under the exigencies of the forced march Maitland had become more of a loner. The other men acknowledged his chirpiness, were perhaps even glad of it, but he had no special companion. Willard had become surly and sick. In the absence of anyone else, Butler found himself falling into step beside Maitland, magnetised by hatred.

'Believe in this tiger, do you, sir?' asked Maitland on one such occasion. They were slithering and stumbling along a section of path high above the river Kwai Noi, on the approach to Kinsayok, their halfway point. They seemed alternately to be clinging like human flies to a ribbon of mud above the drop, or wading through the rocky gulleys where swollen streams hurtled into the river. But they were out of the thick of the jungle and some of the attendant menaces, real and imagined, had receded. The guards, in anticipation of a meal and a dry bed in one of the better camps, had resumed their positions on the flanks of the column.

'Certainly,' replied Butler. 'There must be plenty around, and they're hardly likely to ignore a ready food supply.'

'Can't say it bothers me too much,' said Maitland. 'Stick together, eh sir, that's the thing.'

'Together we stand,' agreed Butler. 'It's all we can do – the Nips aren't going to protect us.' A few minutes elapsed as they slithered and skidded down into a gulch where rocks were just visible through a boil of white water.

It was hard going. The column had got strung out and a lot of the men were scarcely able to walk, let alone negotiate a savage knee-deep current and jagged rocks. One of the guards stood on the far side screaming with impatience, aiming blows indiscriminately at his charges as they clambered out on to the bank.

'Bloody hell,' Maitland moaned. 'I hate bleeding water.'

'Hang on to me,' suggested Butler.

'Thanks, don't mind if I do.' Butler had to stop himself gagging as the skinny, filthy paw grabbed at his shoulder.

'You stick to the rocks, and lean on me,' he said. 'I'll wade alongside.'

Maitland didn't answer. Even through the rushing of the water Butler could hear his breathing, loud and sharp, and smell his fear.

In front of them Willard, who had been more or less carried for the past ten miles, collapsed short of the bank and was tossed and rolled by the current, gargling and flapping his arms, too weak to help himself. Only his bulging, terrified eyes signalled his panic. Butler stopped and braced his legs, keeping his eyes on the far bank so as not to lose his balance. This was not his problem. Willard's two companions snatched at his arms and legs and eventually hauled him to safety. He lay on the mud, cut in several places by the rocks and with a thin stream of yellowish fluid coming from his mouth. But the guard made them get him on his feet and the three of them wove away like drunks. Willard's feet, in huge, split, waterlogged boots, trailed almost comically on the end of his stick-thin legs.

Butler pushed forward again. The strap of his pack cut into his shoulder where Maitland's weight pressed on it. The gully was only a few yards wide but it felt like miles. At one point Maitland stumbled and yelped with terror, his fingers biting into Butler's shoulder. Butler derived a fierce, perverted pleasure from the other man's discomfort, and his dependency on him.

They reached the other side, scrambled out and managed to pass the guard without being struck. Both of them were shaking and gasping from their exertions. Maitland was white as a sheet.

'Thanks,' he said at last. 'Thanks, sir. Couldn't have made that otherwise. I can't fucking swim.'

'No one could in that.'

'Willard . . . the poor bastard nearly drowned.'

'Might have been kinder to leave him.'

'You're a cool customer, aren't you, sir?'

Butler was pleased to see he'd shocked Maitland.

'A realist.'

'Putting a bullet through someone's head is one thing, but leaving someone to drown . . . that's torture.'

Butler shrugged.

About a mile further on they caught up with the others and found there was a *yasumi* ordered while the tail of the column caught up. The sun had come out for a while and they were down beside the river again, this time on a quieter inlet with a flat muddy beach and some rushes and puddles. Willard lay sprawled in the sun, his face ghastly.

'Prisoners want to swim – swim!' The guards, with one of those characteristic mood switches, indicated the river and pantomimed removing clothes and a rapid breaststroke.

'Don't mind if I do,' said Butler.

Several of them began to pull off their boots and shorts. Jumbo, still impossibly modest, had decided to go in in what remained of his clothes when someone near the front threw an arm up.

'Steady the Buffs! Crocs!'

There was a collective groan fading into a murmur of curiosity. Jumbo plumped down on the ground next to Tidy. 'I was looking forward to that.'

134

Tidy said caustically, 'I wouldn't put it past them to select the most croc-infested stretch to suggest swimming.'

Out of a habit of politeness, Jumbo said: 'Oh come on, surely . . . '

Butler joined the group of rubber-neckers, some of them stark naked, near the water's edge. What they saw were tracks: huge splayed footprints leading from the rushes to their left into the water. They lifted their eyes from the prints to the oily swell of the river, but could see nothing.

One man said: 'What the hell? There's no need to go far out. Let's swim.'

But no one took up his cry and in the end no one swam either. Maitland sat down next to Willard with a protective air. Butler went over to Jumbo and Tidy.

'Are there really crocodiles there?' Jumbo asked.

'Yes, there are fresh tracks.'

'One has the feeling,' remarked Tidy, 'that the entire natural world is lying in wait for the unwary.'

'Or the unfit,' agreed Butler.

Jumbo had another of those intimations of horror. He shuddered and lay down on his side, his back to the river.

A little later a couple of small boys aged about nine or ten appeared on the far bank, leading a water buffalo, and waved to them. Some of the men waved back. The boys led the buffalo into the water and swam with it, sometimes alongside, sometimes lying over its back. Their shouts and laughter, and the gloop and splash of the water as they played, floated across to the prisoners.

The man who had first noticed the crocodile tracks stood up and tried to warn them, but they simply waved back at his gesturing arms and carried on, absorbed in their games.

After a quarter of an hour or so they waded out on to

the bank, dragging the protesting creature behind them on its length of whiskery rope, now festooned with waterweed, and disappeared back into the jungle.

The last men in the column and their furious guard arrived at the inlet and were allowed no *yasumi*. Butler roused first Jumbo then Maitland. Surprisingly, Willard's partner got him back on his feet. They moved off.


Kinsayok was beautiful and malarial. Two waterfalls several yards wide poured down into the river, and in the thick bamboo jungle beyond there were strange outcrops of twisted, mossy rock, some of them concealing the entrances to bat caves. From these caves the bats streamed out, millions strong, at dusk, making the air shiver and vibrate with their cries and filling it with the fine dew of their urine.

The camp itself was about a mile from the riverbank. There were sturdy huts in a compound, even some basic furniture and utensils made from bamboo. Every mod con, said Maitland.

The men of F Force spent only two nights there, making contact with the occupants of the HQ lorry which had waited for them. It was a breather, of sorts. They were under cover and there was edible food, rice and something the Aussies called 'doovers' – a kind of rissole made up of anything that was to hand. It was disgusting, but it had a nodding acquaintance with protein. It tuned them back in to the possibility of survival.

After the first evening they spent their time helping the resident prisoners cut bamboo for construction work. They went into the deep gloom of the jungle, where the bamboos grew to the height of telegraph poles and some two feet in diameter. They cut the poles and were showed by the old hands how to carry a twenty- to thirty-foot length on one shoulder, perfectly balanced so they could manage the weight. Jumbo found the whole business incredibly hard and painful. He felt humiliated by his ineptitude. He kept collapsing beneath his burden, and only the good offices of others, especially Butler, prevented him from getting a flogging. Far smaller men than he, Maitland for instance, seemed to manage, trotting like rickshaw boys through the undergrowth with their outsize loads. When they'd assembled a large enough pile of bamboo the lengths were fastened together and dragged by an elephant the mile or so to the river.

It was at Kinsayok that Jumbo was vouchsafed a baffling insight into the Japanese mentality. He was coming back into camp on the second evening when he saw a group of Thais carrying something slung from a pole. Seeing him watching them they came over, very garrulous and cheerful, and showed him their catch. It was a huge king cobra, about nine feet long and as thick as a man's thigh. They stretched wide its jaws to show Jumbo its fangs, and pulled out its hood so he could see the black spectacle markings.

'What are you going to do with it?' he asked, without much hope of being understood. But one of them did.

'Take sell to Japanese officer. Very good sex!'

And off they went with their mammoth, deadly aphrodisiac. Jumbo followed at a distance. The camp was sprawling and F Force were accommodated on the edge of it. Jumbo had not been anywhere near the Japanese centre of operations.

The Thais carried the snake through the camp to the commandant's house, which was so surprising that Jumbo quite forgot himself and stood staring in wonder. It was the garden that took his breath away. For here, in the thick, steaming jungle, where every plant rampaged towards the distant canopy at many times the normal rate of growth, a space had been cleared and a perfect oriental garden created. Here were harmonious spaces, and tiny streams dividing them, paths picked out in stones, arches, bridges and trellises of bamboo – a miracle of human vision and effort over nature's blind, thrusting force. Through the garden went the Thais, with the king cobra sagging and swinging from its pole. Jumbo turned away.

He did not find the garden's beauty comforting. On the contrary. For what might a race with such a single-minded desire for order and control be capable of? A race who could create a willow-pattern garden in a malaria swamp, but who believed in the aphrodisiac powers of a snake?

On the third morning they set off on the final leg of their march. The sickest men were left behind at Kinsayok, and some had died there. So, yet again, they were fewer.


They could feel now that they were getting further and further away from the well-established camps, from all that had helped them keep their tenuous hold on reality. The jungle grew denser, the terrain steeper and less hospitable. And the rains, which had been patchy for the past few days, returned with a fury and insistence that stunned them. They put one foot in front of the other, and looked no further than the next step.

They'd almost forgotten the tiger when Butler saw it. There was too much to bear without worrying about something which might not even exist. Besides, the old India hand said, it would have stopped short of the camp at Kinsayok. Even the boldest man-eater wouldn't venture near where cooking was being done on open stoves.

And yet Butler was certain it was the same animal. They were negotiating a stretch of path barely a foot wide that cut across a bend in the river. They'd long since given up marching only at night because they were behind schedule, so now it was march, march, march, and *yasumi* (if they were lucky) when the guards felt like it. Most of them had lost track of the time, but Butler reckoned it must be early evening. It was terribly dark because of the thickness of the giant bamboo and the heavy cloud cover.

They were sheltered from the worst of the rain, but there was an angry wind on the prowl that made the great hollow trunks groan and reverberate hideously.

There must have been some kind of incident further up because the column straggled to a halt. None of them spoke. Some sank to the ground at once, a few even lay, curled like emaciated foetuses on the saturated ground. Maitland, a few yards ahead of Butler, got down on his haunches, head sunk between his knees. He was shivering.

From habit, Butler stepped into the undergrowth beside the path to relieve himself. He winced. His testes were red-raw and weeping. When he had gingerly replaced himself he raised his head as he did up what remained of his fly buttons, and looked straight at the tiger.

It was standing only about six feet away, and motionless. Its face, jaws closed and ears erect, was calm and almost placid. But its liquid yellow eyes glaring back at Butler were like the open doors of a furnace.

For perhaps five seconds Butler felt no fear whatever. He returned the tiger's stare with interest and a sense of recognition. Then, as a delayed wave of panic hit him, the tiger turned away with a heavy swinging movement and dissolved into the tumultuous darkness.

Butler returned to his place in the column. The rest of the prisoners were exactly as he'd left them, but one of the guards was on his way down, laying about him with his rifle and yelling. In a minute they'd be off again. Butler stepped forward and placed his hand in Maitland's armpit to hoist him to his feet. He said nothing about the tiger.

After this, though he didn't see it again, he could always sense its silent, watchful presence, never very far away. After that one brief spasm he no longer feared it. The tiger was evidence of another, more enduring world outside the narrow one of man-made pain and misery they inhabited. He felt privileged to be the one who shared its secret. It conferred a kind of kinship on him.

The condition of his balls, due to vitamin deficiency, was quite agonising. It made walking difficult, but he wasn't too sick otherwise and they were within a day's march of their final destination with the promise of some kind of shelter and an improvement in rations. He forced himself on.

Maitland, on the other hand, was flagging. His small frame was badly weakened and he had left only those mental resources which had stood him in good stead in the past. Willard had pulled round, but was keeping his distance. Butler, as Maitland's ex-officio aide, found that they were more and more often at the back of the column, struggling to keep up. If they fell too far behind one of the guards would run and drive them forward with a hail of blows and abuse.

Jumbo and the padre had stopped carrying out their informal Christian burials. No one had the strength for the lifting and digging. There were generally a few Thais in attendance who appeared like shades out of the jungle and were prepared to bury the dead for a small consideration. They looked different up here, within range of the Burma border; they were darker and swarthier, a forest people. Women, too, appeared with baskets of poor, unappetising food, mostly the same glutinous rice balls and shreds of fibrous meat that the prisoners got anyway.

Without the funeral services, Jumbo was nearing the end of his tether. Tidy began once more to get on his nerves. He sought out Butler, who for some while had been bringing up the rear with Maitland. The appearance of both men shocked him, though for quite different reasons. Maitland was a wraith. Next to him Butler appeared almost indecently vital. It was no more than a look in the eyes but it made the difference, Jumbo noticed, between the possibility of life and death . . .

'Will he make it?' he asked. He had fallen in on the other side of Maitland so he was supported between them. The shorter man was slumped forward, sometimes muttering to himself. They spoke over his head.

'Don't see why not,' said Butler. 'There isn't far to go, and he hasn't given up.'

Jumbo wasn't so sure. 'You mean you haven't. He'd have been a goner long since without you.'

Butler's mouth was a thin line. 'It's given me something to think about.'

'Yes.' Jumbo understood that. He glanced at Butler, wanting to say something more, to express admiration and friendship. But he couldn't, and they continued in silence.


There was no *yasumi* and no food that evening. The guards kept yelling 'Speedo!', as if they could have gone any faster if they wanted to. They got particularly impatient with the men who couldn't walk, and though the others tried to keep the worst cases in the centre of the column, it was inevitable that some should fall behind. Butler and Maitland were among these, and when Jumbo was called to the front to help Tidy with some dispute, the gap between them and the rest widened.

Every step was a fight, now, for Butler. Maitland, though still nodding and muttering, was becoming an increasingly dead weight. Butler had jettisoned most of the other man's pack except some string, a mug and a singlet. But he was getting terrible cramps and the rawness round his testicles had spread over the lower part of his body, making every contact with Maitland's dragging weight brutally painful. Sweat streamed down his face and stung his eyes, and a small abrasion on his right shin was becoming corrupt. It was now a pus-filled inflamed patch about the size of a halfpenny. It would be half a crown by morning, he knew, and then – he didn't care to think about it.

He could smell the tiger: a hot, rusty smell, like blood.

141

For a man so far gone Maitland was extraordinarily tenacious of life. How long, for God's sake, could a man continue in this state? Butler asked himself. That night, when it was pitch dark, and all they could see of the man in front was the glimmer of the cooking pan on his back, the answer dawned on him: for quite a while, if supported by someone else.

'Live, you bugger,' hissed Butler under his breath. 'Live, and be grateful.'

Jumbo didn't know what time it was when they stopped. It was far into the night, and they'd only done so because some squabble had broken out between two of the guards. The shade of status amongst those who were already at the bottom of the administrative pecking order were finely drawn. The prisoners, as usual, simply stopped in their tracks, some folding to the ground, most remaining standing. Each man knew that when the guards stopped arguing they'd direct their rage at their charges. There was nothing to be done. You might as well make the most of the break. It was while they stood there, each separated from his neighbour by exhaustion and the dark, that they heard Butler shouting.

'Help! We need help! Quickly!'

Jumbo felt a prickle of adrenalin. It took strength to roar like that. Something must be badly wrong. He began blundering back down the line, bumping into other men. Some of them were out on their feet and collapsed like card houses when he touched them. A couple of others, infected by his air of urgency, and Butler's continued yelling, followed him. The guards, suddenly united by the need to keep order, came crashing after.

Jumbo saw Butler's face, a pale thumbprint on the dark.

'Christ, you took your time! He fell – Maitland – I

couldn't stop him. God alone knows where he is.'

At first Jumbo couldn't understand. Where had Maitland fallen? How had he disappeared? And then he saw, and remembered, the sheer drop by this bend in the path, the flank of the gulley thick with bamboo. It was probably no great distance, a series of steep shelves, but the chances of finding a man, in their condition and in the blackness, were negligible.

'But what can we do?' he asked helplessly. Feebly, as it must seem to Butler.

'If I go down first and you follow at intervals, at least I can find my way back. He may not have fallen too far.'

'I suppose we could try,' said Jumbo.

'Waste of time,' said one of the others.

For a second Jumbo thought Butler would leap at this man's throat. But the guards were on them now, screaming and carrying on.

Butler tried to explain. 'Can we try to pull this man back? He's somewhere down here — ' He stabbed a finger downwards. His face was scored by the intensity of his frustration. The guards were unimpressed. This was the opportunity they'd been waiting for to close ranks once more and stamp their eroded authority on the despised prisoners.

'Prisoner march! Speedo!'

'Bastards! Bloody bastards!' Butler's voice cracked. The smaller of the two guards gave him a terrific straight-armed smack on the side of his head. He fell over, got to his feet, was slapped again. On the fourth or fifth slap he had difficulty getting up and the guards were still prodding at the rest of them with their rifles and yelling, 'Speedo!', so Jumbo and one of the others pulled him upright and staggered along to rejoin the column.

When dawn came they found they were on the edge of the jungle, with the river in sight once more and presumably not far from their destination. They had a short *yasumi* in the pouring rain. Butler had come round, but looked terrible. For the first time Jumbo glimpsed in his face the closed-down look that so many of them wore. But never him, never Butler. Not till now. It frightened him.

'I'm sorry about Maitland,' he said. 'Poor chap. And after you'd lugged him that far.'

'It can't be helped,' replied Butler.

'I'm not sure he would have made it, anyway. I remember you said yourself —'

'I know what I said,' Butler snapped. 'Perhaps I was right after all.'

'You have nothing to reproach yourself with.'

Now Butler looked directly at Jumbo through swollen lids. Somewhere in there was the old, mocking spark.

'Shut up, Oliphant,' he said.

# CHAPTER TWELVE

# 1989

I may have scorned Kranji, but in Kanchanaburi I visited the war cemetery. Because of the season there were no tourists here – I was actually the only guest in the hotel – and I felt less manipulated. The morning after I arrived, after an execrable 'English' breakfast of wet scrambled eggs and leathery toast, I went for a walk. I wanted shampoo, aspirin, a film for my camera, items as rare and unobtainable as the Crown Jewels the last time I'd passed this way.

The girl on the reception desk told me there was a drugstore not two hundred yards from the hotel. She also recommended that I visit the 'real Thai market': I determined I would do no such thing. I had no wish to be jostled and importuned by the locals. I wanted to walk, alone.

I'd come the day before, having taken the air-conditioned coach out from Bangkok as soon as I arrived. From Banpong onwards the Thai train, to which I had transferred in Butterworth for the twelve-hour overnight journey north, had not exceeded fifteen miles an hour. We had been exposed to a slow-moving tapestry of poverty and squalor. On a refuse-strewn embankment not three yards from the train windows were shanties of corrugated tin, plywood and cardboard where mothers put infants to the breast, dogs and children played (and relieved them-selves), and old crones cooked food over bonfires in the large open *kwali* that I so clearly remembered. On a man's back as he trudged along, a *kwali* used to resemble the shell of some weird crab; as an outdoor cooking vessel it offered open house to flies.

Here and there in the mêlée groups of men in tattered shorts and singlets were hunkered down, talking and smoking. These informal conferences had no air of urgency, no sense of the need for change. This was life, and she was a bitch.

As we drew nearer to the centre of Bangkok the train occasionally trundled alongside booming freeways, and was easily overtaken by careering lorries jockeying for position with Japanese commuter cars and motor scooters carrying whole families, bareheaded and beaming. I realised I was witnessing in action a nation more wheel-fixated than the Americans and more speed-crazed than the English. It was a sobering sight.

Bearing this in mind when I boarded the coach, I had selected a seat near the centre. It was only half full, so I sat on the aisle and felt I had done what was possible to ensure a buffer zone between myself and disaster. A pert ste-wardess brought me a coral-coloured cocktail with a straw. I could hear background music – the sort that in record stores is labelled 'Easy Listening', but which induces homicidal rage in the serious music lover.

The driver wore a short-sleeved shirt of brilliant white, a black bow tie and black gloves. His hair glistened like patent leather. High above his right shoulder was a TV of Japanese make, crowned with a picture of the King of Thailand and garlanded with artificial flowers. Here was a Thai happy in his work – actually paid to drive a huge vehicle at speed back and forth along a highway which had never known a traffic cop. I swallowed the drink like medicine.

*

When I had done my shopping the following morning I had an opportunity to observe at first hand the changes that forty-five years had wrought in Kanchanaburi. My memories of it in 1943 were necessarily dim, but I retained an impression of narrow streets teeming with people rather than traffic – Buddhist monks, coolies, beggars, rickshaw boys, businessmen, shoppers, stall holders and sidewalk philosophers. All that had changed. Or at least the people were still there, but had been pushed to one side by a great, wide, thrusting road that shot like a Tyson punch through the centre of town, a monument to Thailand's love affair with the combustion engine. Every side road and alley, when I could find the courage and opportunity to cross, was packed with pick-up trucks, vans, cars and motorbikes; some new and in use, others receiving remedial care.

The first act of every vehicle owner, as far as I could determine, was to remove that effete western accessory, the silencer: the noise was hellish, and the air noxious with diesel fumes and exhaust. These were almost certainly the factors which prompted me, eventually, to enter the cemetery. I spotted, on the far side of the street (though psychologically the distance was far greater), the smooth, ice-cream coloured domes and turrets of a Buddhist graveyard, which at least held out the hope of some peace and quiet.

It took ten minutes and a considerable risk to life and limb to reach the graveyard. I sat on a bench for a while among the *stupas* and then decided to continue on this side, away from the town centre.

I hadn't gone more than a hundred yards, flinching as I was buzzed at close quarters by speeding thuk-thuks and motorcycles, when I came to the war cemetery. Rarely had anywhere seemed more inviting. A great open space of cool, immaculately tended grass, the row upon row of simple memorials interspersed with flowering plants and shrubs and bordered by gracious trees, many of them flame trees in full bloom.

I went in. The pillared entrance took me from one dimension into another. I don't think I only imagined that the din of the traffic, still just yards away, grew fainter.

There were eight people there. Three Thai women in large hats, bent over their weeding, a group of casually dressed westerners with cameras cruising the graves, and a couple of teenagers in school uniform spooning in the shade of a flame tree. It was very harmonious. Live and let live seemed to be the order of the day in this park of the dead.

Not wanting to get embroiled I went to the corner furthest from the tourists and began strolling along the lines of memorials with their simple plaques. Some bore quotations, some verses, some lists of friends and relations reminiscent of the noticeboard at Changi. Others displayed only the name, regiment and date. All, though affecting by their numbers, were frauds. No one was buried here. How could those tens of thousands of bodies, wasted and decayed even before death, have been recovered from the maw of the jungle or the hideous mess of the camps?

The three visitors began drifting towards me. The woman glanced my way and smiled sympathetically. I pretended I hadn't seen. Although the sky was a thunderous purple beyond the flame trees, promising the inevitable rain, it had held off so far today and it was fiercely hot. My head was beginning to ache from peering at the inscriptions. I withdrew to a shady corner in which were massed the memorials of those men unidentified but 'Known to God', and a grave containing the ashes of three hundred more. Some pen-pusher had put a lot of thought into these subsections with, no doubt, the very best of intentions. But it was still a sham.

*

I sat there for some time with my head bowed. I was sure the three Europeans conferred at one point about whether to approach me, but delicacy prevented them.

When I felt cooler and more rested I got to my feet and began to walk back towards the entrance, promising myself that I would try and ring Cary from the hotel that evening. At the junction of the centre aisle I paused and looked down. I don't know what made me do it. Perhaps my ghost, who had been absent lately, plucked at my sleeve. In any event, look I did. And there, neat and unassuming, with no accompanying message, was the name of someone I had known.

I stared for a few seconds, pinned down by one of those hard, bright moments of shock. Then I turned and walked fast towards the road. In the marble antechamber a group of Japanese tourists dripping with photographic equipment stared at the dedication and talked in whispers, baffled by this disobliging reminder of their recent history.

When I got back to my room someone had laid a purple flower on my pillow, and a little card with the words 'Have a nice day'. That reminded me of home, and Cary, whom I was now certain I would not ring.

My head was throbbing. I opened a bottle of water in order to take some aspirins, but I discovered I must have left the polythene bag containing my purchases in the cemetery. I did not go back for them, but crashed down on the bed and lay with my eyes closed, and a steel wire tightening round my forehead.

In spite of the pain I did fall asleep, and was roused by the ringing of the phone.

'Hallo, reception here.'

'Oh . . . hallo.'

'You want your lunch? Is ready for you in the dining room.'

Oh God. I was their only guest. They had asked me

whether I wanted a Thai or western meal at midday. This could well be the high spot of their week.

'Of course. I'll be right down.'

I splashed my face, sluiced my mouth out and ran a comb through my hair. Down in the dining room half a dozen youthful Thais – boys and girls – in pale green and white stood about waiting for me, cloths over their arms, smiles pinned in place. There was nothing for me to do but sit down on the chair they so eagerly pulled back, accept the napkin they laid with a flourish across my knees and attempt to eat the vast meal they brought to the table.

If there's one thing I dislike it's eating when I'm not hungry. This was lunch for six Olympic athletes, not one tired, elderly tourist. It was very greasy and highly spiced. The soup contained large chunks of unidentifiable animal and vegetable matter. I knew that the Thais, like the Chinese, will eat more or less any part of anything that moves: scales, claws, eyes, necks, tails ... My stomach convulsed. I looked up to see six young faces beaming encouragingly.

I ate a few small mouthfuls of everything – the soup, an omelette containing mincemeat, fried vegetables and meat in a thick, hot brown sauce. Then I was defeated. Even as I pushed my plate away, with an apologetic smile to my adoring audience, I remembered how I would once have killed for that meal.

I took my cup of coffee out into the lobby and sat down on a sofa near the main entrance. A large, empty car park separated the hotel from the main thoroughfare and its attendant hazards and racket. The thought of going back out there appalled me, but I wasn't booked to move on till tomorrow and I couldn't spend the afternoon alone here with my thoughts and the eager, hovering staff.

When I'd finished the coffee I got the girl at the desk to call me a cab, and asked to be taken first to the famous bridge over the Kwai and then to the JEATH museum.

The cabbie, of course, knew more about it than I, who had lived through it. He was a Kanchanaburi man born and bred, whereas I'd only passed through on my way to the jungle camps. But at the bridge I disappointed him by not even getting out of the car. It was one enormous rip-off. I knew the original, wooden bridge was gone from its site half a mile downriver at Tha Makham, but I hadn't been prepared for the exuberant exploitation here: the riverside café, the stalls, the gift shops . . . A sign read: 'Board the Death Railway Here! Cross the Famous Bridge Over the River Kwai!' It was grim. Young men on motorbikes roared across the narrow central section of the bridge, T-shirts flapping.

I told the cabbie to drive on, to his obvious chagrin. 'You want to go to Chungkai? To Death House?' I could hear the capital letters in his speech, begging for attention. But he'd picked the wrong person this time.

'Just the museum.'

The museum was housed in a reconstruction of a POW sleeping hut at the end of a side street not twenty yards from the riverbank. The curator was a Buddhist monk. There was no one else there except for two urchins salvaging cigarette butts from beneath the 'sleeping platform' which acted as a shelf for the museum's exhibits.

I moved slowly round, staring and peering. It was an exhibition of atrocities. All the worst material, anecdotal and factual, had been collected together to create a sickening catalogue of suffering. Deprivation, punishment, torture . . . had it been as bad as this? Worse! the museum screamed. Much worse!

I emerged into the sullen afternoon light feeling bad. My knees were like jelly, pain jabbed at my head and neck and my stomach was loose. And, by Christ, did I feel my age! I sank down on a wooden bench. My face and hands were cold and damp in spite of the heat. Any minute now it was going to rain. I was thousands of miles from home. I gave in to the unforgivable self-indulgence of the homesick and felt sorry for myself.

On the way back I collected my purchases, which were lying where I'd left them in the cemetery. At the hotel I told the receptionist firmly that I required no dinner, Thai, European or otherwise, and went straight up to my room. I undressed, spent twenty minutes in the bathroom, and got into bed. I didn't ring Cary. I had the feeling that if I heard his dear voice I might very well cry.

I lay in the dusk with the curtains drawn, listening to the rain hammering down outside. I had what Hilda would have called the horrors. Oh boy, did I have them.

When I closed my eyes I could see only one thing. That neat square of stone with its polished plaque and humble, unassuming inscription:

'Michael Patrick Maitland. Bedford and Hertfordshire Regiment, 1914–1943. RIP.'

# CHAPTER THIRTEEN

# *1943*

It was seven o'clock, morning *tenko*. They stood in the rain, quiet and patient as farm animals. They might have complained, had it been worth it, but they'd already been standing there for half an hour and it might easily be another two before they left camp for work. If you stood very still, you could sometimes fool yourself into a tranced state where pain, cold, exhaustion and sickness became peripheral. The part of you that was the sentient, thinking being withdrew to a place deep inside you till it was no more than a secret glimmer.

Jumbo had not yet reached that state. From the look of him, neither had Butler, who kept glancing edgily back and forth along the row in front. It was a mannerism he'd developed recently. Jumbo, always susceptible to Butler's moods, found himself doing the same. Not that there was anything new to see. Lines of skeletal men, ragged, mostly barefoot and filthy. The lucky ones still had a pair of shorts. Most wore only a Jap-happy – a makeshift loincloth. None of them would have qualified for anything more than sick parade back home. And even by the standards of this camp at least half were unfit for work here. Yet the delay, as usual, was caused by the protracted wrangling between the chief engineer and Symington, the MO, about whether a further fifty could be found to go and work on the road.

'No work, no *meshi!*'

This phrase, another stock feature of morning *tenko*, floated across the lines. Jumbo saw Butler twitch with irritation. They were all so tired of hearing it. Japanese logic, warped but rigidly applied, ruled that if you didn't contribute to the keeping open of the road which brought supplies, you didn't eat. So sick and starving men who couldn't work were starved still further and could only be kept alive by the eking out of the other men's subsistence rations. The pressure on all of them, and especially on Symington, was intense. If the MO had been a lesser man they might have wound up taking the line of least resistance. As it was he continued to fight. His thin, nasal Edinburgh voice was rarely raised and his manner was just civil enough to pass muster with the Japs.

Jumbo thought him a really excellent man. He told himself repeatedly that when (he tried not to think 'if') he got home he would make a point of telling people about Symington. He pictured himself with his father. 'We had this absolutely first-rate MO, a Scottish chap. Everybody respected him, even the Nips in a funny sort of way. He never lost sight of his standards, even when he had no drugs, not even saline solution, nothing . . . '

It was a happy and recurring daydream this: himself as a veteran, safe and sound, with nothing to prove. He liked to think of the fund of stories he would have, how the good would be subtly enhanced and the bad – well, he wasn't sure it could be any worse. But at least it would be over.

He caught Symington's voice, sharp and implacable. 'I'm sorry, these are sick men. I cannot allow them to work. If they work they will die, and be no good to anyone. The railway will not be finished if too many men die.'

'The railway will be finished no matter how many die!' barked the engineer. He wore white gloves, and Jumbo

154

could see a flash as one of them rose in the air in a grandiose gesture. Butler's shoulders jerked again. Every morning they went through this. Someone along to Jumbo's left muttered, quite audibly, 'Fuck the bloody railway, fuck the rotten pay, fuck the stinking *meshi* and the fucking IJA . . . ' Jumbo recognised the voice of Vernon Willard.

There was a ripple of reaction, an almost-laugh. Jumbo's lips twitched and he glanced at the Korean guard who stood out in front. But he was as cold, wet and miserable as the rest of them. If he'd noticed he chose not to make an issue of it. Butler looked over his shoulder at Willard; he seemed angry. Jumbo lowered his head and stared at the ground to avoid catching Butler's eye.

That was the last diversion. The chief engineer, bored and infuriated by Symington's persistence, decided to deliver a further tirade on the virtues of the samurai code, the honour of working for the Emperor and the complete worthlessness of all prisoners. His voice rose to a screech. The white gloves flashed. A man in the front row slithered to the ground and was carted back to the huts. The rest of them continued to stand there.

Half an hour later the chief engineer withdrew, the guards fetched a further twenty men from the sick lines and they numbered off. They began in Nippon-go, taught them by Steward: '*Itchi! Ni! San! Shi! Go!*' After twelve they shouted anything, ace, king, queen, jack, point, half, fish, chips – Butler shouted 'bollocks!', Willard 'sex!'. The last man was primed by Steward with the appropriate number. By the time they'd completed this ritual they actually wanted to get to work. Anything was better than standing here in the pissing rain. The Koreans felt much the same, so for a few moments they were in an unspoken conspiracy against the engineer.

When he was happy, they set off for the road. At least half the sick men fell by the wayside before they reached the camp perimeter. It was one and a half hours since they'd lined up for *tenko*.

155

'We must be doing something right,' said Butler to Jumbo as they marched through the jungle. 'Dose of salts this morning.'


Work on the railway had been suspended while the road was completed. They managed to lighten their laoours a bit by reminding themselves that the road was the means of supplies getting through. God knows they needed them. They felt themselves to be forgotten men up here. Because of the ceaseless rain even the bullock carts had to stop well short of their camp, and at present they were subsisting on small quantities of rice pap. A party of fifty men was sent every other day to Changaraya, a few miles north, where supplies came down from Burma via Three Pagodas Pass.

Food was an obsession with them. Getting it, preserving it, eating it, digesting and retaining it. Every other urge was transcended by the overpowering drive to eat. The threats to life were numerous and terrifying. There was nothing much you could do to prevent a tiny abrasion spreading into a suppurating ulcer that could lay open a leg from knee to ankle to a depth of an inch, exposing bone and tissue as the rotten flesh curled back in thick black and yellow folds. Nor could you prevent malaria taking hold of you about one day in five so that you lay quaking and sweating in the hut. Nor could you keep at bay dysentery, which claimed half of them at any one time. Cholera stalked the camp, with its threat of unimaginable suffering and almost certain death. They boiled their cooking and eating utensils, but there was nothing else they could do.

There were no drugs, no dressings, no medication or equipment, not even the means to maintain the simplest hygiene. So all these things had to be borne: to be lived with or died from. But food you could do something about. It was the thread, spider-web thin, that tied you to life. Food could be maximised. It could be stolen, bartered for, occasionally bought, and squirrelled away.

Even the disgusting, watery slop of daily *meshi* had to be approached with the zeal and enthusiasm of a good house-wife. The cooks instituted a system of numbering, so that any second servings could be given out on a strictly fair basis from day to day. Men with a 'good eye' had the job of looking at the day's rations and assessing the size of portions. The numbers were known as '*lekki* numbers'. Years later those of them who made it could still, when they got together, remember and recite their *lekki* numbers. They were engraved, someone would always say, on their guts.

So far, Butler and Jumbo had been lucky, depending on one's definition of luck. They had been here six weeks and were still alive. They had had dysentery, malaria and the various scourges resulting from malnutrition, but they had not wound up on the ad hoc operating table with a wad between their teeth. Nor on the bonfire on Cholera Hill.

Butler attributed this success largely to the Marmite he had purloined at Banpong. He had lost one jar during the forced march, but tiny quantities of the stuff he'd so loathed as a child, used to flavour rice pap, had kept 'wet' beriberi at bay and been an invaluable source of vitamins. The squat brown jar had assumed an almost religious significance.

It also had a considerable trading value but Butler did not intend to capitalise on this. He was not above a little dealing on the black market, but the Marmite was not for sale.

Today on the road Willard approached him. They were laying stones as a base for the log surface. They moved slowly, not only from weakness, but because to finish the quota of work before sunset simply meant extra work. On a return trip to the rock pile shortly after the midday *meshi* break, Willard said: 'I'll give you something for that jar of yours.'

'I beg your pardon?'

'I'll give you something for the – you know.' Willard jerked his head back in the general direction of the camp.

'Sorry.'

Willard glanced around. 'The Marmite, squire. The Marmite.'

'I said sorry.' Butler's face was hard. 'No.'

'I've got a bit of soap. And cigarettes.' Butler ignored this. 'There are sick men who could really do with that Marmite,' Willard added virtuously.

'I said no.'

'All right. Hog it then.' Willard picked up a rock and staggered back with it, muttering something along the lines of 'close bastard'.

When Butler caught up with him, he said: 'Listen, Willard. If anyone's going to make a profit on that stuff, it'll be me and I'll decide when. So don't give me that Florence Nightingale junk, it won't wash.' He dropped his rock, missing Willard's hand by inches. 'If you've got some soap, I'd use it to wash your mouth out.'

If Willard and Butler had not already disliked one another, this exchange would have seen to it. As it was, it set the seal on their enmity. Willard thought Butler a self-serving conceited snob. Butler considered Willard a cheap crook. What was worse, Willard had the insinuating rudeness that Butler remembered from the chauffeur, Milne. In Changi and Banpong, when Willard had been one of Maitland's coterie, Butler had more than once had the feeling he was being sniggered at, and now Maitland's shade seemed to stand between them, grinning at their mutual discomfort. Pity the bugger hadn't drowned when there was the chance.

That night in camp, Butler told Jumbo about the conversation with Willard.

Jumbo frowned. 'I don't know . . . maybe one shouldn't hoard things. I mean, when we know there are men who — '

'For God's sake!' Butler interrupted. 'You don't

honestly believe he has some philanthropic motive, do you? Willard wouldn't recognise a selfless act if it bloodied his nose. He just wants to trade up, that's all. Line his own pockets.'

'I've still got most of the jar you gave me,' confessed Jumbo.

'Good,' said Butler. 'Keep it.'

Jumbo fell silent. Lately Butler's fierce certainty about everything had become rather odd. But everything here was so bizarre, and their hold on life and normality so tenuous, that it seemed petty to dwell on behavioural quirks. Besides, who was he to sit in judgement on anyone? He, who had begun to use his father's prayer book for cigarette papers as he had once sworn never to do? Supplies of anything smokable were lamentably scarce, which was a good thing because he was about halfway through Evensong and had reached the Nunc Dimittis which never failed to move him. He couldn't promise that he wouldn't make a cigarette if the opportunity arose, and he wasn't sure that he could tear out the next page without fatally loosening this one. Besides, it would have the sad beauty of a cut flower outside its natural context. He was awfully afraid it would go up in smoke.

'Keep an eye on your stuff,' Butler was saying. 'The Willards of this world will snitch anything to make a fast bob.'

At this point their carefully husbanded candle – a twist of rag in a tin lid containing palm oil – went out. Jumbo walked back to his place on the sleeping platform and curled up on his side on the two rice sacks there. He thought about his prayer book, his jar of Marmite, his clean, soft bed at home. He wasn't to know that it would be years before he could tolerate a bed like that. Years before he could sleep anywhere, in fact, except on a bare floor.

He no longer noticed the small noises around him – the groans, gargles, whimpers and curses. He dozed.

*

It was not long after this that Jumbo had cause to remember Butler's stern warning about the Marmite. He had for some days been displaying, and choosing to ignore, the first symptoms of beriberi – the puffiness, lassitude and sponginess of the bones he remembered from Changi. There he had at least been able to get hold of the occasional egg, or a handful of peanuts from the canteen: here such luxuries were as remote as moondust. But he did have the Marmite.

There was no chance of getting off work. On the morning he reported sick he was ordered out by the engineers with sixty or so other men who could just stand. But happily for Jumbo he collapsed halfway through the morning and had to be taken back to camp.

Symington came to see him. 'Bad luck,' he said. 'I'm afraid there isn't much I can do.' Jumbo nodded. He knew that was an overstatement. 'But you know the score,' Symington went on. 'You've had this before unless I'm much mistaken.'

'Yes. In Changi.'

'So you realise you need vitamin B. An egg. Yeast. That sort of thing. I'm doing what I can to harry Oshiru about supplies, but it's an uphill struggle.'

'I understand.' Oshiru was the camp commandant. On a sadism scale of one to ten he rated only three or four to the chief engineer's eight or nine, but he was a weak, unpredictable man who would occasionally take out his sense of inadequacy on the nearest prisoner. With regard to supplies, Oshiru's hands were tied.

'Rest while you can. I can't promise you won't be sent out again tomorrow,' said Symington. He gave a flinty smile. 'I shall have to work on my bedside manner. It'll soon be the only curative at my disposal.'

When he'd gone, Jumbo dragged himself up, slipped clumsily off the platform and reached underneath for his

160

bedraggled bundle of kit. He found the Marmite, removed the lid and spooned out a small gob of the stuff on the end of his finger. Carefully, holding the finger aloft he replaced the lid on the jar and the jar in the bundle and crawled back on to the platform, exhausted by the effort. He put his finger in his mouth and closed his eyes.

The 'no work, no *meshi*' rule meant he could not officially eat that evening but Butler, Tidy and one or two others contributed a proportion of their own rations and Butler brought it to him in the hut.

'Got the Marmite?' asked Butler.

'Yes . . . ' Jumbo couldn't face any of it. He wished Butler would go away. 'Underneath.'

Butler set the mess tin on the edge of the platform and crouched down. A moment later he stood up again.

'It's not there.'

'No . . . it is.' Jumbo propped himself wearily on one arm, his head swimming.

'I'm telling you,' said Butler harshly. 'It isn't.'

'Oh God.' Jumbo fell back. 'But I had some earlier.'

'It's been pinched.'

'It couldn't have. I've been here since midday.'

Butler snorted. 'You're hardly in any condition to give a determined pilferer second thoughts.'

That was true. Jumbo could say nothing in his own defence. He felt he had let Butler down. That it was he, and not the unknown thief, who was responsible for the Marmite's disappearance. And now he would have to pay for it.

Butler glanced towards the door. 'I suppose you haven't seen Willard?'

Jumbo shook his head. Butler was paranoid. He himself couldn't believe Willard would do any such thing. Neither, if he was honest, did he care. Blasted Marmite . . . he thought he might very well die anyway . . . how much nicer to be in heaven . . . Except that he had started smoking his prayer book – would that make a difference?

Queer his pitch with the powers that be? Surely not. He had only reached the Nunc Dimittis . . . Lord, now lettest Thou Thy servant depart in peace: according to Thy word . . . Lord, please Lord, now lettest Thou —

'Oliphant! Listen! Wake up, can't you?' Jumbo's shoulder was being roughly shaken and he could smell Butler's sour breath. He opened his eyes. The face that confronted him was that of a lunatic, dark with stubble, hair standing up in stiff, black spikes, eyes glittering. Hard fingers bit into his shoulder. 'Oliphant!'

'What?'

'Are you sure Willard wasn't in here?'

Jumbo gave in. He wanted to sleep. 'I don't know – he might have been. There was someone . . . it could have been Willard . . . '

It worked like magic. Butler disappeared.


Very few men watched the fight. They were all exhausted and not many had the energy to do more than lie in their huts. Also, no one wanted to run the risk of guilt by association and the consequent beating by the guards.

So it was only about half a dozen spectators who watched Willard and Butler staggering about in the dark between the sleeping huts and the river. No one spoke or urged them on. The only sounds were the squelch and hiss of their feet in the mud, the rasp of their breath and the occasional dull slap when a blow made contact.

Queensberry rules did not apply. Both men had been youthful boxers of some distinction, Butler at public school and Willard at a boys' club, but the present skirmish owed nothing to their early training. They were so weak they couldn't do much more than charge each other, flailing and swinging. Every so often they joined in a sticky embrace, leaning on one another for relief, each hoping the other would fall first.

Willard was a couple of inches taller than Butler, and

under normal conditions much heavier. But the big men had tended to lose more mass more rapidly in captivity. Butler's lean, wiry physique was the one best suited to endure privation, and now he just managed to outlast his larger opponent. It was Willard who went down with a crash in the edge of the water and failed, this time, to get up.

Butler stumbled forward, fell to his knees and groped clumsily for Willard's neck. He didn't have the strength to strangle him, but he could drown him: hold his face beneath the surface of the poisoned river where the dead coolies, victims of cholera, had been jettisoned. Men did drown from time to time; one more wouldn't arouse comment or suspicion. And Willard was due a drowning.

He didn't notice one of the spectators running back towards the huts. It was not the guards but Symington who returned.

'What the hell is going on here?'

Galvanised by his anger, the spectators moved forward in his wake to separate the two men. Butler shook off their hands like a dog. His eyes never left Willard as he was dragged, gurgling and retching from the shallows.

'What is this about?' hissed Symington.

'Nothing much,' said Butler. 'Food.'

'There isn't any. Do you think this sort of thing is going to help?'

Willard, on all fours on the ground, spluttered without lifting his head: 'He attacked me for no reason.'

Butler sneered. 'He knows that isn't true.'

'Who attacked who is of no interest to me,' snapped Symington. 'And you need not expect my support if you're unfit for work tomorrow. Idiots like you can rot as far as I'm concerned. Get out of here before the Nips find you.'

They straggled back to the huts. Symington first, brisk and fierce. Then Butler, with an unco-ordinated lope, tripping and scrambling in his haste. After him the handful of spectators, two of their number bringing up the rear supporting the dripping Willard.


The man to Jumbo's left in the sleeping hut, Hapgood, was an oddity. He had some playing cards he'd made out of cardboard in Changi and somehow preserved. Every night, when they'd got back from the road, eaten *meshi* and endured the grinding tedium of evening *tenko*, Hapgood would get the cards out of his kit and sit cross-legged on the platform playing a form of patience. He made strange sounds to himself as he played. He was a loner, and the cards were the closest thing he had to a friend. Jumbo thought him slightly potty.

Some time after Butler had disappeared in search of Willard, Jumbo was dimly aware of Hapgood returning. There was a good deal of bumping and rustling as he went through the usual ritual of spreading his rice sacks and retrieving the playing cards from his kit. Then, a creaking as he climbed up next to Jumbo who felt the touch of something smooth and hard against his face. Without opening his eyes he put up his hand to brush it away and encountered a familiar, solid object.

'Found it in my stuff,' muttered Hapgood. 'Don't know how it got there. Nothing to do with me.'

'It doesn't matter.'

Jumbo clasped his arms around the jar and slept. He was one of the few men in the hut not to witness Butler's return. Had he done so he might have been less content with the reappearance of the Marmite.


Jumbo recovered within a few days, and was put on camp duties. It was a relief at first not to be continually exposed to Butler's edgy ill-humour. He and the others cut wood for burning and bamboo for building; they did what was possible to clean and maintain the huts; they fetched copious amounts of water from the river for boiling utensils and cooking; they dug latrine bores and filled in old ones. They tried, against overwhelming odds, to make the camp habitable.

But even with the novelty of lighter work and Butler's absence it was impossible to ignore the grisly facts of everyday life.

On their first morning in this camp, they had awoken from a death-like sleep to find themselves billeted in a coolie burial ground, scattered with the rotting bodies of cholera victims and alive with rats and flies. Since then Jumbo had striven to avoid confronting too directly the march of the epidemic. They'd moved out, and cleaned up. The place they left became Cholera Hill, with the isolation hut and the pyre that burned continuously: a column of smoke by day and a column of fire by night . . . Jumbo averted his eyes. He had nothing but admiration for Symington and the other MOs and orderlies who worked there. Tidy went up several times a day to visit the dying men and to say a few Christian words next to the blaze.

When he noticed Jumbo on camp duties he put him on the spot. 'We could do with some more help on the hill, you know. The longer the bodies are left the greater the risk.'

'You mean – burning?' Jumbo went hot and cold at the thought of what he was being asked to do. But Tidy was brisk as ever.

'Certainly burning.'

'I don't think I could. I'm sorry.'

'Of course you could! Anyone can. It's a job, it has to be done.'

'I'm responsible for getting the water . . . '

'It's all right.' Tidy put a hand on his shoulder and gave him a small, sad smile. 'I understand.'

Jumbo was scalded by relief and shame. That evening he punished himself by wrapping a pinch of foul, heavily adulterated tobacco in the Nunc Dimittis, and smoking it.

He was unworthy anyway, so what did it matter? It would have been better if he'd died. His father would not be proud of him.

Carrying the water was hard, and they worked at a snail's pace. But for the prisoners outside the camp the work was harder still. The road was finished and the engineers had turned their attention to the bridge. It had been a simple road bridge, a mere six feet above the water. To bring it in line with the future railway embankment it had to be raised to a height of thirty feet. The men's only tools were chunkels, a few hammers and steel 'dogs' which joined one log to another. A 'speedo' phase was in progress to get the bridge ready to receive the railway. Sick and crippled men were turned out every day. Even the 'gondoliers' were made to work, men whose feet were so badly ulcerated they could only propel themselves along on their backsides using a bamboo oar. They were carted to the site and harnessed to the pile driver. Here, for twelve hours, they would pull and release a rope lashed to a cast-iron weight of some six hundred pounds. Men frequently fell from the scaffolding and were drowned.

Each day when the bridge party returned to the camp, Jumbo noticed a change in Butler. He was becoming a figurehead, a sort of mascot for the men. No cause was too vain for him to champion. His recklessness was without limits and he seemed to invite and relish punishment. He even upped the ante by ignoring the unspoken rules of verbal engagement with the Japanese, by being aggressive and overbearing. Hardly a day went by when he didn't get a beating for making some wild representation or other to the engineers. His once-handsome face was scribbled with something close to madness.

Most of the men on the bridge did not see the futility of Butler's self-appointed one-man crusade. Nor did they care that as often as not it was counter-productive,

166

resulting in harsher treatment for them all. They saw only a bloke prepared to stand up to the Nips, who didn't care what he said or how much punishment he got for saying it. When Butler downed tools and headed towards the guards to take issue with them, the men stopped working and nudged each other and grinned. 'Here he goes again,' they said, 'the crazy bastard. Good luck to him.' Jumbo, proprietorial, felt that Butler was demeaning himself. Not that he presumed to sit in judgement. He was aware that by keeping his head down, doing his work and inviting no trouble of any kind he had managed to hang on to a relatively cushy number.

It became less cushy when the camp guards, on account of some insult from a prisoner, inflicted a 'no tools' regime on them. This meant what it said. No ropes, chunkels, pulleys, axes – and no yokes for carrying the water containers. So now Jumbo and his team had to lug the heavy, slopping oil drums, one between two men, up the slippery slope from the river to the cookhouse. Invariably they lost most of the water on the way or fell over and spilt the lot, this to the huge amusement of their overseers.

Jumbo was one of the more senior men on camp duties. He knew it was only a matter of time before he would have to make an approach to the commandant. The men on wood-cutting and building had torn and bleeding hands which would turn septic, and without adequate supplies of water the risk of cholera spreading was greatly increased.

After three days of it he screwed up his courage and approached Steward. 'I wonder if you'd accompany me to see Oshiru? We can't let this go on.'

Steward gave him a cold, unfriendly look. 'I thought you'd never ask,' he said.

'I'm relying on you to translate in whatever way's appropriate. Not to let me make any gaffes.'

'I'll do my best. But remember Oshiru has some English, so you have to be careful.'

'I'll try,' said Jumbo. Humility came easily to him, but he

had difficulty being humble before Steward.

The two of them went to the commandant's quarters during the midday break. Oshiru was sitting cross-legged on a low platform on the verandah. Behind him, a curtain was drawn across the entrance. His sword lay beside him, unsheathed. He ignored their arrival.

Jumbo cleared his throat. 'Tell him I greet him respectfully and wish to make a request.'

They were both standing with bowed heads. Steward said: 'You wish to beg a favour.'

'Whatever you say.'

Steward straightened up and spoke in Nippon-go. About halfway through his speech Oshiru's eyes focused on the two of them. When Steward had finished there was a pause. Then Oshiru lifted his chin slightly.

'Your turn,' said Steward.

Jumbo hesitated. 'I wish to apologise on behalf of the prisoner who was impertinent. He has been punished by you, and severely reprimanded by our officers.'

Steward spoke again. Oshiru's head inclined a fraction.

'Is it now possible,' went on Jumbo, 'for us to be allowed to use tools once more? We fear the spread of disease if prisoners cut themselves, and if there is insufficient water for boiling.' He wasn't sure whether to add anything to this, but Steward covered his uncertainty by translating at once.

Oshiru grunted. His gaze shifted to Jumbo. For the first time he spoke, a few words in Japanese. He appeared to speak from the throat rather than with the tongue and lips.

Steward said: 'He says the punishment is decided upon by the victors. They decide how long it will last.'

'I understand,' said Jumbo. 'But the punishment for one man is being borne by many. It's hardly fair — '

In the next few seconds Jumbo experienced a time-slip so that his brain re-ran almost at once the sequence of events. He heard Steward's hissing intake of breath – saw

Oshiru jump to his feet, sword in hand, his face bulging and contorted with fury – heard his voice break as he screamed something at them in Japanese – felt Steward's hand tugging at his wrist so that he fell to his knees.

As they knelt there, Jumbo knew what was going to happen. The screaming, feral and high-pitched, continued above their heads. Spittle rained down on their necks and spattered Oshiru's polished riding boots. The point of the sword which he held in both hands trembled on a level with their eyes. When Oshiru raised it both men felt the rushing displacement of air, and waited for the second rush which would be the last sound they would hear.

Jumbo experienced not fear, but a desolating disappointment. His life had been nothing. He'd been cowardly, idle, clumsy and disloyal. He had not lived up to the Christian ideal. He had created nothing, would leave nothing, and had been loved by no woman except his mother. He had never even cracked a good joke – and his last sight on earth was to be a pair of saliva-stained Japanese boots.

Steward was saying something, over and over, like a mantra. Jumbo assumed he was praying. He tried to catch the words, but couldn't. The sword was still aloft, up there somewhere; they didn't dare look and Oshiru was breathing heavily with little grunts. All Jumbo could think of was Lord, now lettest Thou Thy servant depart in peace, which now that it was inevitable no longer seemed such a good idea.

Steward continued to say the words, over and over, his head down, his shoulders hunched. His voice was scarcely more than a keening whisper.

The boots, so firmly planted, moved slightly, as if Oshiru were steadying himself for the *coup de grâce*. Steward was now speaking so rapidly that the words were a rattle.

Jumbo couldn't see Oshiru's face but suddenly he knew that the moment had passed. One of the boots took a step back. There was a long, hoarse sigh. The point of the sword lowered, waveringly, back into their range of vision.

Oshiru spoke: just one word. Steward fell silent. The fingers with which he touched the inside of Jumbo's wrist were wet with sweat.

They rose. Oshiru was standing still, holding the sword with its point now resting on the ground. His shoulders were slumped and his whole face, which only seconds before had seemed about to explode with violence, sagged heavily. He was looking towards them but no longer appeared to see them.

Copying Steward, Jumbo began to back away, bowing with each step, hands clasped in front of him. Not until they were twenty yards from the commandant's quarters did they turn and walk slowly away. When they were out of sight and earshot of Oshiru the reaction set in. Steward slumped to the ground, curled forward over his knees, head in hands. Jumbo began to shake uncontrollably, his teeth chattering. They had been close to the probability of death for over a year now, but this was different. The thin veil between life and death had been abruptly torn aside to reveal the howling black abyss and for a few terrible seconds they had been suspended helplessly over it.

When they had recovered some sort of composure, Jumbo helped Steward to his feet.

'I have to ask you,' he said. 'What were you saying, back there? When he was going to' – he made himself say it – 'kill us?'

'Oh, that,' said Steward. 'You made a bit of a mistake, didn't you?' He let Jumbo flounder for a moment, and added: 'You can't go around accusing Nip officers of being unfair, you know.'

'Christ! I'm sorry!' Jumbo struck his forehead with his fist. 'You told me he had a bit of English.'

'That's right.'

'What an idiot I was!' Jumbo felt utterly humiliated.

Steward had removed his spectacles and was polishing them carefully on the corner of his filthy singlet. 'So what were you saying?'

Steward replaced the spectacles and gazed at Jumbo with watery blue eyes.

'I was asking him to forgive you,' he said.


That night Jumbo sought out Tidy.

'If you still need help on the hill,' he said, 'I'll do it.'

Tidy thanked him. 'What brought on the change of heart?'

'Nothing really. I just realised how foolish it was to be squeamish under the circumstances.'

Tidy accepted this explanation, but did not believe it.


Butler had set up a deal with some Mon villagers, small dark men who appeared swiftly and silently, emanations of the forest.

The Mon had killed a sick buffalo and were prepared to sell off some of the meat to prisoners. They had no idea what the creature had died of, but no one was fussy. The POWs themselves were harbouring more potentially lethal diseases than a humble yak could dream of. Butler had arranged to make contact with the villagers, offer them the few things they had to trade and collect the meat.

This sort of liaison was surprisingly easy. There were no perimeter patrols here, and even if a man were fit enough to attempt escape a day or two in the jungle without maps or survival gear would finish him off. If he was brought back, the penalty was decapitation. So Butler met with no hindrance when he wandered into the edge of the forest to meet his contacts. It was early, before morning *tenko*. The trees dripped and creaked. Ragged banners of mist curled through the tangled branches. The cries of birds and monkeys rang harshly in the distant canopy.

Butler didn't go too far. He knew how easy it was to get lost, and how tiny were his chances of survival if he did so. He had an ulcer on his leg, the same one that had begun on the march north. It had waxed and waned since then, but never healed, and now it was spreading rapidly. Each day it was a bit bigger, blossoming and opening like some fleshy tropical flower, blurry with maggots.

It also hurt. He leaned against the trunk of a tree to wait. It was the first time in weeks he had been utterly alone. He could feel the tension in him splitting and splintering as though his body were made of glass. He was about to slide down the tree trunk and sit when he heard the faint chuckle of native voices.

With an effort he pushed himself away from the tree and stood in the centre of the path.

A group of three men appeared out of the mist. They were smiling and talking. They were not the men Butler had come to meet. His presence did not perturb them. They beamed at him as they approached. Two of them were young Mon Thais, dark-skinned, black-haired, fine-boned. The third man was white. Shorter than Butler but cleaner and healthier. His hands were loosely bound, but he walked jauntily just the same and gave Butler a sideways nod of the head as he passed.

Butler watched them go on their way in the direction of the camp. Thoughts of yak meat and trading were driven out of his head. He felt the hot sting of urine down his leg, agony as it trickled over the thin dressing on his ulcer.

Two sets of eyes. The man was Maitland.

# CHAPTER FOURTEEN

# *1989*

The little wooden train plying the route between Kanchanaburi and Nam Tok on the 'Death Railway' went rather faster than the overland express on its approach to Bangkok. We rattled along at quite a jolly speed, jolting about on the hard benches. A small party of Australian tourists had got on at the back of the train, but apart from myself my carriage contained only locals. They smiled at me. Several of them carried baskets and platters of the usual luridly coloured greasy food which I politely refused. I had achieved an uneasy truce with my stomach, but it wouldn't take much for hostilities to break out once more. The mere sight of bananas and sticks of marinaded meat being deep fried on the station platform had been enough to make my gorge rise in protest.

I kept my attention firmly on the landscape going past the window. It was changed beyond recognition, and was much less like what I remembered than the paddy fields and mountains of the journey from Singapore. For miles there was no sign of jungle. It had been torn out and replaced with endless fields of tapioca, banana, custard apples and kapok. We slowed down once to go through the pass at Arrow Hill. The rock face was heavily scored with names and initials, mostly of people who'd visited since the war.

After that we were in flat farmland again, with those characteristic pointed hills like witches' hats in the distance.

I was glad to be leaving Kanchanaburi. Coming across Maitland's grave like that, being reminded of him for the second time in two weeks, had upset me badly. He seemed to be taunting me with my hubris, in supposing I could come back here and remain untouched. I felt as though I'd been roughly smashed up against my past, my face pressed in the dirt, my nose rubbed in it. It was days since I'd spoken to Cary, and it felt longer because of my travels. From now on, until I got back to Bangkok, there would be no way of calling him. Perhaps it was as well. I badly wanted to tell him everything, to explain about Maitland. I knew that when I was home, face to face with Cary, he would not only understand but be wonderful about it. If anything it would bring us closer together. But the phone didn't suit us: we'd barely exchanged a civil word since I'd left. An admission of weakness from me now would probably lead to unseemly crowing on his part and undignified ranting on mine . . .

At Nam Tok there was a courtesy bus to the hotel for me and the Australians. It was obvious these were ex-POWs and their wives. They seemed like nice, friendly, honest-to-goodness folk and I wanted nothing to do with them. I acted the stuck-up Pom to fend off possible advances. At the hotel I hung back while they checked in and enjoyed themselves being chummy with the reception staff. They were staying in the main complex, which was fine.

I decided to skip lunch and followed the boy with my bags down through the garden, and then along a treacherous duck-board path to the floating rafts.

My spirits lifted almost at once, as they always did when I was on or near water. I'm a Pisces, of course; it's my element. The slight lilt of the raft, and its enchanting privacy with the little verandah looking out across the river to the steep green wall of jungle opposite, were perfect.

I spent the next couple of hours reading and sleeping. As I gradually relaxed I realised how fraught I'd been over the past few days. I simply sank into a blissful inertia and drifted there, weightless and witless, luxuriating in the isolation.

There were sounds. The cheerful chatter of hotel staff and rivermen on the landing stage twenty yards away . . . the occasional hoot and shriek of some bird in the jungle . . . the pluck of the slow river around the edges of my raft . . .

When the first long-tailed boat came by I nearly fell off the bed. Not just with surprise, but because the spreading wake set the raft bobbing and rocking like a dinghy in a gale. I went out on the verandah and saw the offending craft zooming away upstream, the water whipped white behind it, the tranquillity ripped to shreds by the snarl of its engine.

It didn't matter. I glanced towards the landing stage and saw the young men there laughing unmaliciously at me. I smiled and made a gesture that said 'Who cares?' After all, why should the speed- and noise-infatuated Thais make any exception for water vehicles? The long-tailed boat was their own particular invention, a shallow gondola steered by means of a fifteen-foot metal rudder with a powerful outboard attached to the end: a miracle of noise nuisance and environmental pollution, and – I had no doubt – the most tremendous fun.

I went to the hotel for supper, which was served out on a large verandah. Suicidal insects of every shape and size zoomed and pinged against the overhead lamps and fell flailing to their deaths on the tables. Lizards darted and palpitated on the floor. The waiters were utterly charming, although they thought I should sit nearer the Aussies (their term) so as not to feel lonely. I remained adamant.

There was only one sitting, so we were all at the coffee stage when there was a shout from down below and the waiters flew to the edge of the verandah and peered over, shouting and waving in great excitement. The youngest was dispatched, *con brio*, to fetch something, and sprinted between the tables, his eyes starting from his head with the thrill of it. He returned almost at once carrying a concrete paving stone. This was too much for one of the Aussie matrons, who joined the waiters by the balustrade.

'Oh my God!' she said. 'I don't believe it! Jack, take a look at this!'

This was the cue for the Aussies to rise *en masse* and join in the fun. I remained seated. The tallest of the waiters was holding the slab aloft at head height. The others seemed to be offering helpful advice, waving fluttering hands that said 'wait' and stiff ones that said 'now!'. When he finally dropped it on to the ground below a tremendous cheer went up. They then left their posts to a man and could be heard reassembling in the garden, talking animatedly.

The woman who had first gone to investigate looked in my direction. I could feel her debating with herself whether she should fill me in on what had happened. I continued to sip my second coffee and gaze into space.

Her deliberations resulted in her coming over and leaning close to the side of my face as though about to tell me my flies were undone.

'I have to tell you – you know what was down there?'

I started like a man whose pleasant reverie had been rudely interrupted. 'I beg your pardon?'

'You know what those young men were doing just then?'

'No, I can't say that I do.'

'Killing a snake!' She straightened up, eyebrows meeting her hairline, chin pulled in, mouth grimacing in one of those foolish 'did you ever?' expressions.

'Well,' I said, 'we are in snake country.'

'This was a big one,' she assured me. 'Huge. Ugh!' She shuddered exaggeratedly. 'I can't stand the things!'

'That's one less for you to worry about then.'

I could see her wondering whether I was appallingly rude or merely a bit of a character. By now the rest of her party were drifting back into the lounge.

'I must go.' She opened and closed a hand in a childish wave. 'Byee. You will join us, won't you, if you fancy a bit of company?'

'If I do, I will, yes.'

I finished my coffee completely alone except for the kamikaze insects. I wasn't especially proud of the way I'd handled the situation. But I wanted solitude. And that woman, with her chainstore clothes, her beads, her bag and her huge spatulate hands and feet with their red-painted nails, was doubly dreadful after the seclusion of the river raft.

Cary would not have approved. He would have played it differently, expressed a lively fascination with everything the woman had to say, charmed her half to death and then spent a hilarious half hour after she'd gone pulling her to pieces and picking over the entrails.

I was the dark side of our partnership, no question.

On the way back through the garden my curiosity got the better of me and I made a detour to take in the patch of grass and shrubs below the verandah. There was the snake all right. And it was huge, as the woman had said. A king cobra some six feet in length and as thick as a strong man's bicep. The middle of it was burst open where the paving stone had landed, but the rest was chillingly whole and perfect.

I glanced down at my feet. I was wearing light canvas sneakers, and no socks. If this had been the States there would have been signs everywhere warning people of the dangers of snakes, giving detailed instructions about protective clothing, where not to walk and what to do if bitten. Here they let everyone wander about in blissful ignorance and shied paving stones at the snakes. I smiled to myself, but I looked where I was going.

Next day I hired one of the long-tailed boats to take me upriver to Kinsayok, famous now for its waterfalls and 'forest walks'. Mindful of snakes I wore socks and my only heavier shoes, oxblood brogues which looked pretty silly with my cotton slacks. Discretion, I had decided, was the better part of elegance.

It was strange to be roaring up the Kwai with the spray in my face, taking not much more than an hour to get to the place we'd known as the 172k mark and which had cost us so much pain, and so many lives, to reach.

The landing stage and the steps cut into the steep bank were still there, and much the same. It was a charming place, with the falls tumbling down in shining folds from woods to water. At the top of the steps, all was changed. I wandered aimlessly about the broad tracks, occasionally following signposts directing me to 'the bat cave', 'the jungle path' and 'the falls view', but it was all pretty tame. There were picnic and camping areas, an information centre and lavatories like log cabins. Halfway through the afternoon it poured with rain. Even standing under the trees I was soaked to the skin.

I'd left the boatman down at the riverside bar, drinking whisky and chewing the fat with his pals. I decided to cut my losses and go back. I must have taken a slightly different route, for suddenly I was in an area crisscrossed by bubbling streams. And here by the path was a patch of ground fenced off, and a notice in Thai and English: 'Japanese cooking stoves from Prisoner of War period'.

I paused. There were four horseshoe-shaped depressions, edged with blackened brick. The Japanese cooked with heat from above, not from beneath like westerners. I passed on. Not much further along there was another fenced area, and here were the prisoners' stoves, built up like backyard barbecues in three sets of four. Twelve stoves for three hundred prisoners: four stoves for twelve guards. The ghost was at my shoulder as I stood there. Beyond the stoves was an area of jungle overlooked by the enthusiastic planners of leisure facilities. It seemed to vibrate with silent, unseen life, staring back at me. This was where the camp commandant, in his willow-pattern garden, had bought a dead cobra, bigger even than the one the boys had killed. I remembered his face, swollen and febrile as he negotiated the price, as though he were in the process already of achieving that mythical potency. And here in Kinsayok the tiger had fallen back into the forest and waited, patiently, until the column moved on . . .

I headed back towards the river. There were no tigers left in Thailand now, and yet I felt something at my back every step of the way.


'We're going to Hellfire Pass this arvo. Would you like to join us?'

It was the sort of question I would like Cary to have heard. Going to Hellfire Pass – they do a great brunch there.

'It's just that we'll be using the bus, and there'll be plenty of spare seats.'

It was the same woman naturally. I was sitting by the pool, reading, and the kind soul had taken pity on me.

'We have special permission,' she went on. The men in our little group were there, you know. And would I be right in thinking you're an old POW as well?'

She cocked her head coaxingly. Of course I should have denied it right away, but some atavistic need to keep up with the other fellows made me admit that yes, she was right.

'I knew it.' She clasped her hands together, then held one out. 'Tina Murchison. How do you do?'

I shook the hand, which enveloped mine like an enormous paw.

'So ycu'll come?'

By now it would have seemed simply churlish to refuse. I thanked her with a rather poor grace and said I'd be there.

That afternoon the bus disgorged us at the top of a precipitous flight of wooden steps. Because the other men had to assist their wives, I reached the bottom long before anyone else. I found myself on a kind of broad ledge, along which ran a track, stony but overgrown. Here and there the old wooden sleepers showed through like the bones of a dead animal.

Successive choruses of cicadas buzzed as I walked along. The voices of the Aussies sounded faintly behind me. To my left the ground sloped away in wave after wave of dense bamboo. Then the track burrowed into a granite hill. Sheer rock faces towered on either side and the bamboo growing at the top had arched over the aperture, making a sort of natural tunnel. The light was dim and aqueous, and my footsteps echoed slightly.

At the far end of the tunnel there was a still-intact section of line and then the ground fell away as if it had been dynamited. A great gulch, foaming with jungle, yawned at my feet. On the corner of the rock face was a stone plaque commemorating the Australian POWs who had worked here day and night by the light of burning torches. Alongside the plaque hung an Australian flag, dirty and rotted into holes.

I hung about, not quite sure what to do with myself in this shrine to other men's suffering. The Aussies grew silent as they drew near and began to whisper, as if they were in church. The women hung back with a sort of respectfulness and their husbands gathered round the plaque. One of them read the words aloud in a hushed voice. One by one they removed their peaked caps and sunhats and bowed their heads. I could see tears shining on the heavily creased face of the man nearest me. I looked away. All that rugged, honest emotion was a reproach to my mean-spiritedness.

I walked very slowly back to the bus. There seemed to be twice as many steps on the return journey and I was breathless and trembling when I reached the top. The driver was eating *rambutans* out of a brown paper bag. He glanced at me sympathetically, mistaking my physical distress for something deeper.

I didn't disabuse him. I went straight to my seat at the back of the bus and closed my eyes, pretending sleep.


The following morning the Aussies left. Again, I was the only person in the hotel, the focus of all that eager service and attention. It was my last day and I'd hired a car and a driver to take me up to Three Pagodas Pass.

Even as a prisoner I'd thought what an imposing name that was, and it sounded doubly magical to us because it was the railway's end, the place where our stretch would link up with the line from Burma and we could down tools. I pictured fold upon fold of steep, misty hills rolling into the west, a broad valley and three huge pagodas like benign gods overlooking the scene from some lofty vantage point. In '44 I'd come through the Pass at the dead of night, so it had retained its mythical status for me.

I sat in the back of the car to discourage conversation, but happily I seemed on this occasion to have hired the only genuinely sullen man in Thailand.

When I mentioned the name of my camp he shrugged. 'All camp gone now.'

The journey took about three hours. We travelled first through undulating domesticated country with patches of forest, and then began to climb steeply. It was a new road, and there wasn't much traffic. Occasionally a lorry or truck would come hurtling the other way at a reckless speed, its cargo of fruit, vegetables and young men bouncing around in the back. Once we had to stop so sharply that I flew forward and banged my face on the front passenger seat.

The driver managed his first and only smile. 'All Thai like to drive fast.'

When we at last turned off, near a place called Sanklaburi, the road deteriorated sharply and we jolted along in a cloud of grey dust. At one point we passed two elephants, a large one ridden by her *mahout* and a perfectly adorable baby trotting alongside, ears flapping. The man was very dark. We were close to the Burma border.

We seemed to be travelling along the top of a plateau. As we began to descend we came to some buildings on our right – a café, a petrol station, a couple of empty-looking shops. There was no one about and the atmosphere was desolate. In the far distance I could see the rolling hills of Burma.

'Phra Chedi,' said my driver, nodding his head. 'Three Pagoda Pass.'

To say it was a disappointment would be like calling Marilyn Quayle unfortunate. It was – pathetic. A patch of scrub like a traffic island with four tracks converging on it. The three pagodas were small, sorry-looking things rather like those South American termite hills you see in the geographical magazines, and made from some substance that resembled papier-mâché. There was the inevitable covered stall selling lacquer work and brass and teakwood animals. It was manned by stolid, sad-eyed Mon girls who didn't move or smile as we approached, and did not speak when I purchased a little covered box. Who on earth provided them with trade I couldn't imagine. It would have been hard to imagine a more dismal, disenfranchised place.

'You want see typical Mon village?' asked the driver.

I said why not? We'd come all this way. He pointed down the northerly track and I wandered along till I came

182

to a straggle of broken-down wooden houses, some of which seemed to have been gutted by fire. A few staring children followed me at a distance. The adults watched listlessly from doorways and steps. The only cheerful creatures were the ubiquitous curly-tailed dogs trotting about and lifting their legs on the verandah stilts.

I went to the end, then turned and came back. I felt awkward and embarrassed.

'They've had a fire there recently,' I said to the driver as we got back into the car.

'Always fire in this village,' he agreed. 'In all Mon village. Burmese people come over, they want to own this part.'

I was glad to get away, to escape from this lonely place with its squalid feudings and unhappy people. It could not have been more different from the broad and breathtaking mountain pass of my imagination. And of the IJA's great railway whose completion it had marked there was no sign. Not a trace left by those thousands of wretched men.

I should have been glad that the railway had been so utterly erased. But I wasn't. I felt cheated and depressed. It seemed like the last in a whole succession of cruel tricks played on us.

'I take you place for lunch,' said the driver.

He turned off the road a little further south and we began to descend quite sharply along a bumpy track flanked by jungle. I could not imagine eating a thing.

Afterwards, I wondered whether the driver was more sensitive than I'd given him credit for: whether he'd intuited something about me and my feelings and was trying to help. The village he took me to was only a few houses, but I was welcomed, seated on a verandah and offered a dish of homecooked mutton or goat, hot and spicy with a trace of aniseed. It was not at all bad. My hosts and the driver retired to the back of the house, and no one stared at me. It was a humble place, no more affluent than the village of Phra Chedi, but there was an atmosphere of well-being. A bullock tethered to graze, a smell of cooking, the sounds of laughter, women walking from house to house. My clenched spirit unfurled a bit.

I ate more than half the food. When I put down my spoon and fork my host appeared, took my plate and smiled. He pointed, nodded, and mimed walking. He said one word: 'River'.

They probably wanted me off the premises for a while. I proffered a fistful of baht and he chuckled indulgently, took some and folded my fingers back round the rest. Then I set off in the direction he'd indicated.

I was out of the village almost at once, and the path curved to the left so that the trees seemed to close behind me. And then there was the river, flat and sluggish, slithering between steep banks. Two small boats were marooned on a muddy inlet on the far side, and I could see a scattering of white plastic bottles used as floats for fishing nets. There was no one about. Down river there was some sort of jetty and I headed towards it. I had a childish urge to sit with my feet dangling in the cool water.

It wasn't a proper jetty, only a couple of sodden black timbers sticking out of the water like rotten teeth. I took off my shoes and socks, rolled up my trouser legs and stepped gingerly into the edge. The silky mud threaded between my toes and clouded the water so I couldn't see my feet. I put out a hand and grabbed the nearest upright to steady myself, then took a long step to the next one. I was now in to just below my knees. The cool water and the slippery mud felt wonderful.

Hanging on to the timber I turned around to look back at the bank from this new angle.

And suddenly I knew where I was. The view spun, shimmered and revealed itself. The jungle had reclaimed some of it, and near the village the people had planted kapok and maize. But the essential configuration was still there, lying in wait beneath its flimsy disguise, ready to ambush me.

This was the camp. The slimy wood beneath my hand was all that remained of the bridge. The river round my feet had carried death, and the mud had swallowed up the corpses.

And on the gentle slope above me, where the forest had been cleared to plant crops, the fire had burned, day and night.

# CHAPTER FIFTEEN

# 1943

Oshiru paid the Thais their reward for returning the deserter and then had Maitland attached by a chain to a stake in the centre of the camp as an example to the other prisoners before his execution.

Maitland did not seem especially cowed by this treatment, and the fact that he was in considerably better health than the rest of them added to an impression of almost indecent chirpiness. He behaved, thought Jumbo, like someone who didn't believe it was really going to happen. He was not supposed to receive rations, but Steward and Willard risked a similar fate by smuggling him a small amount of their morning *meshi*.

When they dispersed after *tenko* Jumbo watched with the gravest misgivings as Butler, limping heavily, went to see Oshiru. After his experience with Steward nothing would have induced him to make further representations to the commandant. He marvelled at Butler's singleness of purpose, and this on account of a man whom Jumbo was still sure he had never really liked.

He went to work on the hill with no great hopes for the success of Butler's mission.

Butler intended to see Oshiru on his own. He didn't like

the thought of being dependent on Steward, but the interpreter fell into step beside him as he lurched along.

'If you're going about Mick, I'll come with you.'

'It's all right. I can manage.'

'I doubt it. Not if you don't speak Japanese. He'll be waiting for you to slip up. Ask your friend Oliphant.'

Butler stopped. When he did he could smell the ulcer gnawing into his shin.

'Very well, if you think it will make a difference. But don't alter my words. Say exactly what I say.'

The two men stared at one another. Butler was obliged to take Steward's silence for agreement. He limped off, and Steward followed.

Oshiru listened attentively as Butler spoke, and then turned towards Steward as he translated. Butler stared past the commandant. The curtain across the door of his quarters was drawn back, exposing the wall opposite on which had been hung a piece of grey wood of a curious natural shape like a hieroglyph. The rest of the wall was blank: no shelves, no clutter. The whole thing struck Butler as very odd. The impulse to hang a piece of wood on one's wall, especially in a place like this where wood was a creeping menace and only fit for burning, was incomprehensible to him.

Steward stopped talking. Oshiru spoke. Steward turned to Butler. 'He wishes to know how you know that Maitland suffered a fall.'

'I was with him at the time.'

Steward spoke. Oshiru replied. Steward turned to Butler again. 'The commandant suggests that you were this man's friend and helped him to escape.'

Butler kept staring at the piece of wood. 'I was his friend. He fell and I wanted to help him, but it wasn't possible. We had to leave him behind.'

Steward translated. There followed a silence while Oshiru walked slowly to the end of the verandah and back. Butler shifted his weight, trying to ease the pain in his leg. He wanted to be done with this charade. He wished he knew exactly what Steward was saying on his behalf. He seemed to be talking more, and with greater emphasis. What was he up to?

Oshiru returned. Unexpectedly he addressed Butler in English: 'You left your friend to die?'

'I had no alternative.'

Steward remained silent. Oshiru studied Butler. 'And now?'

'Now he has returned I want to tell the truth, in order to save his life.'

Oshiru looked at Steward, who translated. He nodded, and took another turn along the verandah. When he returned he spoke in Japanese.

Steward said: 'The punishment is not your concern. But your remarks have been noted.'

A wave of the hand dismissed them. As they left Butler saw Oshiru take out a handkerchief and press it to his nose and mouth.

'Well?' he asked Steward. 'What chance?'

Steward pursed his lips and shook his head. The pain in Butler's leg faded momentarily. They parted.


The bodies were stacked outside the isolation hut, like logs. They tried to swaddle each corpse in a rice sack, but since dead men were in good supply and the same could not be said of rice, this was not always possible.

Jumbo was used to the work now. It was a job – not exactly like any other – but a necessary one, and with a certain routine. There was also the bonus of not being harried by the Nips all day long. The Japanese had a hysterical fear of the disease. They seemed to think they could catch it by merely looking on its victims, and were only too happy to leave the prisoners to do their own dirty work on the hill.

More than three hundred men had died from cholera

already, and between ten and twenty were dying each day at this time, many of them from the Lancashire regiments who had received only half their prophylactic injections while at Changi. The chances of survival were one in five, but most victims were dead within two days of passing the first ominous rice-water stools. Jumbo had grown used to admitting young men in the early morning who, by sunset, were identifiable only by their position in the hut. Violent vomiting and cramps wrung every ounce of liquid from their already wasted bodies. They wound up pallid, dehydrated husks.

When the moment came they died quietly, with the simple acquiescence of animals. Jumbo ceased to be shocked when a dying man's friend asked for his toothbrush or boots. Practicality equalled a kind of dignity.

Just occasionally a man pulled through, emerging with a haunted expression which Jumbo recognised. This was a man who had glimpsed the abyss, as Jumbo had done during those interminable seconds in the shadow of Oshiru's sword.

Today, the day of Maitland's return, Jumbo's neighbour Hapgood was there. It was shocking to see such a secretive man jack-knifed and gagging in the grip of the illness, lying in his own slime and unable even to play cards. Ambushed by death without ever having known life, reflected Jumbo, but checked himself. What arrogance! What vanity! If he himself were to go now the same could be said of him.

During one of Hapgood's quieter moments Jumbo went over to him. 'Sorry to see you here,' he said. Woefully inadequate words. 'Anything you'd like?'

Hapgood's eyes, yellow and sunk deep in cavernous sockets, seemed dead already. Jumbo produced his prayer book. He'd used most of the services now, but the hymns remained.

'Anything from here be a comfort?'

189

The papery lids drooped slightly. A slug trail of vomit trickled from the corner of Hapgood's mouth and was accumulating in the hollow of his ear. Jumbo wiped the ear clean with the corner of his vest.

'John Bunyan,' suggested Jumbo. He read the first verse of 'He Who Would Valiant Be' in a confiding tone, feeling rather foolish but also proud because he knew he was behaving for once as his father would wish.

As he closed the prayer book Symington's sharp nasal voice made him jump. 'Oliphant, we need some clearing out here. Can you see to it?'

Jumbo stood up. He said: 'By the way, Hapgood, it was good of you to return that Marmite I put in your kit. A lot of blokes would never have given it back.'

There was no response.

Jumbo went outside. He and the four men who worked with him began shifting the corpses from the pile by the door to the fire. He was continually surprised by how well human bodies burnt. But then, of course, these were mere dry twigs of bodies, leached of moisture.

As the flames took hold of them the corpses twitched, writhed and gestured. Some sat up as though they were alive.

That night Jumbo went down into the camp. The chain was still attached to the stake, but Maitland was not at the end of it. So it had been hallo and goodbye after all. But at least there wouldn't have been too much suffering. Not like cholera.

He hurried to see Butler. He was lying on the platform with his hands behind his head. His ribs stuck out like a toast rack. The stench from his leg was atrocious and Jumbo had to struggle not to retch.

'What happened to Maitland?' he asked. 'I'm sorry you got no change out of Oshiru. Did they behead him?'

Butler gave a short, coughing laugh. 'Did they hell!'

'What, then?'

'Bugger all is what. I was triumphantly successful. He's free.'

Jumbo was awestruck. 'I never thought you'd pull it off.'

Butler dragged long, dirty fingers down over his face so that his lower lids gaped redly.

'Oh ye of little faith.'

How true that was, thought Jumbo.


Butler could hardly walk now. An enfeebled immune system and a complete lack of drugs meant an ulcer simply rioted through skin, flesh, sinews and joints. Maggots from the latrines were introduced into the gaping hole to eat away the corrupt tissue. It didn't look nice, but it disposed of some of the mess. There was no thread of any kind for sutures. Symington and the others used the mandibles of red ants to hold the edges of wounds together. The pitiful rags of bandages that were left had been used and boiled and reused so often they were like muslin, and couldn't contain the incessant ooze from an ulcer.

Butler was one among several who resorted to ad hoc curatives in the hope of escaping the operating table on the hill. A couple of days after Maitland's return Jumbo went to camp for the midday *meshi* and found him sitting on the riverbank. Not far away stood Steward, hands in pockets, staring at the water. Jumbo went and squatted down next to Butler with his mess tin.

'Have you eaten?' he asked. The old, social formula, ludicrous when applied to the few ounces of weevily rice pap.

Butler shook his head. He gazed down at his stick-insect legs, which hung over the bank so that from the knees down they were submerged. The stained and sodden piece of bandage lay on the ground next to him. Jumbo tried not to look at it.

'Want some?'

191

Butler shook his head again.

'What are you doing?'

Butler pointed at the water. 'Food for fishes.'

Several tiny fish were clustered around Butler's ulcerated leg, nibbling greedily. Shreds of tissue floated in the water. Jumbo looked away quickly. 'Does it work?'

Butler glanced at him for the first time. 'Does it matter?'

'That leg ought to be properly cleaned.'

' "That leg ought to be properly cleaned"!' Butler mimicked.

'You'll lose it,' warned Jumbo.

'There's not much of it to lose.'

Jumbo shovelled in the last mouthful of rice. As he did so he saw Maitland, with Willard, sitting in the shadow of the nearest hut. Maitland raised a hand.

Jumbo touched Butler's shoulder. 'There's Maitland.' Butler did not respond. 'I hope he's suitably grateful,' Jumbo added stoutly. 'He owes you his life.'

This time Butler grunted, pulled his legs from the water and began to wrap the tattered cloth around the ulcer, which now stretched from ankle to knee. When he'd done that he struggled to his feet and lurched away. He looked frail and unsteady, as if the least contact would cause disintegration.

Jumbo got up. As he did so he caught sight of Maitland, smiling broadly. For the first time Jumbo was unmoved by the smile and did not return it.


Butler could no longer work. He lay in the ulcer ward, inhaling the smell of decay, waiting for something to happen. He didn't talk to anyone and soon they stopped talking to him. He hoped that if he stayed still and silent for long enough his haze of pain would materialise and hide him from prying eyes. Particularly those of Maitland.

Once or twice he was sure he had seen Maitland in the doorway of the hut, a small bony figure like a marionette in his Jap-happy. He always wore that smile which made his face still more skull-like, and was peering in, looking for him. Butler had turned his back to the entrance and closed his eyes, and when he'd looked again Maitland had gone. But he was conscious of him out there. He was being stalked by Maitland, and he had gone to ground.

Symington was adamant. 'You'll lose that leg if it's not cleaned up. We'll have to scrape it.'

'No!' said Butler.

'You want an amputation?'

'What the hell do you think?'

'Then we have to do it. It's perfectly simple. Hurts a bit at the time, but when we've got rid of the muck we can close it up and we stand a good chance of saving the leg.'

Butler had no option. It wasn't the pain of the operation he dreaded, it was being carted out into the light and up to the table on the hill like a bloody human sacrifice, exposed to what he most shrank from – the public gaze. And especially that of Maitland.

But the leg had to be dealt with, and he was in no state to raise any serious objection. Two men came to collect him and carried him bodily out of the hut, sitting on their laced hands, legs dangling. Outside they transferred him to a bamboo stretcher for the journey up the hill. He didn't like having to lie down since it made him feel vulnerable. He kept trying to lean up on his elbows which made it hard for the porters.

'Lie down, sir, you're rocking the boat.'

He did so. The sky above was dark blue, with great balls of cloud rolling across it like tumbleweed. He actually looked forward to the pain because it meant he wouldn't be thinking of Maitland. No one could get at him when he was on the hill.

They put him on the table, and Symington pulled the length of tattered mosquito netting along the overhead cross bar so it overhung the table on either side like a ridge tent. The heat was stifling. Butler could hear the fluttering of the flames not fifty yards away. Symington leaned over him.

'I'll get a couple of fellows to hold your wrists and ankles. It's going to be painful for a little while. All right?'

Butler saw Jumbo Oliphant to his right. Down near his feet Symington was holding the sharpened edge of the tin spoon in the flame from a lighted twig. He blew out the flame. Butler felt Jumbo's hands – still moist and cushiony after more than a year in captivity – closing over his right wrist and ankle. Two more hands, smaller and harder, gripped him on the left.

Butler's scream, not of pain but of horror, startled Jumbo so much that he loosened his grip and Butler's right arm flew up and struck out at Maitland, on the other side of the table.

'For Christ's sake!' shouted Symington. 'Hold on to him, can't you?'

'I'm sorry!' Jumbo grabbed wildly at Butler and managed to re-establish his hold. Maitland, in spite of Butler's fingers clawing at his face and chest, had not let go. His pointed, peeling knuckles were white.

'Get him away! Get him away! Let go! Don't let him hold me!'

Butler was almost sobbing. Symington, with absolute concentration, began his work with the sharpened spoon. Butler gabbled and wept. Jumbo was horribly distressed. He'd hoped to be of some support during this, a minor but excruciatingly painful operation. As it was he felt like a torturer.

'It's all right, old boy. It's all right,' he muttered. 'Hold on.'

'Forget it,' said Maitland. 'He can't hear you.'

Jumbo looked across at him. The brown eyes in Maitland's monkey-face were brighter than ever, and his mouth carried a hint of an impertinent smile.

Butler gave a final spasm and fainted. Jumbo felt a surge of tenderness for his friend. For the first time, perhaps in

194

his entire life, he, Jumbo, was needed. And by Butler, who had never needed anybody.

It didn't take long. Symington closed the ends of the wound as best he could and wrapped it in a cleaner bandage. Before transferring him to the stretcher Jumbo fetched a couple of medical orderlies.

He said to Maitland: 'He doesn't seem to want you, does he?'

'Can't think why.' Maitland shrugged. 'We were mates.'

At that moment Jumbo knew it wasn't true.

'What are you doing up here anyway?' he asked, as Butler, regaining consciousness, was carted away.

'Hadn't you heard? The Nips were bum-stabbing round our section yesterday.' Maitland referred to a rudimentary test employed by the Japanese – a glass tube was thrust into the anus and withdrawn with the evidence from which to detect cholera-bearers. 'I'm a carrier.'

He sauntered off. He seemed proud, thought Jumbo, to be a harbinger of death.


Symington managed to keep Butler back on camp duties for a few days. He did this not so much on account of Butler's physical condition, which was considerably better than that of many men working on the bridge, but because of his mental state. Butler, it was clear to everyone, was breaking down. The espouser of wild causes and champion of losers had become a shambling, mumbling scarecrow. The engineers didn't mind using the last of a prisoner's bodily strength, but a man in Butler's condition was a liability. He hobbled about the camp and the others, out of loyalty to the man he had been, covered for him.

Butler himself felt perfectly sane. Indeed he had never remembered things so vividly nor understood them so clearly. His days were spent in a state of agonisingly heightened sensation. When he saw Maitland he experienced a pang like an electric shock.

At night he scarcely slept. He was certain that if he closed his eyes Maitland would lay hands on him, as he had on the operating table, and he would not be able to escape. When he did doze, it was to dream, over and over again, of the march.

*He's more or less carrying Maitland. Every step's painful, a labour of hate. He wants him to live and carry the albatross of debt around with him. They always seem to be at the back, in danger of being left behind. Sometimes Oliphant, that old woman, comes along and gives them a hand, but he's got his work cut out assisting the padre.*

*They can often smell the tiger. An acrid smell, like a pissoir, like blood. He begins to confuse it with his own smell, the smell of his body. He doesn't see the tiger again but he knows it's there, like his familiar, just out of sight in the jungle. It's night when Maitland falls. He somehow becomes a dead weight and Butler can't hang on to him. They're on the side of a steep slope, and Maitland's head and shoulders are over the edge. He flaps around with his arms, but there's nothing to grab because Butler stays out of reach. Maitland's like a beetle turned on its back. The others are way in front. It's raining, but the smell of the tiger is strong. It pours up into Butler's head and fills it, like fumes, like a drug.*

*Maitland's making short, helpless groaning sounds. They're exactly like the sounds he made before, all those years ago, and they enrage Butler. He's excited; he can actually feel a stirring in his red-raw groin, a sensation that transcends everything else. He lets Maitland lie there, half over the edge, as he feels for something – a stone or a stick – but there isn't anything to hand. Then he suddenly feels a smooth, solid weight in his kit. He fumbles in the dark, finds the jar, places one hand on Maitland's throat, and strikes a single clumsy blow to the side of the head. The stringy tendons beneath his hand go slack, like broken strings. The jar slips from his fingers and rolls away. With a tremendous effort, he pushes Maitland over the edge. At once the*

196

*body is swallowed up by the darkness. He can hear it slipping and crashing through the thick bamboo. It's ten seconds or more before it comes to rest, somewhere far below. The stink of the tiger is very strong. It's almost as if he, Butler, has become the animal. He crouches, panting for a few seconds. His shorts are sticky, he's ejaculated.*

*Then he gets to his feet and calls for help. His voice is loud and thrilling in the night, like the roar of a tiger.*


Jumbo didn't sleep much, either. He was used to the noises of the hut; they were simply part of the night, a buzz which he had learned to ignore. But sometimes he could hear Butler's dreams and then he would go over to him and nudge him awake before he reached the really bad part.

He wanted to help, but it was beyond him. He had no idea what to do. He smoked the first page of *Hymns Ancient and Modern.*


So we, when this day's work is o'er,
And shades of night return once more,
Our path of trial safely trod,
Shall give the glory to our God . . .


Jumbo doubted that he had the means of grace. And there was precious little hope of glory. But the path of trial stretched stony and uncompromising before him.


Maitland was admitted to the cholera hut at midday a few days later. It was unusual for a carrier to contract the disease, but he was presenting all the characteristic symptoms – the watery stools, continual vomiting and violent cramps.

He lay near the door, but Jumbo avoided looking at him and continued stolidly with his work outside. It was raining and the fire spluttered and smoked sullenly. In the afternoon a man had his leg amputated above the knee. The entire leg was ulcerous, a chunk of rotting meat. The man wailed when Symington hacked it off, like a mother being parted from her child, but he was still quieter than Butler had been. The orderlies wrapped up the leg and threw it on the fire.

That night Jumbo told Butler the news.

'He's got it – Maitland – the cholera.'

For a moment Butler didn't seem to have heard. Then he looked confused, as if he hadn't understood.

Jumbo repeated himself, and was rewarded by a flicker behind the other man's eyes that was like the old, bad Butler.

'Bugger me. Will he die?'

Jumbo didn't hesitate. 'Yes. Poor chap.'

' "Poor chap," ' parodied Butler. 'Poor little Maitland.'

Jumbo returned to his sleeping space and lay with his arms over his face, praying. For Maitland, sick in body; for Butler, sick in mind; and for himself, a miserable sinner.

He walked up the hill next day with a strange and thrilling sense of dread. In some curious way he felt he held Maitland's fate in his hands.

He met Symington outside the hut. Already five bodies lay there, only partially wrapped. It was a fine morning and a large swallow-tailed butterfly sat sunning itself on the grey, bare foot of one of the corpse. It was peacock blue and white edged with a tracery of black, like lace. The eye markings blinked up at Jumbo as its wings opened and closed. Jumbo's throat filled with tears.

'Not good, I'm afraid,' remarked Symington crisply. 'But not all bad, either.' He nodded his head towards the inside of the hut. 'There's one who's going to turn the corner.'

This was such a rare occurrence that it never failed to

give their spirits a lift. If this could happen, anything could. Together they went to take a look at this one man who was proof against the killer.

'Doesn't look much, I know,' said Symington. 'But I think he may make it.'

They stared down at Maitland, drinking him in. He seemed deeply unconscious, his eyeballs oscillating as he dreamed – of what? His pale, dry lips were slightly parted over stained teeth, but his breathing was even. His narrow, delicately-shaped hands, like the paws of a monkey, the nails deeply etched in black, lay loosely on the soiled bamboo beside his head. He certainly didn't look much. It was incredible that such a small, wizened man could have defied successfully the agonising onslaught of cholera.

'It makes you wonder,' said Symington reflectively, speaking for both of them, 'what the difference is between life and death.'

That morning the work was fiercely hot. For the first time in many weeks the smell of the melting flesh made Jumbo feel physically sick. He streamed with sweat and his legs and arms ached. The *meshi* they were getting at present was unusually disgusting – the boiled-up residue of some crates of rotting fish which had been delayed at a staging camp mixed with what rice there was. The stench of it wafted up the hill. He could not be bothered to stand in the queue for it. The others drifted away, and he raked over the fire and hauled on a couple more branches.

Two bodies still lay by the door. There were no rice sacks left, so they were bare. Even their Jap-happies had been stripped from them. Jumbo had probably known them by name a few days earlier, but now they were just so much inert carrion.

He wandered into the hut. There was the familiar sound of a man spewing up his vital juices.

Maitland lay exactly as they'd seen him earlier. Jumbo stared in admiration. He looked astonishingly peaceful. Except for the minute flutter of his lower lip, you'd have taken him for dead.

As Jumbo lugged the bodies on to the fire a couple of Nips came up the hill. They always surprised you with how fast they moved, three times as fast as any prisoner. Symington and the interpreter Steward trudged, panting, behind them. It must be some kind of check. Symington made a 'God Almighty' face at Jumbo as they got closer.

They paused on the far side of the fire, their quick conversation mingling with its busy crackling. One of them took out a cigarette case and offered it to his companion. They didn't belong to the camp. Visitors – brass, Jumbo surmised. The first man put the cigarette case away and tweaked a twig from the edge of the fire to light the cigarettes.

Symington and Steward stood to one side, waiting, Symington with visible impatience, Steward impassive as usual, removing his spectacles, rubbing his eyes, cleaning the lenses, replacing them.

One of the Japs pointed at the fire, made some observation. The other replied. They both laughed immoderately. Jumbo poked at the edges with his *chunkel*. He felt tired and ill. The four figures opposite wavered and shimmered beyond the flames. They began to walk round towards him, towards the hut.

He didn't care about the Japs; their visit was a mere formality. And he didn't relish having to tell the MO that Maitland had died.

Butler, though – Butler would be pleased.

# CHAPTER SIXTEEN

# 1989

It was clear Oliphant didn't remember. And I didn't help him. His face took on the look of someone awaiting a pleasant surprise. I felt almost sorry that I couldn't oblige.

'I'm sorry,' he said, getting to his feet with a visible effort, 'you're going to have to help me.'

He held out his hand anyway, and as I took it I introduced myself. You can tell a lot, I find, through skin contact. I was grasping his hand as I said my name, and I could feel not the slightest tremor of unease. He even tightened his grip a little as if not to appear unfriendly as he said:

'Go on. Please go on.'

I laughed. 'My God, I know I've aged, but this is embarrassing. I recognised you at once.'

I could see he was blushing beneath the sunburn. He was such easy meat. He let go my hand, replaced the sunhat and shook his head, gazing down at his shoes. They were brand new. Bought specially.

'It'll come to me in a minute,' he muttered. 'Just give me a minute because I'm such an old fool these days, my brain has gone . . . '

I gave him the minute. I was playing dirty. It's not ageing that changes people, it's style. Some people – and Jumbo Oliphant was one of them – are, in their seventies, simply older versions of what they were at seventeen, or twenty-seven. Others, like myself, are totally altered human beings.

He looked up. 'No,' he said. He was pitifully honest. 'The name rings a bell, but I simply can't place it. Anno domini, I'm afraid.'

'We were prisoners together,' I said. 'In Changi, and then again on the railway. Almost to the border.'

'Good heavens!' Now he did look shocked. 'Good Lord!' He took the hat off again and wiped his forehead with it. He gave me a brief, distracted smile. 'Forgive me . . . you've really knocked me for six with that one.'

'But you do remember now?'

'Yes, of course . . . ' I could tell there was nothing more to it than dismay at being reminded of those awful times. 'Of course I do, now. My dear chap.' He took my hand again, and this time enfolded it in both his. 'I'm so very glad to see you again.'

He seemed it, too. Behind us I heard the vicar exhorting the Christian Travellers to get back in the coach.

'Bethlehem this afternoon, remember!'

Oliphant obviously hadn't heard. 'I can hardly believe it,' he said, staring into my face and beaming. His colour was better, he was coming round.

I nodded in the direction of the Christian Travel Inc. bus. 'I think you're wanted.'

'What?' He looked without focusing.

'Your friends are waiting for you.'

'Oh!' He chuckled. 'They're used to it. We've only been in the Holy Land for two days and already they know that this silly old fool is always going to be last.'

I stood aside. 'You'd better go.'

'Yes, I suppose so.' It was as though he couldn't take his eyes off me. He touched my elbow and I walked beside him in the direction of the bus. 'Look, we simply must meet up. I'm a bit tied to my group, but we're allowed some time to ourselves.'

'Time off for good behaviour?'

'Yes . . . yes!' He chuckled again. He had come by more grace and confidence along the way. Learned to make a virtue of his weaknesses. He was a hard man to dislike, but I'd been working on it for years.

We paused at the foot of the coach steps. 'So what shall we do?'

'For a start – where are you staying?'

'The St George, do you know it? It's modest, but in a wonderful position. Only five minutes' walk from the Damascus Gate.'

Christian Travel Inc. would have been proud of him.

'I'm in the new city, all modern and impersonal. They do, however, stock bourbon. I suggest you come over and have dinner with me. I'm here for another couple of days.'

'How very kind. But I don't know.' He looked worried. 'We've been warned against going out at night.'

As if to reinforce his anxiety there was a knock on the coach window and there was the vicar, his baseball cap wagging in agitation, urging the lost sheep to get in.

'Look,' I said. 'We'll make it tomorrow night. I'm at the Calipha. You get the receptionist to call you a cab, say where you're going and bob's your uncle.'

He was terribly fussed, but I ushered him aboard and watched as he moved down the aisle, flapping his large hands in apology. The coach moved off, the camel sat down with a tremendous fart and the Mount of Olives put itself once more on hold until the next bunch of lambs presented themselves for slaughter.


Our erratic journey home from Thailand had brought us through Jerusalem. It was like a dream, all of it. Those of us who'd been in the jungle camps had got dispersed on the way back, and came home in dribs and drabs. I'd wound up travelling with a bunch of men I scarcely knew. We wandered about in a daze. Food, beds, soap, music, clothes – these were enough to bring on shortness of breath, and as for aeroplanes! It was like black magic. Gorgeously scary.

I remember not being able to sleep. None of us could. Every night, from the transit camp onwards, I fell into bed in a kind of ecstasy, luxuriating in the mattress, the clean linen, the blankets, the pillow . . . and every night, after an hour or two's heaving and rolling, I'd get out and lie curled up on the floor, wrapped in a single sheet.

And the odd thing about being clean was that it made you realise how unclean you were. No amount of slathering with scented soap and slooshing with hot water could get rid of the skin eruptions, and the jiggers and the hookworm. And you couldn't scrub your brain out.

I was as close to mad, then, as it's possible to be without being a certified lunatic. I'd always been something of a loner, and I came out of those camps feeling I'd lost everything. It's a terrible thing to have to say, but I almost wished I hadn't survived. I didn't know what I was going to do with the life I'd managed, against the odds, to hang on to.

I guess the worst thing is feeling there's nobody waiting for you. Hilda had died while I was on the railway and her husband, Arthur, had never liked me and regarded it as his sacred duty to keep little Milly as far away as possible from my contaminating influence. There had only been one other person I'd cared about, and who'd given a damn, and he was gone now too. I dreamed about him every night. Still do.

So I came back into the world a lost soul. Sick, deranged and loveless. It was America that saved me. Big-hearted, bullshitting, brassy America, who didn't give a fuck for my neuroses but spotted my modest talents and handed me back my self-regard. And threw up, in the process, Cary.

It was in the interests of an authentic re-creation I'd come back via Jerusalem now. But it was a very different experience. I wasn't dazed this time. On the contrary I was so sharp I was in danger of self-mutilation. And Jerusalem itself, sullen and jittery in the grip of the Intifada, was astonishing. Cary had been quite right to point out that I was no church-goer, but you'd have to be made of stone not to be affected by this place with its layers of history, and belief, and myth, and massacre . . . this was powerful ju-ju. To move from the cold, claustrophobic darkness of the bottle-neck cell where the Son of Man had spent his last night alive to the hot, noisy streets with their boarded-up windows and screaming, spray-paint graffiti was a breathtaking experience, both shock and affirmation.

I like to walk. I couldn't have stood that tour bus, whisking me from place to place, turning the city into a slide show. I wanted to understand the journeys, the distances. What it meant to go from the pool of Bethesda, which must in Christ's time have been a noisome, flyblown bedlam of a place, through the Sheep Gate and down across the Kedron valley to the peace of Gethsemane with its gnarled grey olives.

The Via Dolorosa, too, was something else. I didn't get such a rush out of Pilate's palace and the famous pavement with the King's Game marked on it, and the striations of chariot wheels. No, for me the thrill was the walk through the narrow, scruffy streets, besieged by hawkers and opportunist kids, buffeted by the sounds and smells of a tough, callous life carrying on regardless. And knowing it must have been exactly like this.

I found a very elegant, expensive shop on the edge of the Jewish quarter, and bought a superb silver horse for Cary. A mere suggestion of a horse, all fluid energy and line. Touching it made me want to be with him, and glad that it wouldn't be long.


In the evening I returned to the Calipha, had a good dinner and eavesdropped on other people's conversations in the bar. It was a sleek, characterless international hotel, serving western cuisine. Delayed reaction, I guess, against that Thai garbage.

Until I bumped into John Oliphant I'd regarded my trip as pretty much of a failure. It had stirred up memories and muddied the waters with bad, old feelings, but to what end I couldn't say. The ghost had appeared at intervals but no answers had emerged. Until now. I couldn't believe my luck. Here, among the holy places, it wasn't gentle Jesus who'd come to my aid, but a hirsute, scowling old Javeh, red-hot for vengeance. I was really looking forward to my dinner with Oliphant.

Curiously enough, I saw him again the next day, only he didn't see me. I went to the Holocaust Museum and the Christian Travellers were there mob-handed. Even the pitcher for Jesus was pale and quiet in the presence of so much evidence of what men can sink to. Oliphant looked an old man. The fabulous elegance of the place only added to its pathos. It made you think of all the creativity that had gone up in smoke, all the art, the music, the words, the ideas, the life that had been immolated. The children's memorial, with its thousands of reflected candles glowing in the gloom, and that disembodied voice reading out the endless list of names, was almost too beautiful. It said, unequivocally: Eat shit.

I came out and strolled in the hard white sunlight for a minute or two. There was a superb statue in the garden: the simple figure of a woman weeping, her face in her hands, a little larger than lifesize. Beyond her the ground fell away so that she was outlined against the unforgiving blue of the sky, impossible to ignore.

I stood looking at the statue, and as I did so I saw someone else. Oliphant was much closer to the statue than I. He was in tears, mopping his eyes and nose with a huge white handkerchief, his heavy shoulders heaving with distress.

I watched him for a bit. Then I walked through to the

cafeteria and had a cappuccino.

He arrived at the Calipha on time, and clearly pleased with himself for having struck this blow for independence in the face of dire warnings from the pitcher. To my astonishment he was wearing a light grey shirt with a dog collar, beige polyester slacks and a navy blue blazer. A man of the cloth, forsooth: what a delicious irony. I had on a Lacoste sweatshirt, white trews and moccasins. We must have made the oddest couple.

We went to the bar, and he asked for passion fruit juice with ice 'if you've got it', a proviso which would have marked him down for a Brit in any part of the world you care to mention. I had a large Stoli. They brought a dish of black olives and another of pretzels, both of which he exclaimed over in delight. It made me wonder what kind of a dump he was staying in.

'So,' I said, 'you're a priest.'

The word obviously embarrassed him. 'Oh . . . well. I'm retired these days. I have a sort of first reserve's job in North London. Cricklewood. Do you know it?'

'Only by name.'

He nodded. 'Pretty much of a sinecure. I'm out to grass really. But when the rector's on holiday, or ill, I get a chance to "do my thing" at parish communion.' He put the inverted commas firmly in place. 'And what about you? You look tremendously fit.'

I knew what he meant. He was being polite. The phrase he would use at home would be 'well-preserved'. My appearance probably frightened him half to death.

'Thank you. Yes, life's pretty good. I live in the States now.'

'Ah!' His tone implied that this explained everything. 'What took you there – job?'

'Caprice, in the first place. But it suits me down to the ground. I've been there, oh, nearly forty years. It's home.'

'I thought I detected an American twang.' He put an olive in his mouth, bit on the stone with some force and made quite a business of ejecting it, eyes watering, into his fist, looking for somewhere to put it. He resorted at last to the ashtray.

'Do you have a family?' I asked.

'A large one,' he said, with evident pride. 'Too large, some might say. Four grown-up children and ten grandchildren. Two lots live abroad, but we see a great deal of the others. Sadly my wife couldn't come on this trip,' he added. 'She doesn't care for the heat.' He put out his hand for another olive, hovered, and withdrew it. 'You?'

'No,' I said. 'Not my style.'

'Oh,' he said. And then: 'Ah. But happy? Settled?'

'Yes, as a matter of fact. Unless the situation's changed while I've been away.'

He laughed nervously. He had a full complement of prejudices and phobias, but was keeping them pretty well corralled.

'And do you still work?' he asked, as if I were some defunct clockwork toy.

'Certainly I do. I'm a freelance writer. I contribute to quite a few magazines – articles and short stories.'

His eyes widened and he was evidently about to say something of pith and moment when the waiter came to tell us our table was ready.

We ordered – or I ordered on our behalf – a nice light dinner with absolutely nothing middle eastern in it, and a bottle of Pouilly Fumé. When we both had a full glass I said:

'Here's to coincidence.'

'Yes. Yes, indeed.' We chinked glasses.

'You seemed about to say something, in the bar. When I said I was a writer.'

'Oh, no.' He went absolutely puce. 'It was nothing.'

'Please.'

'It's just that I've been writing, too.'

'Really? But that's so interesting. May I ask what?'

'It's a personal memoir. About the railway.'

'Good for you.' I believe I concealed my apathy well, but I couldn't resist adding: 'You don't think that's rather a crowded market?'

'It is, of course it is.' He was painfully quick to admit it. 'But one always feels, somehow, that one has something new to say. And I do find it tremendously therapeutic to, you know, unburden myself.'

'So it's going to be the truth, the whole truth and nothing but the truth?' I smiled benignly.

He returned the smile, unfazed. 'As far as my poor memory can manage. I shall allow myself a little artistic licence.'

'Naturally.' Our smoked chicken salad arrived and he made yummy noises about it. I watched him rummage with his fork. 'And do you have any publishing interest yet?'

He had just put in a large mouthful and held up his hands to show that I must wait. I watched placidly as he munched, and dabbed with his napkin at some vinaigrette on his shirtfront.

'Sorry . . . this is delicious, by the way. No, I haven't exactly got a publisher yet. On the other hand FEPOW have been very supportive, and they seem to know of various small outfits which specialise in this kind of thing.'

'Good.' I bet they did. All those old buffers wanting to get things off their chests. A vanity publisher's wet dream.

'How far along are you?'

'About halfway, I think. I seem to reach a number of false crests. But one of my problems – one of my many problems – is that I don't type. Or hardly. I have an ancient portable, but I'm strictly a two-fingers man, so in the interests of getting finished I muddle along in longhand. What I really need is an amanuensis. Some nice, inexpensive girl to give me a hand.' He caught my eye. 'Oh dear, that didn't sound too good, did it?'

I smiled in acknowledgement of his little joke, but not only for that reason. I felt good. The jagged fragments of memory, hate and desire had drifted and settled into place. Nothing is so soothing as harmony. I saw now that it had been pre-ordained, and that my journey had been guided by unseen agencies. The God of Vengeance hovered beningly over us.

'Maybe I could help you there,' I said.

'No – honestly?' He chased the last few fragments of curly lettuce round the edge of the plate, and speared them. 'I could only afford a very nominal payment.'

'Yes, I understand that. But, after all, what would it involve? You're only looking for someone to do the typing, surely.'

'That's right. And to correct my spelling. And who can cope with my terrible handwriting – No.' He shook his head despairingly. 'Such a paragon doesn't exist.'

'No such paragon,' I agreed. 'But a student would probably be delighted.'

'I don't have an 'in' with any students. Or at least there's my grandchildren, but they find my book something of an embarrassment so I don't like to . . . '

'Don't worry about it. I think I know someone. A friend of my greatniece. That branch of my family live in north London – not that far from you, as a matter of fact, and I'll be staying over with them on the way back.' I reminded myself to ring Milly as soon as possible. 'It wouldn't be any problem to put this girl in touch with you.'

The waiter collected our plates, mine half full, Oliphant's polished. He patted his diaphragm appreciatively and then said: 'It would be so kind of you. But I couldn't put you to any trouble — '

'No trouble. The reason I have this particular kid in mind is her grandfather was on the railway. I'm sure she'd be interested.'

'It sounds,' said Oliphant, 'as if it was meant to be!'

210

*

We passed the rest of dinner happily enough. Now that everything was complete and well ordered I found I could put up with him very easily, and he became quite merry and expansive under the influence of the Pouilly Fumé. He said that he and Judy, his wife, had promised themselves a trip to America, perhaps next year. They had friends and relations there, so they were hoping to be able to stay with them.

'And now perhaps we can add you to our list,' he said, scraping up the last of his *crème brûlée* and smacking his lips. 'We don't know anyone else in New York.'

'Of course you must come and stay. We'd love to have you,' I said, safe in the certain knowledge that he would do no such thing. Mind you, the picture of Cary entertaining the Oliphants had rich possibilities . . . We exchanged addresses.

We went back into the bar for a nightcap, brandy for him and bourbon for me. There was something I had to know.

'Tell me,' I said. 'What became of that man Butler? The one who went bananas?'

'Terribly sad,' he said. He looked it, too. 'He was a marvellous man, you know, before he went to pieces like that. Marvellous. I was at school with him, idolised him a bit actually. And I wasn't the only one. The men would have done anything for him.'

'I didn't know him that well,' I said. 'And I was moved on to Burma.'

'He got killed on the way back. A whole pack of us were holed up at Kamburi, and he bought it in one of the Allied bombing raids. Sickening irony.' He shook his head.

So it had all been for nothing. 'I'm sorry. I know you were friends. You must have missed him.'

'I did. I did. He wasn't himself after the cholera camp, but you never know. He might have recovered back in civilian life.'

'I doubt it. That type needs the army like oxygen. Or better yet, war. I should think that bomb did him a kindness.'

Poor Oliphant. Perhaps that had been below the belt. I might have said something, but at that moment I was paged for a phone call at reception.

He brightened. 'I must go. It's been simply marvellous talking to you.' Greatly daring, he added: 'That'll be your friend back home.'

'I dare say.'

We went to the reception desk and he ordered a cab, and then thanked me again for my stupendous generosity.

'It's okay, really. My pleasure. And I'll see what I can do about some secretarial help.'

'Yes, yes . . . mustn't keep you.'

He wandered off and sat down in an easy chair near the door. One of the girls behind the desk held aloft a white phone.

'Mr Steward? Your call from the States.'

# CHAPTER SEVENTEEN

# 1989

Galilee was more to Jumbo's taste than Jerusalem. Not so exhausting. And it was easier, in these more rural surroundings, to imagine oneself back in time and following in the steps of the Master. Also, there wasn't the undercurrent of violence that had underpinned everything in the city. They had frequently been shouted and spat at, and on one occasion when they'd had to take a detour through narrow unmade streets, they'd been stoned.

Here, there was more of a holiday atmosphere. The Jewish hotel in Tiberias had a large swimming pool, a disco bar (not patronised by the Christian Travellers) and a 'leisure patio' where coffee, cocktails and assorted snacks could be taken beneath coloured parasols which leaned and quivered in the stiff wind that blew off the Sea of Galilee. This wind arose every afternoon between two and three, turning the glassy surface of the lake into a racing, glittering expanse of waves, spattered with white horses. It made Jumbo think about the 'cloud no bigger than a man's hand' and the suddenness of the storm which had so terrified the disciples. It was all most affecting.

It was true that in Nazareth some wet cement had fallen off scaffolding with astonishing accuracy on to the shoulders of one of their party, a young woman in a sundress. But then, as the Bible said, nothing good ever came out of Nazareth (with One notable exception).

You could picture the Lord walking from place to place at the head of a dusty, enthusiastic crowd, practising His ministry wherever there was a place to stop and people to listen. You could picture Simon Peter, gruff and short-tempered, running his fishing business from the bustling Roman-occupied town of Capernaeum. At the site of St Peter's primacy there was a tiny church right on the lake-side, and a statue of Jesus handing His crook to the big fisherman, with the water almost lapping their feet. When the Christian Travellers arrived, there was a young monk standing in the doorway of the church, reading. Jumbo wondered if the monk lived and worked there, and envied him. The possibility of real goodness seemed greater here, in these surroundings that one shared with Christ.

They held their own communion service at the Church of the Beatitudes, set amongst peaceful gardens overlooking the water. The words of their service harmonised with the singing of a group of Italian pilgrims outside, and the cheep of small birds in the high dome. Jumbo was deeply moved.

He didn't forget the meeting with Steward but it didn't occupy the forefront of his thoughts. It had been a pleasant and surprising diversion from the otherwise rather fraught atmosphere of their stay in Jerusalem. It had also enabled Jumbo to cut something of a dash with the other Christian Travellers. He didn't think he merely imagined that they held him in rather higher regard after that. He was a man with a past, with some pretty unlikely friends.


It wasn't until the last full day of their trip that Jumbo recalled the meeting and its implications with any real force. They'd had a whole day out in the hills and made some delightful stops. At Caesaerea Philippi they'd wandered by the upper reaches of the River Jordan, and seen a kingfisher like a blue spark darting into the water. They also came across a little group of Scottish fundamentalists conducting a baptism in the river. A great tall man with a red beard was standing with his huge thighs braced against the current and calmly immersing a boy of about fourteen. The pitcher urged his flock to hurry by with eyes averted from this showy extremism, but Jumbo loitered, fascinated. He could not imagine being held like that, so uncompromisingly, and pushed backwards into the rushing water. He didn't think he'd have the courage – he'd struggle, or shout, or raise his arms. But the boy submitted, and emerged with closed eyes, the water streaming back off his face. It was like a birth. Jumbo had not been present at the arrival of any of his children, but he had seen births on television, and looked at his son-in-law's artistic black and white photographs of Tessa's first confinement . . . He stared. The congregation on the bank burst into song, and helped the new Christian up the riverbank, wrapping him in towels and embracing him. A couple of them saw Jumbo watching and smiled.

'John! John . . .?'

It was the pitcher calling. Jumbo hurried on.

They'd continued – to Cana, where several of their number bought bottles of 'Cana wine' to take home; to Nazareth, and the upsetting incident of the wet cement; to the Mount of Precipitation where wild taxi drivers rushed them round hairpin bends at sixty miles an hour; and finally to a kibbutz on the eastern side of the lake, for lunch. Many of the Christian Travellers, stomachs unsettled by the morning's eventful drive, refrained from the main course of 'St Peter's Fish', but Jumbo was not among them. He was still dazzled by the Jordan baptism, its physicality and force, which made the Anglican rituals of his own group seem timid and bloodless. He ordered the fish, and having failed to interest the rest of his table in a bottle of wine, ordered a glass for himself.

The fish, when it arrived, looked as if it had but recently

been terrorising small fry in the depths of the lake. Pop-eyed, spiny, snaggle-toothed and finned like a Cadillac it occupied the whole plate, dwarfing the mixed salad that accompanied it. Jumbo was more used to fish coated in a comforting blanket of sauce or batter, but conscious of the sceptical gaze of his fellow diners he tucked in with a will and pronounced it tasty, which indeed it was.

After lunch there was an opportunity to swim off the stony beach. Not many of them availed themselves of it, but the girl who had been the victim of the cement-droppers in Nazareth went in, in a black and white bikini, and her daring inspired a couple more of the younger ones to do the same.

Jumbo watched indulgently for a while, and then strolled to the quayside where they were due to board the boat for the return to Tiberias – at present no more than a smudge on the far shore. He sat down on the stone wall, overwhelmed with impressions. Though he had been sad to leave Judy behind, he realised that he was able to absorb more in her absence. He gave a deep sigh of guilty satisfaction.

The lake rippled as the first gusts of the afternoon wind chased across it. Ten minutes later it was rough. The Tiberias boat came into focus, dipping and rearing through the waves. As it drew nearer the Christian Travellers arrived on the quayside in ones and twos and sat in irregular groups along the wall, like swallows congregating for migration.

Jumbo felt aloof, a man who had got that bit more out of this trip than the rest of them. This sense of superiority was so unusual for him that he had to give himself a ticking off. If he'd learned anything here, it should be humility. Nonetheless, he smiled to himself as they wobbled over the gangplank and up to their seats in the prow.

The pitcher explained that they were going to weigh

anchor in the middle of the lake and hold a short service, to give thanks for the fellowship and spiritual adventure of their pilgrimage. Jumbo wondered about the boat's other passengers, who were a noisy lot, men with loud voices and teenagers with a ghetto-blaster. But perhaps they were used to it.

The boat turned in the small harbour, gently rocking on the swell. Jumbo sat right at the front, over the driver's cabin, staring out to sea.

When they hit the open water the whole tenor of the voyage changed. The boat seemed to go at twice the speed, smacking into each wave and bouncing off it, sending fountains of spray back into the faces of the Christian Travellers. The wind pummelled the tattered green canvas awning overhead. Everything creaked and squeaked. Jumbo had to hang tightly on to the side to stop himself sliding about on the narrow wooden bench. But still, he told himself, it was exciting. Inspiring, even. A fitting end to a marvellous trip.

By halfway across he was less sure. His stomach felt queasy, and in spite of the brilliant sun his face was cold and his bare arms covered in goose pimples. Tiberias still looked a long way off.

The pitcher staggered up to the prow and addressed them, shouting above the wind.

'Because of the high sea we're going to go rather closer to shore than we usually do. I hope no one will be too disappointed. You'll still be able to get good photographs of the lake and the hills if you look back the way we've come. Thank you!'

Jumbo gritted his teeth. For a second there he'd thought they were going to skip the service (to which, only half an hour ago, he'd been so keenly looking forward).

When the engine did shut down they were tantalisingly close to Tiberias. They could even see their hotel, a lego-like cube up on the hill.

The pitcher rose unsteadily to his feet and drew their

attention to the appropriate hymn in their *Christian Travel Holy Land Companion*. It was 'Dear Lord and Father of Mankind', one of Jumbo's favourites. At this moment, it looked terribly long. The other passengers, with a world-weary air, turned off their ghetto-blasters but continued to chatter. The pilgrims started to sing, used by now to striking up a capella in the key which suited them all.

Jumbo tried to sing without opening his mouth too wide. He was now in the grip of full-blown seasickness. If he had stood the remotest chance of making it he would have plunged over the side and swum for Tiberias.

It was the words of the final verse which conjured up, with shocking suddenness and clarity, a scene he had been at pains to forget.

'Breathe through the heats of our desire,' he mumbled. 'Thy coolness and Thy balm; Let sense be dumb, let flesh retire, Speak through the earthquake, wind and fire — '

His face was icy. The sun dazzled on the water. The boat creaked and boomed around him. The flickering reflected light and the noise suddenly transformed themselves into something else, and he was standing by a fire. He was both hot and cold, unwell, not happy. On the far sides of the flames, three figures shimmered in the heat, one of them Steward —

'O still small voice of calm!'

Unable any longer to hold on, Jumbo leaned as far out as he could and was horribly sick. At a distance, he heard indulgent laughter.

'I did warn him,' said a woman's voice, 'about the St Peter's fish.'


Some ten days after his return he received a telephone call.

'Hallo, John.'

'Sorry, who — ?'

'It's Tony Steward here.'

'Hallo!' His voice sounded loud and forced.

218

'I'm calling from my niece's place in Hampstead.'

'Ah!' Jumbo hoped he was not expected to extend some kind of invitation. He added guardedly: 'How much time have you got?'

'None,' replied Steward. 'I fly back tomorrow.'

'That's a pity,' said Jumbo. 'We might have got together again.'

'And we will. You're going to come to the States, remember?'

'Of course, yes.'

'I'm just calling because I managed to contact that girl I was telling you about, the one who could help you with some typing.'

Jumbo relaxed a little. 'That's awfully good of you. I didn't really mean . . . '

'When I say I'll do something I do it,' said Steward, in a brazen way which Jumbo took to be typically American. 'Her name's Janet Dimitos. Don't worry, she's entirely English, reading history at Bedford College, but I believe her father's of Greek extraction. She's very keen. Her semester doesn't start till early October so she could give you nearly six weeks as of now, and maybe a few hours at a weekend after that.'

'That sounds splendid,' said Jumbo. 'Did you explain about funds?'

'I put her in the picture. You'll have to see her, and make sure you suit each other, and you can give her the details then. But I said it wouldn't make her fortune. I think she's hoping she can call herself an author's PA, or a researcher. Something that'll look good on her CV.'

'She can call herself whatever she likes,' said Jumbo enthusiastically. 'Can you give me her address and phone number?'

Steward did so, adding: 'You see she's in Camden Town, which is convenient for you both, and she wouldn't be spending much on fares.'

'I do appreciate this. I can't think why you should go to

such trouble on my account.'

'No trouble. For old time's sake,' said Steward.

When Jumbo had put the phone down he felt tremendously relieved. All the little sights and sounds of his everyday life, kept at bay by the conversation with Steward, rushed back to enfold him: Judy hoovering in the sitting room, the faint smell of Irish stew, the dog barking idly at something in the garden, the safe, familiar clutter of his study. Everything was all right. Better, in fact, because he was going to get this nice, keen student to do his typing. The book would begin to look like a book. And Steward was returning to the States.

He got up stiffly from his desk, and stretched. He had a fancy to wander along to the kitchen and make a cup of instant coffee for Judy and himself. Through the long sash window of the vicarage he could see the grey spire of St Cuthbert's pointing like a missile at the heavens above the massed aerials of Cricklewood. In the Oliphants' narrow, unkempt garden there was already a pile of sodden leaves and other arboreal debris from the gale a week ago. And there was the dog, standing in the middle of the oblong of tussocky grass, still barking with his head lifted like a wolf at some imagined danger.

# CHAPTER EIGHTEEN

# *1989*

Phyllis got the chocolate fudge cake out of its box and put it on a plate. It was her favourite and she got it whenever her granddaughter came to visit. They were both chocaholics. In fact, it was Phyllis's proud and justifiable boast that she had reached an amazingly spry eighty-two on chocolate, cigarettes and strong tea, and without recourse to any vegetable save the potato. She was active, she was happy, she had a smashing little semi-detached bungalow in the old people's complex in Willesden.

'Tray's ready,' she called. Jan came through from the lounge, picked up the tray and carried it back, putting it down on the low table in front of the settee. The TV was on with the sound down – *Teenage Mutant Whatsit Turtles*, which Phyllis enjoyed, but Jan asked: 'Mind if I turn this off, Gran?'

'No, no, you go ahead, sweetheart. And help yourself to cake.'

Jan did so, while Phyllis poured the tea. Part of the charm of these infrequent get-togethers was their shared sense of indulging in forbidden pleasures. Phyllis's daughter, Shirley, was a great one for a healthy mind in a healthy body and Phyllis respected her for it. Shirley had had a tough life, never knowing her Dad and then deserted by her husband. She'd had to stay healthy to cope, and had done so admirably. But it was pleasant to share a packet of Marlboros, sip Typhoo and eat fudge cake beyond the reach of Shirley's censure. Phyllis finished her cake, and ran a well-manicured finger round her mouth to pick up the crumbs. 'So what news have you got for your old grandma today then?'

Jan kicked off her fringed boots and drew her bare feet up next to her on the settee. 'I've got a job.'

'You're never leaving university!'

'Of course not. But I don't go back till next month, and I haven't any cash left since we went to Greece, so it's turned up at the right moment.'

'Smashing. What sort of a job?'

'I'm going to help this old guy who's writing his memoirs,' said Jan. 'He's a vicar, would you believe.'

'You'll have to watch yourself there,' agreed Phyllis. 'So what's the book about?'

'That's the thing. It's about when he was a prisoner of the Japs. On the railway, like Granddad. It was Laura's uncle from the States who put me on to him. He said there was even a chance he might have known Granddad, because they were both in one of those camps near the border.'

'In one of the cholera camps, was he?' said Phyllis. 'That sounds like an interesting job. I hope he's going to pay you well.'

'The money won't be fantastic, but he's not far away so getting there and back won't cost me anything, and at least it's something that's good experience. It might even stand me in quite good stead, you never know.'

'When do you start then?'

Jan stubbed out her cigarette. 'Soon, I hope. I'm going to see him tomorrow.'


An hour or so later Phyllis went to the gate with her granddaughter and watched her as she walked along the road in the direction of the bus stop. Seventy in the shade, and apart from the boots she was wearing black woolly tights, a leather jacket and dainty black gloves with open-work over the knuckles. But still and all, she was a good girl – bright, sensible, hardworking, and found time to come and visit her grandmother. Phyllis thought there was far too much criticism of the young.

She went back inside. Jan had taken the tray through to the sink, but she'd told her not to bother with the washing up. The young led such busy lives, people to see, places to go, whereas old women had time that needed filling.

She was pleased about Jan's job. She'd always been interested in the past, in her Granddad. It was funny. You'd think it would have bored her rigid. Phyllis always regretted that she couldn't tell her more about the railway. The wives and families had only received two postcards during that whole time, and those had been no more than formulas printed by the Japs and signed by the prisoners. She'd found out more about it since the war, talking to one or two people who'd been put in touch with her by FEPOW, and by reading books and seeing films. She'd enjoyed *The Bridge on the River Kwai*, but she'd read somewhere since that it wasn't very authentic. That the real thing had been worse. She went to the mirror over the mantelpiece and patted her hair, which was still dark with only the merest hint of grey. 'Touch of the tarbrush,' Mick used to say. 'Stolen by gypsies. That makes two of us.'

And he used to give her that bright-eyed, saucy grin. She could never say no to him.


Janet Dimitos was not due till three o'clock, but after lunch Jumbo couldn't settle. He'd once heard an author on the wireless saying that writers lost most time and concentration through the expectation of interruption. This he now found to be true.

He was also a little anxious. He didn't know what to

expect, and he was an inexperienced interviewer. How should one broach the question of payment? He could only hope that Tony Steward would have done most of the groundwork for him. It also dawned on him that if the girl was awful or unsuitable in any way, it would be difficult to turn her down because of Steward's warm recommendation. He would have to resort to – well – half-truths.

'I think I'll go and do a spot of clearing up outside,' he called to Judy, who was clattering about in the kitchen. 'Give me a shout when she arrives.'

They were neither of them great gardeners, and he wasn't in the mood for fiddly jobs. He got the rake from the shed and began combing through the long grass, collecting up more leaves and twigs for the bonfire. The dog bounced about, barking at the rake. It was hot and sunny, and there was a traffic smell from the cars in the Kilburn High Road. Quite soon Jumbo was sweating profusely. It was not really how he wanted the girl to find him. A reflective pose at the desk would have been better.

Too late. Judy appeared at the top of the steps by the back door.

'John! She's here!'

He stood leaning on the rake, catching his breath. The girl didn't wait, but walked briskly down the steps and across the lawn. The dog ran around her, leaping boisterously. She greeted it calmly, offering one hand and saying 'Hallo, hallo' in a soothing way.

She stopped on the other side of the bonfire pile and said: 'Hallo, I hope I'm not early. I'm Janet Dimitos.'

She had coal-black hair worn in a sort of bird's nest, and thick dark eyebrows. She was small, with thin, muscly legs, but she had an imposing bust. Jumbo couldn't help noticing, because it had the words 'Save the World' written across it.

'Of course you're not early. At least I have no idea what time it is . . . ' He glanced at his watch. 'And it doesn't matter anyway. Shall we go to my study and have our chat?' The words sounded like the invitation of some musichall bounder, but she said 'Sure' and they walked back together towards the house.

It had gone well. As Jumbo accompanied Jan (as she had asked him to call her) to the front door about twenty minutes later, he was more pleased than he could say. And grateful to Steward for having had such a bright idea and following it through so conscientiously.

She might look typically modern, but Jumbo detected quite an old-fashioned young lady in there somewhere. That would be the Greek blood, he had no doubt. Continentals were like that. She could type, she was keen, she said she would have no trouble coming over on her bicycle each day and would bring her own lunch because she was a faddy eater. She asked if it would be all right if she had the occasional cigarette, if she went into the garden with it. He was touched both by her addiction and her concern.

He hadn't liked to pry about her grandfather, though she did mention him. Time enough for that when they got to know each other better.

He opened the front door. Indian summer flooded in, a warm, buzzing cocktail of petrol fumes and pavements and fast food.

'It's going to make such a difference to my work, having you here,' he said.

'Good,' she said. 'I hope so.'

He watched her go. As she closed the gate behind her she looked back at him and gave a wave, and grinned – a collusive, slightly wicked grin.

Jumbo shivered. Someone had walked over his grave.

I was so pleased with myself I travelled back Club Class. Pan Am, too, to get me re-oriented before I saw Cary. I ordered a large Stoli and tonic, and tilted the seat back. The stewardesses wore name-tags: they were called Sherilyn and Dallas. I was going home. Mind you, reaction had set in. I was absolutely bushed.

But then I had nothing to do, now. Nothing to do but drink and doze and think about Cary and how much he would like the silver horse, which nestled among my socks and shorts in the baggage hold.

I closed my eyes, the vodka lying in a little hot puddle in my mouth. I was content. I thought I would tell Cary about Mick. You didn't do someone you cared about any favours by pretending there had been No One Else. Mick Maitland had been my first, great love. More than love, my first great adoration. I had been completely besotted with him, because he was everything I was not. Easy about himself, his ambivalent sexuality, his effect on other people. The only purely and utterly amoral person I've ever met. All through the time in Changi I'd been like a man with a fever, just living, waiting for the next time, and the next, content with whatever he was prepared to give me. I was hooked. It was funny living through that intense, agonisingly wonderful experience at a time when life generally was so dire. It was terrible but thrilling, like a dream.

To come back from the dead – twice. Just like Mick to saunter back into camp with fat on his ribs and a smile on his face, and then escape execution. That had had nothing to do with Butler. I was already beginning to understand what was going on there. His defence of Mick was to save his own skin. I fleshed it out and couched it in the terms that would persuade Oshiru what the honourable course was.

But a third return would have been too good to be true. A little man, as Mick had been, couldn't cheat death again. It was against the natural order. Class and prejudice and envy and snobbery stretched out long fingers all the way from England. We thought he was dying. Hardly anyone survived cholera anyway. I had hoped perhaps when I took the Jap brass up to the hill that afternoon that I might be able to sneak a look at him, perhaps say something to him even if he couldn't hear.

Oliphant was there, going about his grisly business. I remember thinking how awful he looked, and that perhaps he would be dead by that time next day. He had just put some bodies on the fire. I was standing to one side of the Japs, between them and Symington. They were provoking us, lighting their cigarettes from the fire. It was that movement that made me focus, for a second, on the three bodies.

I saw that one of them was Mick. I could tell because of the tiger-eye tattoo. His mouth gaped and his arms rose beseechingly at the flames took hold.

And then I heard one of the Japs say, in Japanese:

'That man is alive.'

It was no joke. And yet they both laughed.